Breathing Fire

R.K. Lilley

This book is dedicated to my mom, Linda, and my sister, April,
for making me want to write the kinds of books we love to read.

CHAPTER ONE

A Doozy

Day 1

My day had already gone to shit when two angry druids stormed into my shop. My blood went cold. The hair on the back of my neck stood on end. My palms itched to hold the handle of a weapon. The presence of druids in my shop was bad. Very bad. Their presence made the rest of my day seem pleasant in comparison, and it'd been a doozy so far.

I'd gotten exactly two hours of sleep the night before, thanks to some new scheme concocted by my best friend/arch-nemesis, Christian. He'd taken me on a police stakeout, claiming to need my help. I'd only gone along because he'd claimed it was an emergency, and I owed him a favor, or ten.

By the end of the long, eventless evening, I was more than a little suspicious that he'd dragged me out just for the company. We'd spent hours in a crowded night club, bullshitting until four in the morning, before I'd realized I'd been duped.

When I'd confronted the mischievous Christian, he'd only shrugged, saying, "I was bored. It's not like you had a date." I'd gone home in a rage, which hadn't helped me get to sleep any faster.

I'd still managed to stumble into my shop relatively close to opening time. Even at seven a.m., the day had already been a scorcher. Just being outside, even at that early hour, felt a lot like being assaulted by nature's biggest hair-dryer.

My dark t-shirt and jeans were wrinkled (but hopefully clean?) my blonde ponytail was messy, I hadn't had even one cup of coffee, and I was in a dark mood, but it was my only day to open the shop, so by the gods, I could manage to at least get there somewhere approaching the right time.

I was none-too-pleased to run into cops and a busted lock as I approached the back entrance of the used bookstore/coffee shop I co-owned with my sister. I came to the obvious, and correct, assumption that our shop had been robbed, yet again.

We were located in a questionable area of town. Though admittedly, in Vegas, every area was at least a little bit questionable. Even posh areas in Vegas got robbed. Vegas criminals were equal opportunity employers.

I'd cursed with gusto when I saw the full extent of the robbery. The robbers hadn't gone straight for the safe, as they had the last few times. The place was trashed, top to bottom. Why would anyone rob a used bookstore? I had no idea. There was never a lot of cash in the safe, not ever. Pickings must be slim indeed for our little shop to be the target of no less than four robberies in the last nine months.

My naturally paranoid mind had worked with the statistics busily. It was not a good sign, I'd concluded. It was starting to look like a good time to move on from our comfy old bookstore. It had been aiming in that direction, anyway. The growing popularity of e-books would have closed us down soon enough. Business had been far from booming, and we had stayed in one place long enough.

We moved often, my sister and I. We were runaways by nature. Drifters by necessity. And we were adaptable. It was our greatest ability, as far as I was concerned. We changed houses, jobs, cars, and cities on a regular basis. We'd lived in several countries, and we acclimated to other cultures well. That was, perhaps, why the states had suited us so well for so long. And the transient population in a place like Las Vegas was a particularly good fit. What better place for two accomplished runaways to fade into the background?

I dealt with the police, sending them quickly on their way, and began the annoying and time-consuming process of cleaning up my mess of a shop.

By nine a.m., both of our full-time employees had called out sick. This meant that on top of repairing the whole shop from its assault, I had to run both the cafe and book portion of the store. On a weekend. Grrr.

Suffice it to say, I wasn't in my best mood come opening time. I didn't even bother to hide it from the customers.

My sister, Lynn, still didn't answer when I called her for the fourth time. 'Personal Jesus' played as the background music for her phone. She had an unhealthy obsession with that song.

"Bastard," I said at the beep, and hung up. She was, in fact, a bastard, but she was about as sensitive about that as I was.

I went back to work still cursing her. One of our regulars walked in, looking around the still messed up shop. He gave me a sort of dazed, questioning look.

I just shrugged at him. "If I tell ya, I hafta kill ya," I told him, straight-faced. I made a cutting motion across my throat.

He rolled his eyes at me, and headed to the mystery section. So I'm only funny to myself. It's really the least of my problems.

The morning rush wound down, and for once I was happy to have an empty shop come early afternoon.

I was repairing one of the few bookshelves that was still busted. I was rather proud that I'd managed to get things back together so quickly. I was mentally patting myself on the back when the entrance bell chimed. Twice.

"I'll be right with you," I shouted from where I was working in the horror section at the back of the store. I didn't mean it. I was going to keep working on what I was doing until the customers either; a. Came and asked me for help, or b. Asked me to check them out. Customer service had never been my strong point.

Was that the lock clicking? I wondered, seconds before someone cleared their throat behind me. I straightened, turning, and dusting my hands off on my jeans as I did so.

Every part of my body tensed in frozen panic when I saw the two men standing in my shop. I was using the term 'men' loosely. For all intents and purposes, though, they looked like clean-cut businessmen in uniform three-piece suits. Even their ties were a matching conservative gray. Most wouldn't notice the guns they carried under their jackets. And almost no one would feel the power radiating off of their skin like steam.

Druids had long held the responsibility of governing the supernatural community in both the U.S and Europe. They guarded the secrets of their own race quite obsessively from the outside world. This, I guessed, was why they felt they had to help keep the rest of us hidden. Help was the wrong word. That made it sound as though any of us had a choice in the matter. We didn't.

The staying hidden from the outside world part had never been a problem for me. The part where they made us submit all of our personal information into their infamous rosters, well, that part had never sat well with me.

We had been scamming their system for as long as I could remember, sometimes more effectively than others. My history with the druids was long, sordid, tempestuous, complicated, and ugly. And that was putting it mildly.

Having two druids walk into my shop was a disaster no matter how you looked at it. The fact that I happened to recognize these two in particular was much worse than just bad. It was an outright cluster-fuck. And, of course, it didn't help that they both just happened to hate my guts. My palms itched badly. My hands just ached to hold a weapon at that moment.

I liked guns. Okay, I *loved* guns. They just felt right in my hands, the heavy weight of infinite comfort to me. Even the weight of one in a holster at my hip, back, or ankle just felt good to me. And firing one. *Mmm*, I loved that, too. The recoil was like an old friend. But they weren't my favorite.

If it had been socially acceptable, or more importantly, legal, I would have had a two-handed axe strapped to my back, or even a two-handed sword. Ahh, but an axe was my favorite. A sword could behead, but an axe was *made* for it. And chances were, if I needed a weapon to kill something, that something needed to lose its head in order to die. I had a gun at my ankle, but with two angry druids invading my domain, what I longed for was an axe.

I had one somewhat close by. It was strapped to the bottom of my desk, because paranoia could be called a religion to some of us. But going for it was really just a wistful fancy at this point. I couldn't kill these druids. One did not kill a druid if one wanted to stay off the radar. A druid's death would not go unnoticed or unexplored. And it would never go unavenged. Even those at the very bottom of the druid food chain were protected.

It was a fact that if you were born supernatural, in any way, you wanted to be born druid. I had wished for the privilege more than once, even though I hated most of them.

I couldn't decide if it was good or bad that they seemed to be as surprised to see me as I was to see them. One thing was for certain. It was damned unlucky.

Michael was the first to recover, cursing fluently. He was relatively short for a druid, no more than six feet tall. His coarse, light-brown hair was cut into a harsh buzz-cut, as though he wanted to fuss with it as little as possible.

He pushed black shades to the top of his head, pinning me

with his angry dark-brown eyes.

The other one, Mav, didn't say a word. He just turned, punching a hole into the nearest wall. I was tempted to tell him he'd have to pay for that, but I really didn't want to bother.

Mav was a few inches taller than his partner, but shared the same coloring. I seemed to recall that they were distant cousins.

"We could kill her now. We could just bury her in the desert," Mav said to Michael, his back still to me. "No one ever has to know. We could just eliminate this can of worms, once and for all."

I flashed a half-sneer at Michael, who'd never taken his malevolent gaze off of my face. "I'd love to see you try," I told them both.

I knew they'd never kill me. That kind of disobedience just didn't happen in the druid world. And there was an order from higher up that I was not to be killed. Not to mention the little detail that they had no clue in the world how to actually get the deed accomplished.

Taking all of that into consideration, I suddenly had an idea. Admittedly, it was not a great idea, but it was the best I could come up with on short notice. Actually, the more I worked out the details in my head, I realized that it was a borderline *terrible* idea, but I was certain it would buy me some time. And time was what I needed.

I would be the first to admit that I was a shameless runner, though even I knew that was nothing to be proud of. But running like a coward meant that I had developed some pretty extensive evasive skills over the years. I could work wonders with a head start. And no one knew better than I did that sometimes a head start had a price.

Michael was shaking his head at me slowly. "No, we won't kill you-" he began, but Mav interrupted him.

"Do you have any idea what he was like when you left?" Mav

asked me, his eyes scary. "He was a mad thing for months. Did you hear what he did in the arena? No one even knew he had that in him. You made him into that! And when he gave up looking for you, he turned bitter, and we all suffered. We all had to pay because of your fucking games!" His voice was a growl by the end.

I was taken aback when I saw that his eyes weren't human any longer. I had always thought that Mav's powers were limited to far below the level of the beastcall.

"Are you even sorry for what you did?" he asked. I couldn't help but notice that he'd given me a better opening than I could have maneuvered for myself. That was helpful.

I shrugged, giving him a pointedly bored look. "He got over it," I told him. "I hear he's doing more than fine. You've never had a younger Arch-"

Before I could finish, he was across the room, backhanding me. The blow knocked me off my feet. "Whore!" His voice was nearly a howl.

It took a lot more self-control than I cared to admit not to retaliate to both the blow and the word, but I made myself at least appear calm.

"I hear he's interviewing applicants to replace me nightly," I dared to say, standing up to face him again. I saw the punch coming, and braced myself. The back of my head hit the wall at the back of the room. I saw stars.

CHAPTER TWO

Happy Place

Not fighting back was much harder than I had thought it would be. My nails dug so hard into my palms that I felt the skin split. My plan would be much more effective, though, if I didn't leave a scratch on either one of them.

I repeated this to myself, over and over again.

I thought that watching me fly across the room actually made Mav feel better. He was noticeably calmer when he said, "You and your sister haven't registered with us for over five years."

Actually, it was closer to seven, but I wasn't going to correct him.

He continued, "I know I don't have to tell you the kind of trouble I could give you for that. In addition, you were both registered as weather-witches. You're gonna have to do better than that this time. You don't have a high-ranking boyfriend to protect you anymore." He was downright smug by the end of his little spiel.

"Are you implying that I'm not a weather-witch?" I asked him. I wasn't, of course. Not even close.

"Don't push me," he snarled.

I tried to smile pleasantly at him, but knew I fell far from the mark. "Would you like me to go make it rain? Or better yet, I could make it about a hundred and ten degrees outside, with no humidity. That one's my specialty."

Yes, it was a bad Vegas weather joke. They didn't laugh, either.

I got a hard punch in the stomach for the comment. I spit out a large mouthful of blood.

"You are going to give us some straight answers, Jillian, or we will be making you very sorry," Michael threatened.

"In that case, I should tell you that my name hasn't been Jillian for years." He slapped me for that comment.

"You're going to tell me what you really are, or I swear I'll make you sorry," Mav said.

"I'm not telling you a damn thing. You couldn't beat it out of me. I doubt you could even hold me down long enough to try," I said, and it was a dare that I knew these knuckleheads couldn't resist. I'd learned a long time ago that if you suggested something to someone, if it was something they had already wanted to do, something they were already considering, they would almost always take you up on it. This was especially true if you were dealing with idiots.

"Hold her," Mav told Michael.

They were cooperating faster than I could have anticipated. They were really stupid. Which was good. I had kind of been counting on it, though I couldn't exactly get excited about having the shit beat out of me.

Michael gripped my wrists from behind, more tightly than he needed to. All the better, I told myself, though the feeling made me want to fight harder.

I let myself struggle against the hold, just hard enough to guarantee that my wrists would be bruised.

"What the fuck are you? And how old are you, anyways? I heard that you met Dom when he was just fourteen! That was fifty years ago…"

I definitely wasn't going near that one. My age was a touchy subject, to say the least. Physically, I could have passed for being anywhere between twenty-five to thirty-five, but that was no reflection of my actual age. My kind did not age physically. Or die of natural causes, for that matter.

Mav proceeded to batter me up. There could be no doubt that he relished the opportunity. Sadistic bastard. He landed a solid punch every time I answered one of his questions with an impassioned, "Go fuck yourself!"

It hurt. God, did it hurt bad. And I'd been through some pretty rough stuff. I'd been alive for a very long time, and my life had never been easy, or painless. Nevertheless, getting the shit beat of you never failed to suck.

I tried to take my mind elsewhere. I thought of other places, better places. Nope. The beating still sucked royally. I tried to make my mind go to a happy place. Did my mind have a happy place? Apparently not.

"Damn," Mav said at one point. "Dom told me about this. He told me that your hair and eyes shifted color during sex. I never realized it'd be so pretty. Does this mean you're turned on?" he asked, leering at me.

I spit in his face. He punched me in the jaw, hard.

"I think it means she's pissed," Michael answered for me.

"It means I think you should go fuck yourself," I added helpfully. Pain had never been a good enough excuse to make me shut my mouth. My breath whooshed out hard. A solid punch to the ribs will do that.

I lost track of time as the beating seemed to last forever. The bastard even made me black out at one point. I had reached my absolute limit when I called a halt to it.

"Enchanter," I finally gave an answer to his favorite question. It was a lie, but not a real obvious one.

"Bull," Mav snarled, and smashed his fist into my ribs. He loved that spot. I coughed up more blood, spitting it in his direction.

"Wait, wait," I said when he went to punch me again. I had really reached my limit. I knew it for certain because the panic in my voice had become very genuine. "I am an enchanter, and I can show you." He paused, and I continued, "I can make you do my will. For instance, you're not going to tell Dom that you ever saw me. In fact, you won't tell anyone that you know where I am."

Mav just blinked at me for a minute. "Now why on earth would we do that?" he asked. "If that was an enchantment, it was pathetic. I had no urge to obey you."

"I'm pretty sure you don't want him to see me like this. And if you tell him that you found me, there's nothing stopping me from paying him a visit myself."

Mav just grinned at me. "I've seen how fast you heal. You'll be good as new by the time you reach his casino. And he won't believe a word that comes out of your lying, whoring mouth."

I clucked my tongue at him, going in for the kill. "I'm no druid, Mav. You've seen how fast I *can* heal. It's a spell, not a natural ability. It takes effort on my part. And neither of you have any healing abilities of any kind. That much I remember. You could probably call in someone that does, but I'd be willing to bet that you won't risk anyone else finding out about this. No one is willing to become an accomplice to you idiots."

"I wonder how Dom would react if he saw the shape I'm in, with not a *scratch* on either one of you. I know from past experience that the proof that you restrained me will make him go apeshit." I held up my wrists. They were red and already turning into a dark, bruised purple. "These little marks alone will trigger his wrath."

Mav was starting to look a little green, but he still tried to bluff his way out of it. "You haven't seen him lately, Jillian. He hates your guts. He doesn't give a damn what happens to you."

My chest hurt a little at what he said, and I wondered how much of it was true. I tried to snort at him disdainfully, but it just made more blood spurt out of my nose.

"You and I both know that he could hate me enough to beat me to death himself, but he's still dominant enough that if he sees me like this, he'll rip apart whoever did it just for disobeying a direct order, and with so much apparent gusto. I have no qualms about giving you two up to him."

Michael finally let go of my wrists. I fell to the floor, glaring up at both of them.

"Fine, you win, for now," Michael said, not looking me in the eye. "We'll report that we found nothing unusual when we went to make inquiries at your shop. But, you know, all you're doing is buying a little time. Everyone has to come clean sometime, Jillian."

"Be careful what you wish for." I flipped them off with both hands until the bells chimed their exit. I tried to sit up. The world went black.

CHAPTER THREE

OCD

When I came to, every part of my body was throbbing. I noticed, as I stumbled around the shop, that my assailants had been considerate enough to put up the closed sign on their way out. How nice. And they hadn't managed to break any bones. When I returned the favor, they wouldn't be able to say the same.

I dug up some aspirin in my office. It didn't do much for the pain. A half pint of my sister's rocky road ice cream helped, though. I more or less passed out in my office chair.

When I next awoke, I noticed a completely different sensation than pain. My skin was literally steaming. I could see the bare skin on my arms glowed gold. My nails changed colors as I watched. Magenta, crimson, scarlet, orange… It went on and on, the colors shifting through the spectrum of every hue. I knew from past experience that my hair and eyes were doing the same.

This had been happening a lot lately. I was pretty sure it wasn't normal, even for my kind. I needed to ask Lynn about it, but I knew nothing like this had ever happened to her.

My body had been acting up for a while now. Pretty much, I was hoping that whatever problems it was having would work themselves out, or better yet, go away. Whatever this thing was, I was really just counting on the whole immortal thing to trump it. A few hundred years of perfect health had made me overconfident, I supposed.

I lay there, eyes closed, until my body had calmed down. I sighed. I was procrastinating. I had some unpleasant magic to perform. My battered body had already begun to heal the damage that had become my insurance.

I had lied to Mav when I told him that my body did not heal quickly on it's own. I did, however, have a way to stop the healing process, for a time.

I unlocked the hidden drawer in my desk, drawing out the ancient relic I kept there. Chanting softly, I stopped my body from healing. This was a spell generally meant for someone other than yourself, and it almost hurt worse than the beating, but desperate times called for desperate measures. And lucky for me, I was on a first name basis with both desperate times *and* desperate measures. Boy, did they love me. The feeling was very much *not* mutual.

My body quickly rebelled, and I emptied my stomach into the wastebasket beside my desk. This was not going to be a fun couple of days, but at least I had bought Lynn and I some time. Now I just had to get up off my bruised ass and make use of it.

The closest thing I had to an informant worked as a cocktail waitress at The Golden Dragon.

The Golden Dragon was a dump casino on the outskirts of the strip. It was, however, the closest casino to The Grove, the monstrosity of a casino that belonged to the druids. It doubled as their base of operations for the west coast.

It was a perverse phenomena, since the druids were notorious for their love of forests and water, and all things green. I had often wondered why they would choose to station so many of the green-loving bastards right smack in the middle of the desert, but I'd learned not to ask. No druid would answer that question. And just asking it tended to make them real salty.

I'd met Casey years ago. She had been sobbing quietly in the cafe portion of our shop. She was a cute little thing, with corkscrew auburn curls and bright green eyes. I'd sat down in the chair across from her and asked her if she needed help with anything. She'd then proceeded to tell me her life story, including the most prominent part, about her having a stormy affair with one of the higher ranking druids.

I'd given her some good relationship advice, knowing a thing or two about the subject, and we'd been friends ever since. I'd also placed a silencing spell on her. If she made a habit of talking too much to strangers about such things, she'd quickly find herself buried in the desert.

And so I found myself dumping some money into a slot machine as I waited for the cocktail waitress to make her rounds. I got lucky. Casey just happened to be working my section of the place. Her face broke into a big smile when she saw me. She nearly skipped her way over to me in her excitement.

Gods, had I ever been that young? Not in this lifetime.

She wore a black and gold cocktail getup that exposed her midriff and left nothing to cover her ass but some fishnet pantyhose and a string. She was sporting the bad boob-job that so many professionals in Las Vegas had adopted.

I was shielding my bruises for the sake of not drawing attention to myself, though people seemed to stare my way no matter what I did. Being blond and around the six foot mark tended to make me stand out.

"Hi there," she said, as she got closer. "Just here for slots?"

I smiled at her. "I came by to see you, actually."

She beamed at me. "One second. Let me go tell my boss I'm taking a break. I have a fifteen minute one coming up, but they won't notice if I slip out for thirty."

She pulled out a smoke the second we stepped outside, lighting it. She offered me one, and I declined. I knew I'd never get lung cancer, but I just couldn't stand the things.

"Some druids came and paid me a visit today. Heard any gossip about anything to do with our shop?" I asked bluntly.

She froze, the cigarette actually falling from her hand. "Shit, yeah, I have. Been meaning to tell you about it. I guess someone who visited your shop claimed that you were magic-users. Some old hag, looking to get a reward, I hear. Joseph told me about it because he knew I went to the shop a lot, wanted to know if I noticed anything unusual." She laughed nervously. "Crazy, right? I figured they'd go check out your place and see that she was scamming them."

I was watching her face while she spoke. She never met my eyes once.

"Why'd you cross me, Case?" I asked her softly.

She burst into tears. "I didn't mean to, I swear. Joseph used something on me. I was talking, telling him things I didn't want to. I figured you'd get out of whatever trouble they made for you. I know you're really strong."

I let my shields down, showed her my battered face and arms. She sobbed harder, apologizing over and over. I put my shields back up.

Normally, I avoided using magic around humans like the plague, but it seemed the damage was already done here. "Why couldn't you at least give us a heads up?" I asked her.

She was shaking her head. "It was like I said, some old w-witch-hag got to them first."

Witch-hag's were a particularly nasty class of witch. They always looked like ancient old hags, regardless of their age. Their youth was the first thing they sacrificed to gain more power. After that, they got even more desperate, sacrificing countless other things. The rogue hags were even less particular, sacrificing humans or even whatever Others they could get their hands on. It alarmed me a bit that one had been aware of me, but not me of her.

Luckily she hadn't been a rogue, or she would have done worse than gone to the druids. If a rogue hag knew what I was, if they had even an inkling, and got the jump on me, with any knowledge of how to bind me, she would harvest me for parts. There's nothing a rogue hag would love more than getting ahold of one of my kind.

Casey continued. "Then Joseph was questioning me. I've never seen him like that. He was ruthless. I'm not sure I ever really knew him at all. I'm so sorry," she sobbed, backing into the side of the building and sliding down into a crying heap.

"What all did you tell them about me?" I asked quietly.

"Everything I knew. Everything you've ever told me, or that I've noticed on my own." She was curled up on the ground now. "What can I do to make it up to you?"

I felt a little sick at heart, but I was too practical to overlook a good opening when I saw it. "You can't, Case. But you can call me if you hear anything. Keep me up to date on anything you find out." I was walking away as I finished, Casey a mess on the ground of the alley behind me.

"Are we still friends?" she called after me.

"You tell me. I don't have a lot of friends. Is this how you normally treat them?" I ignored her pitiful sobs and walked away.

Well, I'd learned two useful and unfortunate pieces of information with that errand. One was that Casey's boyfriend was on to our little chats, probably had been for awhile, if he had resorted to be-spelling her. The other was that, whether they wanted to or not, Mav and Michael wouldn't be able to just forget that I existed. It was obvious that the attention of more higher-ups had been caught.

On the bright side, if Dom was one of those higher ups, I was pretty sure I would know it by now.

I was speeding down Tropicana Avenue when it started again. I started to tremble. I barely pulled over before I lost control of my body. A familiar force pushed against my mind, and this time I didn't fight it.

At first I didn't understand what I was seeing. It was all wrong.

"I should not be looking at you like this," I told my other form. The dragon was more beautiful than I had realized, gazing at it from the outside for the first time. It was all glowing, shifting colors, as its long form writhed in agony. Its eyes were the same palest aquamarine I wore in human form.

"Why is this happening?" I asked it. It didn't answer. It was hard to pull my eyes away from its entrancing beauty, but I did for a brief moment, and I perceived that all that surrounded us was an inky blackness.

Suddenly, all of that blackness turned to a shinning silver. Water seemed to surround us at every angle. It laid its body on the shifting ground, head nearly touching me. Was it going to sleep, or laying down to die?

It rolled suddenly onto its back, showing me its belly. I stepped close, but couldn't touch it.

"What's happening to us?" I asked it. It had clearly brought me here to show me, but I was not as perceptive as I needed to be. It began to moan in pain. A twin pain brought me to my knees, clutching my middle. Suddenly its moan turned to a roar of agony. I tried to shield my ears from the noise, but instead found myself voicing the same agony in my human throat.

As the noise died down I realized I was lying beside my other self, close to mirroring its pose, our limbs almost touching.

I turned my head to meet its eyes. So much anguish floated in their depths that I gasped. Was this what I had always dreaded?

"It can't be the madness." My voice was a hoarse whisper. I was too young, and I'd been doing so much to prevent it.

Surrounding myself with humans on a nearly daily basis, staying in human form more than dragon. Everything we had ever learned about preventing the brain sickness that lived in our bloodline, I had practiced as part of a daily routine. I was damn near OCD about it.   Its tormented roar was my only answer. I blacked out.

CHAPTER FOUR

About That Crazy

Day 2

I woke up in a bitch of a mood. My body hurt even worse than it had the day before, when I had dragged my bruised ass back home late, falling into bed.

I could smell something burning, and I strongly suspected that it was my bed. I just lay there for awhile, feeling odd for some reason. I mentally catalogued the reasons why I felt so weird.

It may have been the fact that I had a spell suspending the powerful regeneration that my body was accustomed to. It could also be that I had more than likely incinerated some of the important parts of my bed while I slept. Wouldn't that be fun to explain? But no, It was something else. I just couldn't put my finger on it.

I finally got up, stomping into the bathroom. I didn't even look back at the bed. I had no desire to see what kind of damage I had done while I slept.

I had just redecorated my bedroom, and I had really liked the fresh new look. It was a mix of orange and brown bedding with a dark, heavy wood bed frame, and matching furniture. It was just the style that I was into at the moment. I hadn't even had time to get sick of it yet.

I slammed my door on the mess.

I just stared at my reflection for a long minute, before what I was looking at sank in. "What the fuck?" I shouted at my reflection. Ok, I could be a drama queen. I could be honest about it. But this was almost too much for my teetering sanity.

My long blond hair had been so straight that it didn't even bend for more years than I cared to count. At the moment, however, I was looking at a head-full of corkscrew curls. They were curled up so tightly that my hair was now a half a foot shorter. I looked vaguely like a grown up, battered version of Shirley Temple.

I just stared at myself, frozen for a long moment. I had the pale aquamarine eyes that were a trademark of my family. They were so pale that, when my pupils were dilated, as they were now, my eyes could look almost completely white. Our eyes had been called many things. Haunting, ghostly, ethereal, other-worldly, beautiful, eery, creepy. Right now mine narrowed with the look of faint disgust on my face.

"What's goin' on?" Lynn's muted voice came from my bedroom, shaking me out of my reverie.

I opened my bathroom door, and just stared at my sister. Her short black hair was sticking up in every direction. This was extremely unusual for her. Lynn's hair usually did precisely what she wanted it to. It was the polar opposite of my hair, which usually did nothing at all. It wouldn't even take to dye. The stuff just washed out.

But the messy hair wasn't the problem. What really bothered me was the shiner covering her right eye. "What happened to you?" I asked her.

"What the HELL?" she asked me at the same time.

"I woke up like this." I fingered my curls.

"You beat yourself up in your sleep?" She raised a brow at

me.

"Oh, that," I said stupidly. "That was Druids. Who gave you the shiner?"

"Hell if I know." She looked disgusted with her answer.

"Druids? Really? That's not good. So Dom found you?"

"Not exactly. It's complicated, but for the moment, I have it under control. Ish. Just avoid the shop for a few days." There was no trail to connect the store to our house, which was no accident. Welcome to the Church of Paranoia. I founded it. "Have your goths call in some of their friends if they need extra help." As I spoke, Lynn noticed my bed. I followed her gaze and cursed. Her jaw hung open. The linens and much of the mattress were charred black.

She kept looking at me, then at the bed, her mouth trying to form words. I was at a loss for words, as well. Finally I sneered at the bed, then shrugged at Lynn. "The bed started it," I told her, then swept past her, out of the room.

Two of Lynn's human goth followers were hanging out in the dining room. I nodded at them as I passed through to the kitchen. They nodded back solemnly. Yes, Lynn has followers. Followers as in, they think she's a goddess and sort of worship her as such. It was a generational gap between us. I had missed out on that whole instinct to be worshipped thing. In fact, the thought of someone showing me that kind of adoration made my skin crawl. It was, however, a constant source of entertainment for me to watch her do it. And to give her shit for it.

Her current legion of fans were young, black-clad goths who, for some reason, seemed to think she was a vampire. Almost nothing could have been further from the truth, but I was willing to bet that they'd gotten the idea from her.

I have to admit the goths came in handy sometimes, like when they made pancakes for breakfast. I piled three onto my plate, sitting across from Lynn at the table. "Would you pass me the syrup, Elvira." I grinned at her. She hid her own half-smile. Messing with her when her followers were around was one of my favorite pastimes. The goths, a girl and boy with heavy black makeup, both glared at me. "Oh, sorry," I told them. "Oh Black Mistress of the Night, will you slide the syrup this way, please." She slid it to me, and I drenched my pancakes. I was a notoriously healthy eater, but I could comfort eat with the best of them, on a really shitty day. This certainly qualified.

"The bed started it?" she finally asked.

"Don't wanna talk about it." I dug into the food.

"You have any training appointments today?" she asked as I ate.

"Two," I said with my mouth full. It's not that I don't have table manners. I just didn't always choose to use them. "First one is Christian." I was a very expensive personal trainer for a few days out of the week.

"Nice. Tell him I said hi. I'm having lunch with him sometime this week."

I nodded that I would. "I need a jump for my car," I mentioned. My beloved Dodge Challenger had barely gotten me home last night. I had been passed out in it on the side of the road, my lights left on, for most of the night.

She nodded to the girl goth. "Sorrow can give you a jump." I tried my hardest not to smirk when I heard her name, but failed. I shoveled more pancakes into my mouth to hide it. "Thanks," I mumbled around my food.

I finished eating and pushed back from the table. "Give me ten minutes, Sorrow." I managed to only half-smirk as I said her name.

I showered quickly, throwing on some black workout clothes. I managed to get through my whole morning routine without looking at my bed again. I smoothed my curly hair into a tight ponytail. Just when I had it tied off, tiny curls escaped to cascade around my face. Ick. I tried again, with the same results. Being used to hair that did what I wanted, I gave up quickly. Christian would make fun of it, but I could hardly blame him.

I was pleased to find my car already jumped and running when I came outside. I smiled and thanked Sorrow. "Your mistress can't come out in the sunlight?" I asked her.

"I am old enough to stand the sun, if I am adequately covered," Lynn spoke from the doorway of the house. I turned to her, and had to choke back a laugh. She wore thick black sunglasses, and a black scarf over her face. She was clad in her usual black leather, gloves and all, despite the heat. What got me, though, was the lacy black parasol her other follower was holding over her head. I rolled my eyes at her laughingly before I put on my own shades.

She nodded to my car. Country music drifted out from a preset station on my radio. "Nice music," she said, smirking at me. I stuck my tongue out at her. "Nice parasol, Queen of the Damned," I shot back. Yes, I liked country music. I used to hide my guilty pleasure, but I'd given up a while back. All I have to say is, Garth is a gateway drug.

I climbed into the driver's seat and rolled down my window. "I'll call you if anything else develops with the situation we discussed earlier." She nodded, and I waved as I drove away.

Christian lived in one of the expensive gated communities up on sunrise mountain. He lived in a mini-mansion. It was a thirty-minute drive from my place, in good traffic. His house was big and luxurious, and there was no way his cop's paycheck could cover such a decedent house. Luckily, he had an inheritance the size of Nevada that more than covered such things. It was also how he could afford my pricey skills, though he had been a friend for far longer than he'd been a client.

His colossal inheritance also helped to support his favorite pastime. Paranoia. There were many reasons why Lynn and I found him so easy to get along with, one being that he was the most devout member of my paranoid congregation. His security systems were advanced and intricate. I had to use fingerprints, eye scans, and three different key code entries to gain access to his fortress of a home. And that was all before I got to the front door. I couldn't really blame him for going to these extremes. Some exceedingly dangerous creatures wanted him dead, or worse, entranced into a devoted slave.

I was shielding hard as I knocked on his heavy front door, though it was only a courtesy. I didn't want to give his neighbors anything to talk about. When people saw a battered woman, they tended to blame whatever man they saw her with. When he didn't bother to answer, I just used my key. "You're gonna have to try harder than that to get out of a workout, candy ass," I called out, entering his huge marble entryway. His house was decorated like a lush desert palace, all stone and marble, in desert hues of tan and brown. I made my way to the coat closet that housed his shoes.

A pair of hot pink, five inch stilettos were perched at the top of his shoe pile. He had the same house rule as us about shoes. No shoes past the entryway. I would actually have to remove my running shoes, carry them to his gym, then put them back on.

I tossed my gym bag into the closet, slamming it shut. Not this again, I thought.

I heard a shower running in the background and rolled my eyes. He'd better not make me wait while he messes around, I swore. But a riled up brunette strode into the entryway a moment later, giving me a 'go die in a fire' kind of look. She eyed me up in my workout getup. My black sports bra and matching skintight micro shorts weren't improving her mood. I gave her a friendly smile, though I was too irritated to really be feeling it. I was just trying to play nice, since this little scene wasn't her idea. Yep, that's me, Miss Congeniality. "Hi, I'm

Christian's personal trainer," I tried.

She wasn't having it. She curled her lip at me, planting her hands on her hips. "A personal trainer with a key?" Her tone was nasty. She was jealous. He'd probably kicked her out of bed when he heard the doorbell. He needed a talking to. This happened way too often. The irony was, I was the last person on earth she needed to worry about with Christian. The rest of the female population was a different story. The man was a slut.

I shrugged at her, my smile only slightly less friendly. "We're old friends. He's like the little brother I never wanted."

She just glared as she collected her shoes and bag, then gave me a considering look as she let herself out. Boy, was that routine getting old. I'd almost swear that Christian was using our training sessions to blow off his dates... I made a note to give him some hell about it.

I made my way to his impressive personal gym, and started warming up. My sessions with Christian were the only ones I actually looked forward to. No one else gave me a real workout.

I was abusing his punching bag when he finally joined me. I stopped working, giving him a nod. It was easy to see what had the ladies so jealous. He had unruly, shoulder-length, dirty blond hair. His eyes were a pale sky blue and always had a twinkle in them. His features were even and perfect. He was also well over six foot and built. He looked like a nordic god. Ironically, he looked like my favorite brother, Sven. Add to all of that his perfect white teeth, always shaping into a mischievous smile, and he was one hell of a catch. I could see all of the attraction. I just couldn't feel it. Not even a little bit. He had full brother vibe for me. He grinned at me. He pointed at my head. "Did you get a perm?"

I gave him a glare and tried to mean it. "Those little goodbye scenes are getting a little old for me."

He shrugged and smiled, looking far more harmless than he was. "Sorry 'bout that, but I've found that most women leave it alone once they take a look at you." His british accent was very faint after all of his years in America. It was just the slightest clip now.

"Pussy," I taunted him. "Just be honest with them."

The P-word made his eyes narrow. "I am, actually. I always have been. It doesn't seem to be enough anymore. Women are getting pushier and pushier. But I've found that seeing another woman, especially one that they don't think they can compete with, makes them back off, as a rule."

"So reject them, then demoralize them. That's heartwarming. Maybe you should just settle down. Then you wouldn't have to worry about so many of them," I told him, half-serious.

He raised his brows at me. "Relationship advice from the infamous Jillian?" he asked archly. It was a low blow, and we both knew it.

I gave him a roundhouse kick to the chest, and he went flying. Normally, he would have been back up in a second, but my flimsy glamour had dropped when I made contact, and he was busy studying my bruised up body. Shielding and glamour weren't my strengths, to be sure.

"What the bloody hell?" he finally asked, his accent more pronounced.

I shrugged at him. "I had a bad day yesterday."

"Anything you need help with?"

"I'll let you know."

"I'd love to see the other guy."

"You'd find yourself disappointed." I was vaguely embarrassed to admit it.

"Really." His voice was soft now. It was a deceptive tone. I saw the sudden glint of temper in his eyes. I had no trouble imagining what he wanted to do to 'the other guy.' "That sounds ominous. You really aren't going to tell me what happened?"

I shrugged and waved him up. "Maybe later. Right now, I'd rather beat you up some more."

He stood up, but hesitated. "You sure you're up to it? You must be in pretty bad shape if that hasn't healed."

"Actually, the bruising's not as painful as the spell I've put on myself to keep from healing," I admitted.

His brows disappeared under his unruly bangs. "This just gets more and more interesting. Is there something I can bribe you with to get you to spill the beans?"

"Maybe later. At the moment, I want you to quit slacking and fight."

He obliged me, taking me to the floor pretty easily. He probably had a good point. If I went down so easily, I probably shouldn't push it. But pushing myself physically had always helped with this pesky rage problem I had. It helped me to focus, and focusing kept it in check.

He was straddling my waist, holding my hands trapped tightly above my head. "You must be in bad shape, girl. I felt almost guilty taking you down -"

I bucked him off, freeing my right hand and landing a blow to his stomach that left him breathless. I rolled to my feet and waved him up.

We were well-matched in strength and speed. Our styles were even similar. Which was understandable, since I had been training him for years. I'd trained him to fight in the style I had been working on for centuries, that utilized the strength and speed of an immortal. Christian had always kept up remarkably well, all things considered. Of course, he wasn't human.

Christian descended from a long line of English dragonslayers. They were the only things on earth that could actually kill dragons. It made them targets to the monsters. Thus, Christian's paranoia. How crazy did you have to be to help train the only thing on earth that could kill you? Yeah, about that crazy. I was banking a whole hell of a lot on that old saying, 'The enemy of my enemy is my friend.'

CHAPTER FIVE

Touché

For better or worse, the only thing more rare than dragonslayers were dragons themselves, so Christian found himself raised in a time where his very specialized skills were nearly obsolete. He still carried around his neck the family weapon that was named appropriately, Dragonsbane. At the moment it looked like a tiny but intricate knife. But in his hands it could take any shape he required. I'd tried for years to get the details of what power a slayer held over dragons, and what power the blade specifically held, but he kept his ancestor's secrets hidden well for the most part. Once he'd gotten drunk and told me that all of the mountains in the world were just sleeping dragons. That's when I'd known that a drunk Christian was no place to get information.

Dragonslayers themselves, though long lived, were not immortal. A five hundred year lifespan isn't a bad deal either, though. And if they could get their hands on some dragon's blood to drink, the possibilities were endless.

Christian himself was a young slayer. We'd never talked about it, but I didn't think he was older than his forties. He didn't look it, of course. He knew I was older than him, but the actual truth would have shocked him. He had always assumed Lynn and I were exceptionally powerful fire sorcerers. I encouraged the assumption. Some secrets are best kept even from the closest of friends. Our friendship with Christian, for obvious reasons, unquestionably required it.

We began to fight in earnest. I did pretty well, all things considered, but I could tell he was taking it easy on me.

"You know, you can hardly complain," he panted at me. He was across the room, since I had thrown him there. "If we were to compare notes on who has taken more shit from the other's love life, I'm well ahead of you, dear." He gave me a half smile to soften the blow, but it still landed solidly.

"Touché," I said softly, stung. It was very true. When I had left Dom seven years ago, Christian had been tortured for information. He hadn't revealed one thing to them, and he'd known plenty. "I did tell you to lay low for awhile." I tried to sound lighthearted, but didn't manage. I knew Christian was long over it, but I wasn't.

He shrugged. "I'm not scared of the druids. Actually, the bastards had the nerve to contact me recently."

His revelation surprised me enough to get me pinned face first to the ground while my mind worked the ramifications out. "When was that?" I panted.

"A few weeks ago. I guess they suspect that the necros have recruited a few new created Others to their cause. Same old shit that's been going on forever." I struggled hard, but couldn't budge him. He continued talking, as though he didn't even notice my struggles. "That age-old debate between the Born and the Created. Sounds as if hostilities have escalated, though. Druids are putting together a team to move in on one of the necro settlements, fry up some of their half-dead asses. They're gonna make an example. They wanted to know if I wanted in on the action. Cheeky blokes. They thought I'd be tempted by the carnage of an all out brawl."

"Does kind of sound like a good time." Panting, I finally threw him off.

"Yeah, I thought so. I agreed to help them," he said, shocking me and effectively ending our session.

"Ok, lift more weights after I leave, candy ass. Training's over for today."

I made our usual after workout shakes. He didn't notice when I put a drop of my blood into his glass. How crazy do you have to be to feed your blood to the only thing on earth that can kill you, in order to prolong its life, and make it stronger? Yeah, about that crazy.

I brought two glasses to the table, handing him one. I went to grab some napkins, and as I turned back, I would have sworn he was checking out my ass. "Were you just checking out my ass?" I was a little baffled that I even had to ask.

"Yes." He took a drink of my less than tasty concoction.

I wrinkled my nose at him. "Why?"

His eyes were pointing at my chest now. "It still just baffles me, even after all these years. Looks-wise, you're my ideal."

"Me and every other woman in the state," I agreed dryly.

He shrugged. "But there is no attraction. Zero. I guess I'll just never understand it. There are women I know, that I can't stand to talk to, that aren't half as good-looking as you, and I'd still screw 'em. What the bloody hell? You know, it would be convenient, if we could like each other like that. They say good friends make the best lovers."

I burst out laughing, and couldn't stop for a solid five minutes. He looked insulted, but eventually started grinning. "Just think of us as blood relations," I explained to him. There was, of course, a very logical answer to the question he was asking, but I'd never be the one to tell him what it was. Not willingly. "Or a cat and a dog. It just ain't right, so leave it at that."

His sardonic look told me from experience that he was agreeing with me. "Fine. So tell me who worked you over?"

I groaned. "It's a mess."

"Tell me."

"Mav and Michael did it. Some witch-hag turned us in for a reward to the druids. She told them about our shop. Those two showed up, as shocked to see me as I was to see them. I let them work me over."

He looked about as surprised as I'd ever seen him. "The bastards actually fell for that?" he sputtered, half choking back a laugh. It never took Christian long to figure out a punch line. Well…almost never. "My god, Dom is gonna kill them if he finds out. And they'll deserve it, for being such idiots."

I gave him a half-smile. "They were never the brains of the operation. But yeah, things have gotten messy, so I bought us a little time. Time will tell if it was worth the blow to my pride. Something is going on with Lynn, too. Not sure what, though. She had a shiner this morning."

"Sounds like you guys need a safe house. I have a few around town. All that is mine is at your disposal."

I inclined my head in thanks. "I'll let you know if we do. Gonna play it by ear. Everything might turn out fine."

"Oh, shit! I almost forgot to tell you. Since we're on the subject of strange happenings. My sources tell me that the druid Council is negotiating a meeting with the dragons. And it's here! In bloody Las Vegas!" His eyes were shinning with anticipation as he spoke. This was about as excited as I'd ever seen him. "Gives me a slayer hard-on, to tell you the truth. I'm half-tempted to ambush one of them. Though it's an interesting move, considering the druids were just asking me for help, don't you think? Not sure I can be in the same city with a dragon without letting my instincts take over." He was grinning, and he did *not* look harmless now.

I grinned back at him. He didn't notice my hands trembled slightly as I set down my glass. "I'm sure you can contain yourself. But it is interesting timing, to say the least. I wonder if they are trying to ally themselves with the druids."

"I'm not too worried about that. Dragons are a savage, violent lot. They think they're gods, above all laws. And druids live and breath to keep the peace. Those monsters won't respect druid law. They may want something from the druids, but mark my words, they won't hold up their end of the bargain."

"I've heard that about them."

"Oh, yeah. As an extra precaution for their visit to town, I had a friend of mine install a new toy he's been working on. You probably didn't notice it, but as you step through the front door, you get scanned now." He smiled smugly, very pleased with himself.

"Scanned for what?" I raised a brow, sipping my wheat-grass concoction.

"It's a dragon detector." I nearly choked on my drink. "It scans anyone who walks through the door. If a dragon ever tries to come in, it'll alert me with a siren that will bring the house down, and set off a very impressive caging mechanism." He sighed heavily. "Wishful thinking really, one of them coming to me. But a man can dream."

My eyes were saucers as I spoke. "Sounds pretty dubious to me. I think you should get your money back."

He looked crestfallen. "Yeah?"

I nodded. "Sounds like you need a bullshit detector more than a dragon detector to me."

He smiled sardonically. "Well, I didn't say he was a *good* friend. C'est la vie, right?"

"So when does the necro roast happen? And how can I get in on it?" I changed the subject to something we would both undoubtedly enjoy more.

"Man! I wish you could. They haven't given me a time. Everything is still up in the air, I think." He gave me a serious look. "You gonna pay Dom a visit? I bet if you ask him nicely, he'll keep you off those rosters."

I cringed, and ran a hand down my face. "I don't know. It's a bad idea, for all kinds of reasons, but it's starting to look like a lesser evil."

He whistled softly. "What I'd pay to be a fly on that wall."

I felt sick to my stomach at even the thought of that meeting. I couldn't decide whether to put it off or just get it over with. For today, at least, I was definitely putting it off. On the other hand, I was gonna be bruised up and crippled until then.

I suddenly noticed the time on the microwave clock across the room. "Ack, I'm gonna be late for my other client." I got up and went to gather my things. Christian walked me to the door, saying, "Call me if you need anything. Sounds like you might."

"I'll do that. Oh, Lynn told me to say hi."

"Hi."

"You guys meeting for lunch this week?"

"Maybe. Probably," he said cryptically.

"Ok, then, I will maybe probably join you. We won't be working the shop for awhile, so my schedule is suddenly wide open." I shielded up, stuck my tongue out at him, and walked out the door.

CHAPTER SIX

Geas

My next appointment was in Summerlin, which was easily a forty-five minute drive away. I had twenty-five to get there. I liked to be punctual, so the entire drive was a teeth-gnashing affair.

This client was also one of the few that I enjoyed training, though she and Christian couldn't be more dissimilar.

She was a stay-at-home mom in her forties who had a compulsive eating problem. Her rich husband had left her for an eighteen-year-old several years ago, and she had proceeded to eat her way to over four hundred pounds.

At the start of our sessions a few years ago, I had started her out with the conventional methods of weight loss. I had soon learned that her need to eat when she got emotional far outweighed any discipline she may have possessed.

She was a sweet woman, and I grew to like her quickly, so it wasn't long before I resorted to a more unconventional approach. I put a very minor enchantment on her. It wasn't much, really. But every time she reached for food for any reason but simple hunger, she felt a sudden and overwhelming urge to go outside and play soccer with her kids. I had to tweak the enchantment slightly, when I realized she was dragging her two boys out of bed at three a.m to play outside. After that, though, it worked like the charm that it was.

Under my very specialized training regime, Sharon had lost over two hundred and fifty pounds and was approaching the best shape of her life.

I was only five minutes late to her house, but no one answered my first couple of rings. I was considering leaving, assuming she'd forgotten the appointment, when a harried looking Sharon answered the door. She didn't look at me once as she ushered me in. I thought that was a little odd, but I followed her to her home gym.

I set her to work warming up, and she followed my orders. She still hadn't said a word. "Everything all right?" I finally asked her. She was stretching, and I automatically corrected her posture.

She hunched her shoulders in a shrug. "Yeah, just had a bad morning."

As the workout progressed, her mood didn't change. She seemed preoccupied, almost frightened. The warning signs were all there, but I didn't see the trap I'd sprung until four druids walked through the door.

"Jillian." Collin inclined his head to me as he entered the room. Three druids I didn't know flanked him. "I had a hunch it would be you." Collin was my infamous Ex's cousin, and one of his closest friends. He was also one of the few druids I had been on friendlier terms with before the big falling out. He had the raven black hair and striking blue eyes that were prominent in his family. He also had the classically handsome, aristocratic features that were common to his bloodline. And he was tall, as most druids were, towering well over six feet. His build, however, was unusual in that he was almost too slender, a trait that the other men in his family did not share. His brother, Cam, was one of the biggest men I knew, with forearms easily the size of my waist. Dom fell somewhere in the middle, build-wise, but I thought he was closer to Cam's bulky physique than Collin's almost frail one. Collin's posture, however, was proud and elegant, which reminded me rather painfully of Dom.

"Sharon, out," one of the druids ordered. He was a sandy haired brute that I didn't recognize. She didn't look at me once as she jogged from the room. I felt the familiar and bitter sting of betrayal.

I had been going over Sharon's food journal and had it clutched in my hand. I set it down slowly, tensing for a fight.

"I have to admit," I began, "I wasn't expecting to see more of you again so soon."

Collin froze, looking more than a little surprised. "More of us?" he asked, his tone deceptively casual. "You'll have to tell me all about that. Who else have you seen?"

"Why are you here?" I shot back.

He spread his slender hands in a gesture of peace. "Not for the reason you seem to think. I just want to talk."

I looked at him warily. "How'd you find me here?"

He waved a hand at the druid that had ordered Sharon out. "Walt here has been dating Sharon for the last few months. He noticed that she had an enchantment placed on her. He came to me for help to decipher just what it was. When I perceived the nature of the enchantment, I asked her to describe her personal trainer. The description sounded uncannily familiar." Apparently our luck had run out a few times over.

Collin continued. "I couldn't let an unregistered Other go unchecked. So here we are. How have you been, Jillian?" He sounded genuinely interested in the answer. Collin had always been one of the more amiable, easygoing druids. His affable manner had always made him a sharp contrast to his cousin, Dom, and especially his own brother, Cam. I supposed I was lucky it was Collin, and not Cam, who I was facing now. Collin, unlike the three men behind him, who were looking at me with loathing, seemed to wish me no ill will. Of course, I wouldn't count on that. "Why don't we go have a seat in the other room and talk?" he asked.

I nodded agreement. "You first." I followed them into the somewhat gaudy dining room. Sharon had a Vegas sense of style when it came to decorating her house, with way too much marble and gold for my taste.

I sat across from Collin at Sharon's glass dining room table. I made a big stink when Walt tried to stand behind me, and they agreed to stay on their side of the room. Call me paranoid. Period. I'm paranoid, but with good reason. Of course, that's what all the paranoid people say.

"I can't keep this from Dom," Collin began. It wasn't a promising start to the conversation. "But I feel that it would be better, for everyone involved, if you pay him a visit yourself."

"Sure, I'll do that," I said quickly.

He gave me a stern look. "You know I'm going to need more insurance than that. I can't let you leave here without a guarantee of some kind that you plan to either register with us now, or go talk to the Arch."

I sighed. I couldn't get a break from anyone, it seemed. "What kind of insurance did you have in mind?"

He pulled a bracelet of bones out of his pocket. I recognized the item, and gave him an unfriendly look. "So I'm a prisoner."

"I can set it for twenty-four hours. If you speak to Dom in that time, the geas will disappear."

"I need at least two days."

"Fine. Two days, then. But how about this. If you see him within twenty-four hours, I'll let you in on one of the biggest battles we've planned in decades. We're mounting a raid on one of the necro settlements. They took out a rather large human town a few weeks ago. We obviously need to remind them what it means to break druid law. It's gonna be a big one."

"How 'bout this? You give me two days and let me in on it

regardless. And I'll let you put that thing on my wrist without killing any of you."

His handsome face split into a grin thick with charm. "Deal. I have to say, it's good to see you, Jillian. You haven't changed a bit."

I looked at him a little warily. "How is he?" I asked seriously. My question made the other druids shift with agitation and hostility. I *really* didn't have the right to ask.

He had no doubt, of course, which *he* I meant. His mouth tightened, all good humor leaving his face. "He's powerful. After you left, he reached his potential and it was even more than any of us bargained for. Killing Declan promoted him younger than any Arch in remembrance. My father couldn't have been more pleased if it was his own son."

"Is he happy?" My voice was more fragile than I preferred.

He shrugged. "He's busy. He's not as angry as he used to be, but I worry he's just pushed all of that rage below the surface. He dates a new girl every night." I tried not to wince visibly. "Though he's been seeing Siobhan again." I don't think I hid the wince very well for that one. "No, I can't say he's happy, but who is?"

Well, that was a depressing question that I certainly didn't have an answer for.

I stuck my wrist out grudgingly. "Get it over with. I hate those things."

Collin chanted a surprisingly quick spell on the geas, then attached it to my wrist with the utmost courtesy not to lay so much as a finger on me. I appreciated his good manners. Politesse with an outsider was not a common druid trait.

The druids finally let me leave, and I beat it fast. Two days. So short a time before I had to face the man who's memory I'd been running from for seven years.

CHAPTER SEVEN

Emo Prom

DAY 3

I awoke to the smell of burning bed again, and started cursing before my eyes had opened. I had relocated to one of our guest rooms, on account of the bed I'd burned to cinders the night before.

I was relieved to find the damage was minimal when I examined the bed. I might even be able to sleep on it again. Maybe. Yippee. My bed burning rate wasn't quite one a night.

I just stared at my reflection this time. There were no loud outbursts, I swear. The good news? It was straight and smooth like it was supposed to be. The bad news? It was a pale but vibrant purple. Violet? Lavender? I glared at my reflection and decided to just ignore the color until it went away, like the damned curls had.

I showered and dressed, trying to ignore the geas around my wrist. I strode downstairs with a bad attitude. Lynn and her entourage were having some sort of gathering in the living room. I was torn between curiosity (Lynn always kept things interesting) and a desire to avoid having to socialize in any way. I ate some of their party food before giving in to the curiosity.

"A party at ten in the morning?" I asked as I leaned into the doorway. A few dozen goths lounged in various stages of emo around the room. Lynn was in rare form today. She was reclining on a large, intricately carved, high-backed silver chair. Or rather, a throne. I'd never seen it before. When had Lynn picked up a throne? Gods only knew. "Some of you kiddos must have very early curfews indeed."

"*Madame Noir* does not accept anyone under eighteen into her following," one sniffed at me disdainfully.

"None of us have curfews," another cried out.

"*Madame Noir*?" I looked in Lynn's direction. She was decked out in full-on, black latex, dominatrix gear. "You're french now?"

She nodded slightly, smiling just a little. "*Oui.* I was just telling my *Adeptes* about the *horeur. Pardon,* in english you say the french revolution. I was just telling them how my whole family went to the guillotine. When did you dye your hair cotton candy purple, *ma soeur*?"

"Don't change the subject. Wow. Your *whole* family, huh?" I raised a brow at her ruefully. "I thought you were a viking." Everyone in the room was glaring at me. Except for Lynn, of course. I was more than half convinced that she pulled this shit just to make me laugh.

"Oh, *oui*, I was a Viking before I was French," she said, as though she'd forgotten. And as though it was perfectly natural to switch your nationality. "Memory can be a tricky thing, as the centuries pass you by."

"Amen, sista." Her last statement was actually pretty true, though I knew very well that she hadn't forgotten that she had never been even a little french. Sure, she'd spent some time there, but certainly not during the revolution.

I was starting to notice that everyone in the room was a little more decked out than normal, even for them. "What's the occasion? Did I miss my invitation to emo prom or something?"

Lynn choked on a laugh. "The Renaissance Fair is in town," Lynn explained. "We're setting up a tent there. It's nice, on occasion, to visit reminders of the past."

"Ohh, that. Hmm, I might have to give Christian a call, so that we can come laugh at you. How long will you be there, O' Mistress of Black Eyeliner?"

"All day. We'll be set up somewhere in the fortune-teller court. Big black tent. So what's with the lavender hair?"

"Awesome," I said with a grin, completely ignoring her question about my hair. "I wouldn't miss it."

"Did you lose a bet?" she tried.

I sighed. "A bet with god maybe. I don't wanna talk about it."

"Is there something I can bribe you with to make you talk?"

I thought about it. I was always at least a little susceptible to bribery. Especially if it was jewels. Or any kind of treasure, really. Of course I loved to hoard treasure. Name me a dragon who didn't. My kind were somewhat famous for it. There was always some truth to every legend, and that particular legend was *all* truth. "I'll let you know if I think of anything." I started to walk away, then remembered. Shit on shingles, I'd almost forgotten. I raised my wrist, showing her the geas there. She raised a brow at me in question. "I ran into Collin yesterday, and ended up with this thing on my wrist."

She rose. All of her flunkies rose with her. I rolled my eyes as she waved them back down. "We need privacy, in the kitchen." She swept from the room, and I followed her.

I told her the short version, then she got me to spill the long version, which wasn't much different. She, in turn, told me about her more than interesting last few days. Our most dangerous ally, Caleb, had come to town, with tales of some major shit about to go down. And she had met a guy, a mysterious guy, who had placed some kind of enchantment on her. A love enchantment, she thought. I didn't like that, especially considering the timing. I told her so. She was equally disgruntled by the entire affair.

"Well, shit. If Caleb's in town, it's bad. He only shows up for the really nasty stuff." I let loose a fluent stream of cursing.

"We need to move?" she asked, after I'd finished.

I shrugged. "I'm not sure. The geas pretty much means I'm screwed, but I have a plan. Kinda."

"Kinda?"

"Yes, I have a plan, kinda-ish."

"Ish?"

"Ish. Worst-case scenario, I'll have to go see Dom. But I should have it under control. Ish."

"Your confidence is inspiring-ish."

"I do need a favor though."

"Sure, what?"

"You know how crappy I am at shielding. Can you do something for me, to cover the bruises? Just for a day or two."

She nodded, pulling a small relic from around her neck, and placing her hand on my forehead. She chanted for a bit, paused to ask, "You don't want to heal at all?"

I grimaced. "Maybe a touch. I need it to look *bad*, though, under the glamour," I explained, and she continued.

She paused, studying her work. I knew from experience that it would be perfect. Shielding and glamour were her specialties. And my weakness. Our magics had some similarities, but more differences. Hers was subtle and powerful. And very dangerous to find yourself on the wrong end of. She was a master of illusion and subterfuge. You'd never see her coming. Me, on the other hand, *not* so subtle. I was more likely to blow the door up on my way in. Oh, and I'd probably blow the roof off on my way out. "So is that why your hair's been wigging out? The strain of shielding?"

"That's as good a guess as any," I lied. Those problems had been going on since long before I'd been shielding. But I didn't want to worry her. Now was not the time.

She studied me, looking worried. "You sure you got this under control?"

I shrugged. "Ish?"

We grinned at each other. "You take care," she said quietly, as I walked her back to her undead ball. I waved at the room full of sullen faces. "Have fun at the fair, Conformists. Take care, Mistress Emo." I took off before they could respond. I could have sworn that I heard one of them putting a curse on me as I walked away.

CHAPTER EIGHT

Renaissance Fair

As it turned out, Christian was available, so we went to the Renaissance Fair together. He picked me up at the house, tossing me a pink t-shirt when I opened the door. I curled my lip at him. "Huh?"

He grinned, shrugging. "I had it made after last year's fair. I thought it would be cute. Nice hair, by the way, Barney."

"Thanks, candy ass. So, what are you gonna give me to wear this?"

"Look at it before you reject it out of hand."

I unfolded it. I couldn't keep an embarrassingly girlish giggle from escaping my lips. It had black lettering above an obnoxious cartoon. It looked like a blond, shirtless, anime version of Christian. The lettering read, "Dragonslayers have giant swords."

"No way." I threw it at him. He flipped it, showing me the back. It read "Dragonslayers do it dragon style."

I raised a brow at him. "You must have some present for me, if you think you can bribe me into wearing that."

He bent down, flipping up his pant leg. He unlatched an extremely badass looking ankle sheath. "It's been blessed by a holy druid. It grows hot against your skin when evil draws near.

And the knife hilt is studded with rubies. I know how you and Lynn like your jewels."

I took it from him, studying it closely. It was beautifully made, and I did love gems. "I've been called evil myself, but it's not hot against my skin now."

"Rather, someone that means to do evil to you." He flipped open his button up shirt. Underneath, he wore his own pink T-shirt. Hot pink. He was secure, I supposed. It had the same cartoon as mine, but his had a hot blond anime chick kneeling at his feet. *Me?* I threw up a little in my throat. It read, 'Level 140 Dragonslayer = Hot Chick Magnet.' I looked from his shirt to the knife. I really, really liked the knife. I had a weakness for ankle sheaths and he knew it. I already had a small gun strapped to the inside of my left ankle. My jeans hid it completely, as they would this knife. "I bet you got that knife at the same time you got those T-shirts made. You've been planning this for a year?"

He nodded, grinning. He knew I couldn't resist the treasure. Which was more than a little alarming, if I thought about it.

I grabbed the shirt out of his hands, glaring at him. I whipped off my navy T-shirt, right in front of him. I wasn't, by nature, immodest. I just couldn't have cared less if Christian saw me in my bra. I pulled the pink shirt over my chest with difficulty. "You get me kid-sized?" I grouched, as I struggled into the shirt.

He nodded. He had no shame. "That I did."

I finally got it on. It didn't even cover my belly button. I felt ridiculous, but I held out my hand for the knife. "I like the video game reference. Level 140, huh? Nerd."

He shrugged. "I'm a renaissance man. Nerd is a title people wear proudly these days. You can't deny you've clocked in a little MMO time yourself." He stuck his tongue out at me.

I sucker punched him in the stomach as I walked by. He grunted, winded. "Let's go, candy ass," I ordered.

The Renaissance Fair took up all of Sunset park this year. It had grown significantly since the last time we'd been. I swear it got a little freakier every year, too. I wasn't exactly into the fair, but I liked to come and laugh at it, and people watch, of course. A lot of the antics going on were just good comedy. I understood a lot of the 'authentic' costumes so many of the ren enthusiasts were wearing. But just as many of the costumes made no sense to me. Like why was there a flock of kids dressed up for Hogwarts? And why were random people in the crowd dressed up like superheroes? And what was with the fat dude dressed up like a hostess cupcake? And why the hell was Lynn dressed as a dominatrix? I'd have to ask her, if we found her tent in the huge gathering.

We didn't get far into the fair before Christian was drawn to some concession stand. I sat down at a picnic table to people watch while he waited in line. He came back with some kind of deep fried confection I'd never seen before. "What is that?" I asked, wrinkling my nose in distaste.

"Guess."

"Donut poop?"

"Deep fried twinkie. Mmmmmmm."

"That's disgusting. Who the hell even thought of that?"

He shrugged. "Iyonno," he said around a mouthful of food. "Try some."

I shook my head. "Uh-uh. If I'm gonna eat something that wrong, it's at least gonna be frosted or dipped in chocolate. Seriously, though, I want to know who was eating a twinkie and thought, 'Hmm, this thing needs to be more fattening?'"

"There's frosting on the inside."

"It's not the same."

He finished off the half dozen pastries, looking around for something. "Now I want a couple of those giant turkey legs. Usually they sell those all over the place. Where are they?" he wondered out loud.

I rolled my eyes at him. "You have a tape worm or

something?"

He grinned. "Or something. I'm always this hungry."

"Boys are weird."

He stuck his tongue out at me, standing up. "Let's go find more food," he said, sounding like a teenage boy. He pulled me after him. I dragged my feet, but followed along.

"Who comes to the ren fair just to eat?" I complained.

"Us. Duh."

"You, maybe. I came to make fun of Lynn and her tent full of emos. I think one of them was trying to curse me when I left the living room this morning. They are so damn easy to rile up."

"Oh, we'll do that, too. But we have all day to find them."

Christian found his turkey legs, eating slowly this time. We were silent for awhile, watching the festivities around us. A group of tight-clad boys walked by, and I nodded towards them. "What would I have to do to make you wear tights next year?"

He smiled around his mouthful of turkey. "Blow me?"

"Iiick. Thanks a lot. I just puked in my mouth."

"Anytime. I don't do tights."

"Everyone has a price." As I spoke, I felt eyes on me. Not your typical 'checking me out' eyes. Or people watching stares. Someone was watching us very intently. I found the man quickly. That was using the term man loosely. He was very tall, with beautiful, long black hair. He was of some kind of Asian descent. I couldn't have said what, but he was very pretty. He sat at a table about fifty yards away, arms folded, as he stared, an unreadable look on his face. As though he had been waiting for me to spot him, he started walking towards me almost as soon as I found him. "You know this guy?" I murmured to Christian, as the man drew close.

Christian turned, his gaze turning cold as the the man approached.

He was taller than I'd realized as he loomed over our sitting positions. He didn't sit. I just stared up at him, raising a brow.

"You two are friends?" he asked, genuine surprise in his voice.

"Do I know you?" I asked.

"Do we know you?" Christian spoke at the same time.

"No. I just find it very strange that you two are acting as though you're friendly with each other."

I gave him a flat stare. Christian told him what he could do with himself.

The man just stared at him calmly. "This is very peculiar and disturbing." He looked at me as he spoke. "What are you doing with him?" he asked me directly.

"Who the fuck are you?" Christian stood up as he spoke. He wasn't as tall as the stranger, but he put in a good showing.

The man eyed him coldly. "You don't know what I am?" he asked softly.

"How would I know what you are? I don't even know who you fucking are!" Christian looked about one second from punching the stranger, so I grabbed his right arm, pulling him away. Christian didn't seem to understand what the strange man was, but I was starting to get a very bad feeling that I did know. This was turning into one bad week.

The man bowed slightly, mockingly. "Interesting," he said, more to himself, I thought. He nodded at us. "Nice T-shirts." He almost smirked. He melded with disturbing ease and speed into the crowd.

"I don't like that guy," Christian muttered.

I smiled grimly. "That doesn't surprise me. Let's go find Lynn."

We covered about half of the fair before we got distracted by food again. It was ice cream this time, and I indulged. "I was surprised to find you off of work today." I made conversation as we giggled at some of the random fair enthusiasts walking by. The pirates were in rare form this year.

"Oh, that. I may have a lot of days off coming up, actually."

"How so?"

"I've been given an extended leave of absence."

I raised my brows at him. "What did you do?"

He smiled ruefully. "Apparently there's a pretty long list."

"Enlighten me."

"Hmmm, I already forget a lot of it. I recall something about collateral damage being mentioned. Willful destruction of property, maybe? The term trigger happy was thrown around a lot. Very very trigger happy was mentioned once or twice. Carrying illegally enhanced weapons on the job? Carrying several illegally enhanced weapons, even. Apparently when enforcing the law, they expect you to abide by it. What the bloody hell is with that?"

My eyes widened. Someone had been misbehaving. Which didn't really surprise me. I was more surprised that he'd allowed himself to get in trouble for it. "How long of a leave are we talking?"

He shrugged. "Forever?"

"Wow. What are you gonna do?"

He shrugged, not looking at all concerned. "Play around for a few months. After I get bored, I was thinking fireman. Maybe. Who wouldn't love a flame-retardant fireman?" I laughed. He really was flame-retardant. What else could he be when he existed to fight dragons? He needed a few tricks up his sleeve for such deadly creatures.

"Well, at least I'll always have some good connections on the force," he said, sighing. Law enforcement was a popular vocation for druids. Christian got all of his inside information on the Other community from some druids he had become close friends with on the force over the years. He, like myself, didn't hate all druids. Just the vast majority of them.

"Now that we're done talking about my jobless self, would you like to tell me about that thing on your wrist?" Christian asked, his tone concerned. I'd had little hope that he wouldn't notice the geas.

I sighed, shaking the thing like I might get lucky and just make it fall off. "It's a mess, of course. Collin found me yesterday. I'm supposed to go see Dom soon."

Christian whistled softly. "Found twice in two days. Looks like your luck has run out, girl. How can I help?"

I grimaced. "I'll let you know. I think I have it under control, though, for now. I have an idea. I may have a way around this geas."

He cringed comically. "Famous last words. Don't hesitate to call me in on the fiasco, whatever it is, I beg you."

I wished I could argue with him that my idea wasn't a fiasco, but he wasn't wrong. Trying to get out of a geas was only the act of a desperate person. Still, I had to try…

"I'll let you know," I assured him.

CHAPTER NINE

Mistress Jillian

Lynn's pitch-black tent stood out like a sore thumb amidst the other pastel ones. A long line stretched out from the gothic, fortune-telling attraction. We waited in line gamely, trying to overhear any gossip about what was going on inside. Only one person was being admitted at a time. At this rate, we'd be here for hours. We killed time by thinking up pranks to pull on Lynn and her followers. When we got bored with that, we just bypassed the line, ignoring the jeers from the crowd.

We loomed over the skinny black-haired boy guarding the door. He looked up at us, wearing the perpetually tormented look on his face that Lynn's emos favored, the one that always made me laugh. "We're here to see your mistress," Christian told him after he'd stared him down for a good minute.

The boy shook his head firmly. "Mistress Noir is only admitting one truth-seeker at a time."

I smirked at him. "We aren't seeking the truth. Move aside, son."

He pursed his lips at me. "Are you acquainted with the mistress?"

Christian and I nodded. "Tell her Christian and Jillian are here." He disappeared inside the tent for a moment. He came back out, waving us in. "She will deign to see you," he sniffed. Christian messed up his stiffly coifed hair as he walked by. The boy gasped in outrage. "Good boy," Christian told him as we walked inside.

The inside of the tent was, of course, as black as the outside. It was broken up into sections by thick black curtains. The first room was, predictably, the fortune-tellers room. Complete with cheesy crystal ball. A young goth waited behind the ball, face aged with bad make-up effects. An old/young goth/gypsy? Whatever. We passed by her, entering the next curtained area. This room was much bigger, and obviously where the real party was going on. Lynn held court at the back of the room, dressed as a pirate now. I nodded in her direction, but quickly got distracted by the tableau being acted out in the opposite corner of the room.

A tiny dominatrix was putting on quite a show for the room. She couldn't be more than five feet tall, with curly black hair down to her waist. She had the perfect face of a doll. It's expression, however, was far from doll-like. She wore a savage look as she glared down at her feet. Her five inch stilettos looked razor sharp, and were currently digging into the prone back of a man easily twice her size. He was moaning pitiably. "You ask permission to speak, worm!" she was barking at him as we entered the room. She used her whip on him with every word she spoke. She didn't even look up as we entered.

"Yes, Mistress Devour," the poor, submissive man moaned. His back was bloody.

I glanced back in Lynn's direction briefly. "That's fucked up," I told her. She smirked at me.

I wasn't ignorant about such things. I'd been hanging around Lynn long enough to see my fair share of it. But I didn't like the look of this little spectacle.

I approached the kinky couple, kneeling down beside the bound man. He lifted his head the barest amount. His long, curly, auburn hair nearly covered his eyes. I brushed it away with one fingertip. His dark blue eyes met mine reluctantly. I was sure eye contact wasn't something his vicious lover encouraged. I could tell with one look that he was truly submissive. "You ok?" I asked him directly. "You're consenting to this?"

"Yes." His hoarse voice was soft. Mistress Devour started whipping him in earnest. "I didn't give you permission to speak!" she screeched. Her voice sounded petulant and childlike. I grabbed her whip easily with one hand, not taking my eyes off of her tortured lover.

"What's your name?" I asked him.

"Luke."

"Well, Luke, my name is Jillian. Your friend here is a little overzealous. If she ever gets to be too much for you, let me know if you need a hand getting loose."   He could always overpower her physically, so that wasn't really what I was worried about. But a bound sub with little to no boundaries in the hands of the wrong dominant could always use a friend. He nodded slightly, lowering his gaze.

Mistress Devour looked ready to throw an outright tantrum. I hesitated, not really wanting to hand her back her whip.

"He'll speak when I say he can speak!" she spat, glaring at me. *Oh great*. I'd probably just brought out her possessive side. She stomped her razor heals repeatedly into his back. "You're little blond can't save you from me!" she was yelling at him. Had she really just called me little? I was easily a foot taller than the little termagant. I stifled a laugh. She continued, "If you speak to her again, I'll wipe the floor with her ass, then beat you both. Is that what you want?"

A few laughs were stifled around the room at that boast. I didn't bother stifling mine, laughing outright. Her murderous glance shot back to me. "You're laughing? You won't be laughing when I scratch up that pretty face!"

I laughed harder.

She flew at me, claws outstretched for a classic girl fight. I had both of her hands behind her back before she could touch me. She didn't even know how to fight. I couldn't stop laughing for a few minutes as she spat curses at me. I could hear both Christian and Lynn, giggling like children, as she went on and on.

Finally, I shook her slightly, saying, "Shut it," in the most serious voice I could muster. "You really don't want to try to attack me like that again. Ever. Next time, I won't just restrain you. This is the only warning you're ever going to get. Oh, and lay off of Luke when I'm near, or you'll regret it." I finally let her go. She was smarter than I'd guessed. She merely stormed out of the tent.

"Thank you, Mistress." Luke's voice was muffled, his face in the floor. I realized he was talking to me.

"No problem. Call me Jillian. You want to be untied or anything?"

"No, Mistress Jillian."

I rolled my eyes. Christian and Lynn started laughing harder. I hadn't seen Christian move, but he was lounging beside Lynn now. I noticed, for the first time since entering the tent, another familiar face lurking in the corner near Lynn. I nodded to Caleb. Even his usually stoic face was split in a grin. He nodded back.

We went way back with Caleb, far enough back that he must have started to seriously suspect what we were. At the moment, he was a nondescript man with a cleanly shaven head, unremarkable features, and an average, if hard, build. And the coldest, blankest brown eyes I had ever seen. It was his favorite form. His 'blend in with the scenery' form. But he could shed it in minutes and take on another. I didn't know the limits to the forms he could take. It wasn't the sort of information he would ever volunteer.

Caleb was a Mimic. The only one of his kind that I had ever met. He was the perfect killer. And, many times for us, the perfect backup. If shit was going down, we called Caleb, and he showed up to join the violence. He claimed that no one could find a good, solid battle like Lynn and I. He may have had a point, but it wasn't something we were pleased about.

We always knew what we were getting when we called Caleb. He was a calm, emotionless, uncontrollable killer. We only called him when things got real bad. Which, sadly, meant we had called him enough that he was a fairly solid part of our lives now. We'd gotten so chummy with the sociopath over the years that he just popped in for coffee sometimes. Rather often lately, actually. It was a little scary... If you started spending enough time around the real, stone-cold killers, you could get too comfortable and let your guard down. That would never do with someone like Caleb.

"I love the T-shirts, by the way," Lynn chortled.

"Bite me, Captain Hook," I told her.

Christian was studying me, a strange look suddenly coming over his face.

"What?" I asked, eyes narrowed.

"Your hair's not purple anymore. What's the deal?"

"She doesn't want to talk about it," Lynn said, laughter still in her voice.

"That's right."

Christian shrugged. "Whatever. It works better with the T-shirt this way anyways. You don't look so much like an easter egg now."

I started to respond when I felt a burst of energy behind me. I turned, backing into the tent wall. Four men burst into the room.

They walked in with an air of authority that meant they were either cops, or druids. I was willing to bet druid by the crisp dark gray suits, and the burst of energy that hovered around them like a mist. I didn't recognize any of them, which was a definite plus.

They barely glanced my way as they studied the dozens of people lounging around the room. The apparent leader of the four stepped forward. He had brown hair and eyes, a hard face, and the tall, brutish build that many of the druids shared. He was also the biggest in the group of men, though not a one of them could be considered small.

"We're looking for the ones that call themselves Solace and Dustin."

Lynn merely raised a brow at him, not bothering to even sit up. "And who are you?"

"We'll be asking all the questions here," another, auburn haired Druid told her sternly. The second-in-command of the task force, I assumed. Druids were big on rank. Even with just four of them, they would have a clear chain of command.

"Why's that?" she asked.

"That sounded like another question," Christian piped in, helpful as always.

"Solace, and Dustin. Tell us where they are."

"Who?" she asked.

"Are you saying you don't know them?" This question came from another druid of the group. Number three was the shortest of the group, but built like a truck.

"Huh?" she asked, mocking them obviously enough that even they noticed.

"Lady, you really don't want to mess with us. If you know something, you'd best tell us now," number one growled.

She shrugged. I could tell she was already bored with the intruders. "I might know a few by that name. Your turn."

"We've heard some charges against them from some of our informers. We're here to investigate."

"What kind of charges?" Her tone was disinterested.

"We aren't discussing that, especially not in this crowd."

"Everyone out," Lynn suddenly addressed the crowd. "I need to speak to these gentlemen. You may all come back in thirty minutes."

The druids started to block everyone from milling out. "If you want to talk, let them leave us."

The druids let them pass, all four of them giving Lynn hard stares. Within seconds, all that remained in the room with the druids were myself, Christian, Caleb, and Lynn. I wasn't well acquainted with Solace or Dustin, but I'd recognized them well enough to note them walking out.

"Both of the ones we mentioned are charged with vampirism outside of our registry. Obviously there were no vampires here, but do you know the whereabouts of Solace and Dustin?"

""Yes," Lynn replied. "They just walked out."

CHAPTER TEN

The Coming Storm

The druids braced as if to go after them. Lynn held her hands up to halt them. "As you saw, no one in that crowd was a vampire. Charges disproved. Be on your way, boys." Lynn, like myself, had always had a hard time with authority figures. Perhaps that was why she was naturally antagonistic when we happened to run into some.

"It doesn't work that way, lady. We need to interview the suspects. And for that matter, everyone in this room doesn't exactly strike me as human. We'll need to interview all of you as well." All but the leader of the group had gotten very quiet, and they had spaced themselves apart, as though preparing for a fight. Greeaat.

Lynn shrugged. "Interview away."

"Are any of you going to try to say that you're human?"

I raised my hand. So did Lynn. Both of the guys didn't bother. They were listed on the druid roster. Nice and legal. No reason for them to hide. Unless they were in some kind of trouble. They weren't, that I knew of, but both had the potential for trouble at any given time, so I couldn't be positive about that. If they hadn't been hell-raisers themselves, they never would have found themselves friendly with Lynn and I. We were, by nature, perpetual fugitives. Birds of a feather...

The druid in charge nodded his head towards me. I gave him my widest, blankest stare. "You're human?" he asked dubiously. "What are you doing hanging out with these guys?"

I shrugged. Lynn spoke before I could. "Look at her T-shirt. She's obviously this slayer's girlfriend."

He looked between mine and Christian's matching shirts, smirking. He nodded at Christian. "You saying you're a dragonslayer?"

Christian smiled, his friendly, innocent smile. "Yeah. I'm on your roster."

"We will, of course, be checking you out. Right after we speak to our original targets." They said the same to Caleb. Lynn claimed to be his girlfriend. They looked skeptical, but didn't press it. None of them were powerful enough to tell if we were human. Few were, for that matter, if we weren't actively using some kind of magic. Our kind was the first race, and the hardest to identify.

Lynn sent for Solace and Dustin. There was no way to make the druids leave until they had their interviews.

The boy and girl walked in, looking guilty as all hell. I made a note to myself to play poker with them sometime.

"Are either of you human?" the druid leader asked without preliminary.

They both looked guiltily at Lynn. She gave them an exasperated look. "Just tell the man the truth."

"No, we're not human," Dustin said.

"We're vampires," Solace said.

The druids just looked at them like they were crazy. So did I, for that matter. The stupid kids looked like they actually believed it.

"Bullshit," the druid said.

"I-it's true. Mistress Noir shared blood with us. We both feel different. Stronger," Solace said in a rush. Shit. That wasn't good. The druids looked at Lynn, who had claimed to be human. Drinking human blood didn't give you special powers. Only Other blood had those kind of perks. Lynn was effectively outed.

Lynn just stared right back, still looking bored. She was going to try to brazen it out. I recognized the glint in her eye. "They answered your questions. You see that they're perfectly human. Can they go now?"

"Not quite. Since you've shared your blood with them, we're taking them in. We have specific procedures for such things. You'll be joining us too, of course." Well, that decided it. Lynn shot me a quick but unnecessary look. I already saw clearly what needed to be done.

I hit the druid closest to me with a hard tackle. It was the auburn haired, second-in-command. He came up swinging. It was a dog-fight after that. Even the lower ranking druids were tough bastards in a brawl, and this guy wasn't half-bad. He backhanded me hard, and I was stunned for a minute. A bitch slap. I had a second to hope that no one had seen. I'd never hear the end of *that.* The worst part was that I really felt it. With my body's healing ground to a halt, I was literally crippled. Everything became harder. And more painful.

My heel connected with his chin solidly enough that I heard something important pop. Probably his jaw. *Crap,* that had been an accident. I was compensating for my injuries by using more brute force. He was up and rushing at me quickly, ignoring his jacked-up jaw. I ignored it too, focusing on landing a solid blow to the back of his head. My goal was to knock him out quickly, but I seemed to just be pissing him off. I finally settled for choking him out, his hands beating at me the whole time.

He suddenly went limp, and I worried for a second that I'd killed him. A quick check showed him still breathing, and I let out a sigh of relief.

My guy made three of the four druids down for the count. Christian was still toying with his. It was the leader, obviously the toughest of the bunch, but that wasn't why Christian was still fighting him. It was completely deliberate on his part. His was simply prolonging his own fun.

"Christian, finish it," Caleb barked at him sharply. Christian complied, knocking the druid out cold with one powerful, perfect kick to the back of the head. He stuck his tongue out at Caleb. Oh yeah, we were a bunch of badasses. Badasses with the maturity of fourteen-year-olds.

We lined the four unconscious druids up next to each other. "Can you do a sweep outside, Christian? Make sure no one heard anything," I asked. He went without a word. Lynn and I shared a look. I got to work on my part.

It was harder than it would have normally been for me to heal each druid, but I worked quickly. Christian would only be outside for a few minutes.

Lynn started working on each druid immediately after I finished. I stood when my part was done. Caleb was watching us strangely. I gave him a questioning look. Finally he asked, "I can tell that you healed them. Lynn is what, wiping their memories? How long will that last?"

I shrugged one shoulder. "Impossible to say, exactly. One day, maybe. Three tops. She can't work them over too hard or they won't recover." Christian returned, and I shut my mouth. He didn't even look at the downed men.

"All clear. We ready to roll?" he asked. He had a hyper, after battle look on his face. Fighting made him perky. Go figure.

"You've got issues," I told him. I was mostly messing with him. I loved a good fight as much as he did. I just wasn't all chipper about it.

He smiled happily, not in the least insulted. "I found one of Lynn's flunkies. They're getting the goth-tard bus ready to go."

Lynn nodded. "Good. Let's get out of here. We'll leave these guys with the tent. My people should have the rest packed up in a matter of minutes."

"Think these guys'll be out long enough for me to grab an elephant ear on the way out?" Christian asked. Caleb gave him a borderline disgusted look. Lynn and I laughed.

As we made our way quickly to the parking lot, I pulled Lynn aside. I held my arm up. It was literally steaming. I was burning up again. She studied me closely, saying, "You ride with Caleb in Christian's car. You'll have to take one of my kiddies with you. We have a full house."

"What about Caleb's car?" I asked her.

"God only knows. He says he doesn't have a car here. I have no idea how he got here."

"The bus?" I joked.

"I have a feeling he didn't take the bus, either." We shared a long look. We had our reservations about Caleb. He was an ally, had even become a friend, but he was a concern. There was so much we still didn't know about him, about his abilities and his loyalties. I could well understand his need to keep his own secrets; we did the same rather zealously, but it was still a concern. He had arrived with the first wave of the coming storm...

I ended up sprawled out in the cramped back of Christian's porsche, with Caleb at the wheel. Luke, the submissive, was riding shotgun. Apparently he'd volunteered to ride with us. I wondered if he'd done it just to get a punishment from his girlfriend, but I sure as hell wasn't going to ask. He kept his face in profile to me. He was shooting me worried glances from under his downcast lashes. Such demure looks from such a large man were disconcerting to me. I thought I had adapted well to this century, but perhaps I was a little sexist, after all.

I gasped as a wave of raw, painful heat swept through me. *Not good.* I started gasping and shuddering involuntarily.

"What's going on, Jillian?" Caleb's voice drifted at me as if from a distance. I held on hard to consciousness.

"I don't know, but I think I might be about to ruin Christian's backseat," I gasped out.

"What can I do?" Caleb asked, always practical.

I could literally smell smoke coming off of my clothes. I tried to answer him. The world went black.

CHAPTER ELEVEN

Dangerous Backup

I came to lying on a hard slab of concrete. I didn't recognize my surroundings, but I knew immediately that I was in a cel. There were no windows, and the lighting was dim, but I could see well enough to know the man looming in the doorway. It was the only way in or out of the small room.

A worried Luke rushed past the still form of Caleb, apparently oblivious of the danger. He knelt by my head, a damp cloth in his hand. He pressed the cloth to my head, a concerned look on his face. *Great.* My own hunky nursemaid.

"Where are we?" I asked Caleb.

"Someplace safe." He shot Luke a cold look. I saw that there was a fresh bruise on Luke's cheek. It hadn't been there before I'd blacked out. If I'd had to guess, I'd say he'd been bitch-slapped. "Luke assures me he'll reveal its location to no one. I've assured him that he had better not, or I'll teach him the true nature of pain. Those little games he plays have done nothing to prepare him for the kinds of tortures I can devise."

Luke looked suitably scared. He was nodding jerkily. "I swear."

Caleb's cold stare turned back to me. His face was its usual expressionless mask, but I could feel something warmer under the surface. Anger, maybe. "It's time for you to give me some answers, Jillian."

I sat up, fury almost blinding me as I felt the shackles on my wrists and ankles as I moved. The bastard had taken full advantage at my first sign of weakness. I gave Luke a murderous look when he moved to help me. He backed off, head bowed.

I schooled my features into passivity, meeting Caleb's cold gaze with my own. My fury would not help me here. I wanted to rip his head off, but I still needed his backup more, and I couldn't fathom the extent of his betrayal just yet. "So I'm your prisoner? Care to explain what you're doing, Caleb?"

"What the fuck happened to you in that car?"

I gave him a disgruntled look. "I told you I don't know what that was about in the car. I've been having...episodes. I can't explain them."

He set his hands on his hips. No, that was wrong. He had them resting on the hilts of two guns riding his hips. "You're going to give me answers, Jillian. I've been kept in the dark for far too long where you and your sister are concerned. I have a real problem with you knowing more about me than I do about you."

I curled my lip at him. "Are you threatening me?"

"I'm determined," he said ominously. Well, that sure sounded like a yes.

I didn't have to feel down my body to know he'd removed my weapons. You know it's a bad week when even your backup turns on you.

"What are you?" he asked.

Well, that was direct.

"Do you have another room that Luke could wait in?" I asked pointedly.

Caleb shifted, waving Luke out. Luke went, casting me sad,

worried glances. I nodded at the door. He closed it softly behind him.

"What are you? Both of you? I know that you have different powers, and I don't understand it. Some shit is about to go down in this town, and I sure as hell don't plan to stay in the dark about the people I'm fighting with."

It was almost a relief that this was all he wanted to know. I'd had the horrible thought that he was in league with my relatives. If they were in town, he could have been holding me for them. I was still pissed, but slightly less worried. I remained cautious, though. Caleb was not someone to take lightly. I debated for awhile what to tell him. He could threaten me all he wanted, but the truth was, he couldn't torture me into telling him anything I wasn't willing to. But we'd known him for long enough, and he'd seen us do enough strange things, that I was considering just telling him the truth. Besides, if he was going to turn on us, it wasn't as though he didn't already have enough ammo to help take us down.

"We are what you must have suspected we are, Cal. We're descendants of the ancient ones. Dragon-kin. All the evidence points in one direction for a reason."

He looked shocked for a moment. It was as off-guard as I'd ever seen him. "But how? You two have lived among humans for so many years. It doesn't make any sense. And what about Christian-"

I shrugged. "He doesn't know. We got to him early on. We figured our best bet was to keep him close to us. We mean him no harm, and we don't have him enthralled. Hell, neither of us ever learned how. And he's a friend now, so we wouldn't, even if we could. He sees a lot of the same clues you have. I guess that sometimes, if something seems so impossible, your mind just doesn't believe it. Obviously, it's for the best if he never finds out."

"Obviously." He was silent for a long time. I closed my eyes, feeling weary to the bone. Finally he spoke, "I want in on it. Whatever shit is about to go down with you two, I want a piece."

I wasn't completely surprised. Caleb had seen it all, and he lived for action. I gave him a level stare. "I'll be sure to call if any shit does."

"Not good enough. I'm shadowing one or the other of you until I get action. Things have been too fucking calm lately. I'm ready for a storm."

I smiled at him. "You think I'm gonna argue? Great, awesome, hang around all you want. We could use the backup. Happy?"

He nodded, his face back to its usual mask. "Yes. You might not see me, but I'll be around."

"Cool beans. Now get these fucking chains off of me before I decide to take exception to the fact that, the second you saw me weakened, you turned on me."

He actually bent to unchain me. It was only then that I breathed a sigh of relief. I had been waiting for the other shoe to drop, as I usually was. Apparently, information gathering had really been the extent of his plan.

"So, how much damage did I do to Christian's car?" I asked, rubbing my freed wrists.

Now he smiled. "You jacked it up good. He's going to have a conniption. How are you gonna explain his charred Porsche and your charred outfit?"

I looked down. Sure enough, my T-shirt and jeans were blackened around the edges. "Hell if I know. He thinks I'm a fire sorcerer. Maybe I'll tell him I had to fry a spider or something."

"You up for moving to the mountain retreat yet?" he asked.

I shook my head slowly. "No. You go ahead without me."

He gave me a questioning look. "What are you planning?"

I stood up, showing him my wrist. Of course he recognized the geas. "Nothing you want in on. Trust me.

He raised his brows at me. "Try me."

I just shook my head at him. "No fighting. No carnage. I need to go try something particularly unpleasant to get this thing off without actually obeying its command, but it's nothing you could help with. Nothing to shoot, sorry. And if that fails," I sighed, dread curling in my belly, "then I have to go to The Grove, and I know you won't want anything to do with the druid casino."

He inclined his head. "You got me there. I want nothing to do with that fucking place. You wouldn't, either, if you had a clue what they keep in there."

I blinked at him. Caleb kept his hand in many games. It was a fact that he lived his life knee-deep in danger, and he liked it that way. Generally, I didn't know what all of his motives or schemes were. I could trust him to do exactly what he said but never to tell me more than he thought I absolutely needed to know, and that was all. I knew that was for the best. But him having insider information on the druids was a real shock to me. Had he always been spying on the druids, or was this something new? I didn't ask him. He wouldn't be telling me something like that. But his wording more than intrigued me. "What they keep in there? Wanna elaborate?"

His face went from that eery stillness to downright dead between one breath and the next. It was unnerving to watch, to say the least. It was almost like getting a glimpse of him changing forms. "No. Drop it. Just trust me when I tell you that some things are dangerous to even speak about out loud. Just be careful in that fucking nightmare of a casino. You and Lynn in particular. Your blood is just too tempting."

I was no less intrigued, on the contrary, I was dying of curiosity after that little spiel, but I dropped it. Caleb wasn't one to waste words that didn't need to be said, so if he said it was dangerous to speak about, I just believed him. He was a walking, talking land-mine of information, but I had learned, over the years, how to navigate his strange depths. So it was a no brainer to drop it when he said drop it, no matter how damned frustrating it was.

Caleb let me take Christian's porsche. I didn't want to know why he was being so helpful, so I just thanked him, nodded stiffly at Luke, and got the hell out of there.

CHAPTER TWELVE

Witch-Hag's Lair

I was a little startled to realize, as I got settled into Christian's car, that Caleb's strange little dungeon of a house was right on the edge of downtown Las Vegas. I shot a disgusted look at the Fremont Street Experience as I dug my phone out of the back of the car. The location was surprising, considering that the house held cages that Caleb must have wanted to keep secret, and the damn place was smack in the middle of a tourist attraction. Surprising, but good, since the nasty little errand I needed to run was less than ten minutes away.

Witch-hags were generally something I tried to stay far away from. Best-case scenario, I kept tabs on where they liked to be, and stayed the hell away from those places. They were, by far, the most unpleasant kind of witch, and they tended to all go rogue eventually, if they lived long enough, which drove the law-loving druids bonkers, since they couldn't kill them before that happened. A rogue witch-hag wasn't always that easy to tell apart from a law-abiding one, though the stories always told it differently. They could disguise the blood-red of their eyes when they weren't actively using their powers, and their fingertips weren't dipped in blood unless they just happened to be in the middle of sacrificing someone or something. But rogue or not, it was all just semantics, in my jaded mind, when it came to witch-hags. If they knew what I was, it would change even the most law-abiding hag in a heartbeat.

I was broke half of the time, though I usually worked a lot, whatever that work happened to be. Most of my money went swiftly towards my deep devotion to paranoia, and my need to stay constantly on the run. Yes, I was broke, but that didn't mean I wasn't worth anything. If harvested for parts, I was priceless. I was many lifetime's worth of fortunes, if used properly. And to the hags in particular, I was limitless power. Even a good hag, if there was such a thing, wouldn't be able to resist such an opportunity. So avoiding hags was usually a gimme.

Today, however, I was desperate. I didn't get to be picky, or smart, today. I couldn't count on both hands all of the reasons why it was a bad idea for me to see Dom. He was a domineering son of a bitch. He hated my guts. He had the power to mess up my life in all kinds of ways, and I tended to think he would use those powers. But the reason I was really desperate was more complex than any of that. Some bad shit was about to go down in this town. All signs pointed to a disaster headed our way on swift feet, and with our names on its smiling lips. Letting Dom find me at this point would be as good as dragging him right in the middle of it, domineering bastard that he was. He would turn Lynn and my issues from an ugly family skirmish into an outright World War, with himself right in the thick of it. I would go through some pretty unpleasant stuff to see that that didn't happen, so I was desperate enough to attempt just about any other way to get the cursed geas off my wrist, and stay a step ahead and away from my Ex. And as ever, my head start would take its pound of flesh.

It was actually Caleb who had given me the crazy idea, months ago. Though it had hardly been relevant at the time, I'd taken note. He had mentioned, in an offhanded kind of way, that there was another way to deal with a geas, aside from just obeying its purpose. Lynn and I had scoffed at the time, though he wasn't one to throw out misinformation. I remembered his words clearly, though. "A witch-hag could do it. It wouldn't be pretty, but a powerful one has the ability. It doesn't even take a human sacrifice, or at least, it doesn't *have* to. I don't know the specifics of the spell they use, but I do know what they charge for that sort of thing. A pound of flesh and a favor, bound by blood-oath. A steep price or a cheap one, I guess, depending on the geas."

I parked several blocks away from the hag's house, as though approaching it slowly would somehow make going into a viper's den less idiotic. It was set up as one of the strange business/houses that were popular in the area. It was a particularly shabby little house, the yellowish stucco of the outside walls missing chunks, the faded red tiled roof missing half of the shingles. Business must not have been booming for the hag. The little sign out front read 'Holistic Healing and Herbal Cures by Ethel'. Yeah, right. Ethel was well-known as the most powerful non-rogue witch-hag in the state, but even the legal hags had no talent for healing or curing. I had a very justified sick feeling in my gut as I opened her front door.

Ethel's place was set up with a small waiting area attached to a tiny window, like a doctor's office. If a doctor's office looked and smelled like garbage, that is. The carpets were stained and ancient, the walls dirty and yellowed. One other 'patient' waited in the surprisingly large antechamber. From the outside, the house hadn't looked as though it could hold even one room this large, and this was obviously only the waiting area, so I guessed there had to be several other rooms. The other patient was a dark-haired girl. She could have been anywhere from eighteen to twenty-five. She had stringy, dirty hair that trailed into her face as she read a gossip mag. She was small and mousy, buried in dark baggy clothes, and she didn't glance up once from her magazine as I passed by her to reach the little window.

I checked the window and found that the little desk and messy office were vacant. I rang the little bell. It barely made a sound. I studied the other patient as I waited several minutes for a response.

Something was off about her, and my suspicious mind quickly started trying to piece together what it was. She was very still, and turned the magazine's pages as though on a timer. I actually began to time her, and found that, sure enough, I was right. She studied each page for exactly one minute before turning the page rather absentmindedly. It was as though she had been placed there as a prop, which did nothing positive to my peace of mind.

I had nearly talked myself into leaving when an ancient looking woman hobbled into the small office space on the other side of the glass window. She smiled at me, a toothless grin. "Sorry for the wait, my dear. My secretary had to step out. I'm Ethel. How can I help you?"

I studied her for a moment before I spoke. She looked ancient, though that didn't mean a damn thing. And her tone was kind, almost maternal. She made a very convincing grandmother type, which was unusual. Hag's were typically as unpleasant as you'd have expected of women who'd sacrificed literally everything in their lives for some magical power.

I met her pale blue eyes as I answered. "I need something removed," I told her frankly. I raised my wrist just enough to show her what I meant, hiding the object from the patient behind me.

Ethel's eyes widened in surprised. "Oh, my, my. You're in luck, my dear. I'm one of the few who can actually help you with that little nuisance. One moment, my dear." Her tone was reassuring, but unsurprisingly, I was far from reassured.

I fidgeted and fought the urge not to bolt as I waited for a solid ten minutes. A door to the left of the windowed office opened to reveal the short hag. She beamed at me, a hideous sight. "This way, my dear. We'll discuss your...difficulty in one of the healing rooms."

I followed her hobbling form down the dingy hallway, studying her back as I trailed her. She was missing a foot, using some kind of prosthetic, I observed. On a witch-hag, that was a bad sign. It may have been missing from an accident, or countless other things, but it still made me antsy. If she had sacrificed body parts for power, it just made it more likely that she had done worse things, evil things, for the same purposes.

She led me into a shabby room that vaguely resembled an examination room at a doctor's office. She waved for me to sit on a hard bench of an examination table. I did so, though every instinct that I had told me to get the fuck out of there. Following my instincts was a luxury on a week like this one.

She sat in a mock doctor's chair, giving me her attention, a kindly look on her face. "As I said, I can help you with the geas, but I'll need some information about it. And the price for such a task can be...difficult."

I met her gaze steadily. "I figured as much. What do you need to know about the geas?"

She brightened. "So cooperative. I like you, my dear. I need to know the nature of the geas, the rank of the druid that placed it on you, and the nature of your own powers, of course. I'm well aware that you're not human."

I stiffened. I hadn't anticipated that she would ask me outright what I was. It was common courtesy, among magic-users not to ask things like that. I supposed that coming to her for something so illegal sort of trumped the whole idea of courtesy. Double-fuck.

I plunged further into the mess. "It's a geas to meet with a specific person within a set amount of hours. One of the druid lieutenants placed it on me."

She blanched. "One of the seven?"

I nodded.

She moaned pitifully, and her voice was suddenly higher in pitch. It made the hair on the back of my neck stand on end. "That will be tricky. The time constraint is particularly troublesome, but I should still be able to do it. My price is non-negotiable, though. I need a pound of flesh and a favor, blood-oathed."

I schooled my features into passivity. "What is the favor? And what exactly do you mean by a pound of flesh?" I asked, absolutely certain that I wouldn't like the answer.

Her eyes twinkled at me, as though we were sharing some funny joke. It made me want to reach for a weapon. "A pound of flesh is exactly how it sounds, my dear. I answer to a master, as everyone does, and he will take a bite of your flesh and blood to seal our bargain. Think of it as a down payment. The favor, on the other hand, is more complicated. You will have to owe me for that. I will call on you, at my convenience, to do me a service."

I gave her my hardest, coldest stare, letting her see the resolve in my eyes. "There have to be conditions to that favor. I won't kill for you, or do anything that helps you take a life."

Her eyes hardened, as well. "I don't need help for that. Not from you."

I didn't believe her, but I didn't need to trust her. I just had to make her agree to a blood-oath, and make the conditions of it airtight, so I plunged on. "And I need to know what your master is. And who. I need a name and specifics, before I agree to anything."

She stiffened, her entire body going rigid suddenly. I began to bolt the instant I saw her eyes go red, but I was already too late. Who knew how long old Ethel had been rogue? It could have happened yesterday, or she may have been fooling everyone for years. Gods only knew. But I had no excuse for falling into such an obvious trap. It was a fact that I was old enough to know better.

Invisible ropes seemed to pull my arms above my head, even as some force pushed me flat onto my back. They held me easily, in my weakened state. I cursed. Ethel was keening like a madwoman. I didn't know if she was casting a spell or calling for backup, but I wanted badly to shut her up permanently.

As she keened, a dark shadow began to materialize beside her. The hair on my body stood on end, and then my skin began to creep. It had been awhile, but I knew the awful feeling. Something demonic this way came. I couldn't believe that I'd never made the connection between witch-hags and demons before it was literally in front of my face. It all made perfect sense. Making deals and sacrifices for power. The pieces were all there but I'd never bothered to connect them. I struggled and cursed futilely as the dark shape turned into a glossy black nightmare before my eyes. The tall, horrifying thing seemed to grin at me through pointed teeth. That could very well just have been its face, though.

It sniffed the air, clicking slick black claws reflexively. Its teeth snapped, and something rustled like wet cloth behind it. Wings. Of course. It shuddered, which made me shudder with fear. I beat it back. If something was going to take me down, my fear was not going to help it.

It spoke, and I was shocked when it was English that came out of its horrible mouth. "This one is good, slave. You will gain much from this offering. I feel that she is powerful, but still, we must know what she is. It will determine whether we should keep her, or drain her now. Bring me the cypher!"

I cursed louder. A cypher was bad. They weren't much of a threat, as far as magical powers went. They were basically just humans who could tell the Other races apart from each other. No one worried about them much, except to find them useful. Except, of course, a fugitive dragon in a witch-hags hands, who'd just watched a demon being summoned to drink their blood. Then they were bad, bad, bad. My only hope was that the cypher had never seen a dragon, which was a good possibility, and that they were just baffled by my abilities in general. I avoided cypher's like I did hag's, because it was the sane thing to do, so I wasn't sure that my hopes were real feasible, but hey, a girl had to hold onto something.

Ethel hobbled from the room rather swiftly to obey her nightmarish master.

The demon continued to sniff at the air and shudder, as though in pleasure. It was disconcerting and worrisome, to put it lightly. I tried not to shake with fear. "A feast," its dark voice rasped. "You are a feast to all of my senses."

It approached me very slowly, claws and jaws snapping with every step. Ethel burst back through the door, a middle-aged, terrified looking man on her heels, long graying brown hair covering nearly his entire face as he bowed low. He was shorter than the hag, and skeletal thin.

"Here he is, master. Yours to command, master," Ethel screeched, sounding terrified herself.

The demon turned its terrible regard to the man, and he instantly fell to his knees before it. I saw that the cypher also had a prosthetic leg from the thigh down. It was no coincidence that they were both missing limbs, I now knew. I wondered if there was any way that the man's leg had been a voluntary sacrifice.

"Tell me what she is, slave," the demon said, in that insidiously terrifying voice.

The cypher stumbled to me, awkward with fear. I blinked as he came closer and I got a good look at his face. His nose was missing, along with all of his teeth. His face was a gruesome sight. He pushed his hair out of his face, an instinctive gesture, as though to hook it back behind his ears, but those were missing as well.

Looking into his panic-stricken eyes, I didn't think that any of those offerings had been willing, as the hag's must have been. He must have been her prisoner for quite some time, since the wounds over all of his missing parts were healed over. The pitiful man placed a quivering hand over my heart, closing his eyes. I watched his hand warily. Even his nails were missing. He placed a second hand on my chest, right over my heart, avoiding my breasts as much as possible. He wasn't trying to cop a feel, which was something, I supposed.

He took a few deep breaths before gasping and falling back with a low, pitiful moan. "She's fire."

Ethel screeched at him. "Master needs a real answer. What does that mean, she's fire?"

The cypher just began to shake his head, over and over. "I don't know. I've never seen anything like her. She *burns,* deep inside, like fire incarnate.*"

That statement seemed to finally snap me out of my stupor. I studied the yellow-stained wall and channeled my rage. Yes, I did burn. I touched a fingertip to the table below me. It was all I could reach, but it would be enough. Burn, baby, burn.

"Stop that!" Ethel screamed at me. I couldn't imagine how she thought that would actually make me stop.

"Blood. If I touched her blood, it might help me know what she is," the cypher gasped, seemingly oblivious to the blue fire that was swiftly engulfing the table I lay on.

"Blood, yes, her blood," the demon snarled, bringing his snapping teeth down to my neck. I screamed, finally unable to hold it back.

The door burst open and the strange girl from the lobby stood there, holding a ridiculously huge gun in each hand. She didn't hesitate, leveling the one in her right hand straight at the cypher, and taking his head off clean with one quick shot. It exploded, splattering the room, breaking my concentration for a long moment while I stared at the strange girl.

Ethel screamed and screamed, but the girl's rough bark of a voice somehow drowned her out. "Banish the demon, or your head is next, hag."

Something about the girl's voice and the words she used triggered some kind of recognition, and I studied her, shocked and stunned.

The demon roared, scuttling towards the girl with its nightmarish gait. "Now or never, hag," the girl barked, and the hag began to chant, her voice breaking in panic.

It was suddenly easier to breath in the room, and I let my flames abate as I realized that the demon had just disappeared.

Ethel chanted for a few more beats and then just stopped, raising her hands in a sign of peace to the girl. "He's gone. Caged away. He'll make me pay for that."

The girl nodded, her face expressionless. It was then that I was positive of her identity. Her next move proved it. She raised her gun and shot the hag in the head, taking it clean off.

I shut my eyes in relief.

"The walls are still burning," Caleb told me, in that strange girl's voice.

I nodded. "This place is going to burn down. I got the fire too deep into the walls to stop it."

I began to sit up, but Caleb was there, in that strange body, picking me up. "You're seriously off of your game today, Jillian. That hag shouldn't have been able to hold you so easily."

I couldn't argue. He was right. My injured body combined with my absent healing regeneration had seriously crippled me in there. It was embarrassing, especially in front of badass Caleb. "The fact that I attempted something like that at all should tell you just how *off of my game* I am at the moment."

"Yes, that was amazingly idiotic. You need to bite the bullet and go see Dom." He carried me out of the building in that tiny body amazingly fast, not even breathing heavy under my weight.

"I can walk," I told him. He set me down, taking me at my word. I sighed, knowing I owed him now. "Thank you, Caleb. You know I owe you."

He smiled, a cold little smile, just as creepy in that girl's face. "Yes. Never a dull moment with the sisters. So what's your plan now? Hopefully it's something better than this fiasco."

I sighed again, tired and unhappy with the way things had turned out. All of that, and I still had this fucking geas on my wrist. At least I had tried. "First, I need to stop by our house and grab some clothes. Then, possibly a quick trip to the spa."

He just kept staring at me, waiting for me to finish. "Spa?"

"Yes. It's a stupid girl thing. Obviously, you won't understand."

"You're right. Ok. Spa. Then what?"

I grimaced. "Then I get this fucking geas off my wrist."

CHAPTER THIRTEEN

Forsworn

The Vegas weather was at its most manic, going from a bright sunny morning, and then switching to a late afternoon of flash floods, lightning, and thunder. It was a particularly violent one, even for the season. As I headed from our house at the lower part of the valley, to the strip, I actually saw some crazy teenagers trying to body board in it. I shook my head at the sight. Crazy mortal humans, always acting like death was so far-fetched.

The drive seemed unbelievably short, since I dreaded my destination so completely. It wasn't lost on me that the mercurial weather matched my mood. Dread and anticipation both had a firm hold on me, warring until I couldn't have said which one held more sway.

I got some strange looks as I pulled up to the covered valet station in Christian's slightly singed, but still whole, porsche.

The thunderstorm raged gloriously behind me, but my hands were steady as I flicked my car keys at the valet. I strode into The Grove Hotel and Casino like I owned the place. I drew plenty of stares in my black latex getup, thigh high boots almost reaching my mini-skirt, and a corset complementing my diamond collar. My face was an alabaster mask with blood-red lips. I wore a pitch-black, jaw-length wig with straight bangs that just touched my eyebrows. Oversized silver hoop earrings completed my ensemble. I had dipped into Lynn's wardrobe for the outing. I reflected ruefully that the Ren fair costumes must have in some way influenced my fashion sense.

In spite of myself, I felt kinda cute in the ridiculous disguise. Which, of course, made me question myself for going to so much trouble. I mean, sure, I needed a disguise for the security cameras. But what purpose did the brazilian bikini wax serve? And getting waxed was *not* something you wanted to do while an anti-regeneration spell was working powerfully on a bruised up body. I would not be doing *that* again.

I kept my eyes and features in their natural state, but wore a pair of dark, heavy, Dior sunglasses. This whole exercise would serve no purpose if Dom couldn't recognize me.

A receptionist was stationed at a desk in front of the elevators that led to the office suites of the hotel. Several security guards stood in front of the elevator doors behind her.

I gave her a smile that was all teeth and blood red lips. She was a pretty young thing, with light red hair and bow-shaped lips. The part of my mind that was a masochist wondered if she was one of the many women he was rumored to be sleeping with.

"May I help you?" she asked in a professional tone. She was eyeing me up and down. The look on her face was not friendly.

I perched a hip on her desk. "Yes, you may. I'm here to see Dom. If you could tell him I'm here..."

She gave me a totally blank face. "I'm sorry. No one by that name works here."

My smile turned unpleasant, and I leaned closer to her. "Give your Arch a ring and tell him that Jillian is here to see him." I saw recognition light her face at my name. And then animosity. "Call him now, or I'll make a big enough scene that he'll see me himself on the security cameras."

I'm not exaggerating when I say she snarled at me. But she picked up the phone and dialed. "Sir," she murmured into the phone, tone suddenly warm and polite. And breathless. "There's a Jillian here to see you." There was a long pause on the other end. I heard a rumble of words from a familiar voice on the other end of the phone. Then a question. "Yes, sir. She's extremely tall. Black hair. Big breas-" She handed me the phone mid-sentence.

I put it to my ear, heart pounding. "Say something," a heart-achingly familiar voice growled in my ear. There was a world of menace in his voice.

The sound of his voice triggered the unwanted memory of the last time I'd seen him.

DENVER 7 YEARS AGO

My body was shaking as I closed the apartment door behind me, leaning heavily against it. The confrontation I'd just had, with the present Arch-Druid Declan, had left me scared and in full flight mode. He'd pushed all the right buttons, threatening Dom and my freedom. What Declan didn't understand was that pushing all of those buttons had only served to open Pandora's box. A plan was already formulating in my mind of how to use his own proposals against him. I was more than determined that he would not take away the two things dearest to me. Dom and my freedom. Unfortunately, almost everything else was about to go up as collateral. Including my relationship. And the identity I'd been able to maintain for more than a decade.

I made a fresh cup of hot decaf green tea and sat down to drink it, and think. My hands shook every time I brought the cup to my mouth for a drink. I was wound up so tight that, for the first time, maybe ever, I considered having a glass of wine. I'd heard many people found a glass of wine relaxing. Perhaps, in spite of the danger, it would have that effect on me. My kind wisely stayed far away from alcoholic beverages. Bad, bad things happened when we imbibed.

I finally decided against it, opting instead to hit the gym. It was my safest stress reliever. Maybe after a few hours of intense cardio my body would stop shaking. I determined to do just that as soon as I finished my cup of tea.

My body tensed as I heard a key turning the lock on the front door. Dom wasn't due home for several hours, and I had no wish for him to see me so shaken.

My profile was facing the door, so it was out of the corner of my eye that I saw Dom enter, and head straight for the kitchen. I heard him pour himself something on ice. Whiskey, I thought. He was having a bad day, too.

"We need to talk," he began.

I tried to stifle a laugh. *Why did that strike me as funny?* I didn't know. We'd been going through a rocky patch for the last couple of months. One thing after another seemed to be putting distance between us. Too many people wanted us apart. Team that up with some very unfortunate misunderstandings and we'd had some big fights that weren't easily resolving themselves, as they always had so easily in the past.

He tried to ignore my rude outburst, starting again. "Declan is sending me out of town for about a week. The timing is bad, but unfortunately I don't have the luxury of ignoring a direct order. My flight's in a few hours, but we need to discuss a few things before I go."

My breath caught at the news of his trip. Of course Declan was sending him away. It was his best chance to snare me in his trap. No wonder he'd gotten so aggressive of late. What Declan wasn't counting on was that it would also create the best circumstances for me to implement my own plan. *A few hours,* I thought. So this was what it came down to for Dom and I. My mind seemed to be moving like molasses, but I understood that part right away. This was goodbye for us, and Dom couldn't know it. I didn't know what to do with the tightness in my chest, the thickness in my throat that felt like it could turn to tears if I let it. I'd never allowed myself to get this close to someone before, so close that they could tear me apart. I'd never even wanted to before Dom.

"Your behavior lately is baffling to me," he was continuing in a hard voice. I tried to pay attention. "Is it too much to ask that you show a little civility, a little decorum, when dealing with my people? If you had set out on a deliberate campaign to systematically alienate yourself from the druids as a people, you couldn't have done a better job. You've put me in an untenable position."

Wow, he thinks I'm trying to ruin his life, I was thinking to myself as he spoke. I hadn't expected him to make this easier for me, to give a speech that would actually strengthen my resolve to get out of his life.

"First, you throw a jealous tantrum and chuck Siobhan out of a twelve story window."

I laughed out loud.

"You may think that's funny, but I don't think you understand how difficult this has made it for me to protect you and our relationship. Where is your self-control?"

I couldn't seem to stop laughing, but it wasn't happy laughter. It was more the hysterical kind. I finally got ahold of myself, wiping my eyes. "You really think that's what happened with Siobhan? She said something to piss me off, and, in a jealous fit, I couldn't stop myself from throwing her out a window?"

For the first time since he'd entered the apartment, I looked at him. He met my wild eyes with his own. His were beautiful, and mismatched. One was a jewel-toned blue so perfect it was almost violet, catching the highlights in his raven hair. The other was golden, and otherworldly. A wolf's eye. They were the legacy of his mothers side of the family, a mark of druid pride carried on only in his powerful bloodline. And he was the last to carry them. They were the most beautiful eyes in the world to me. I could lose myself in those eyes. I had, many times. And right now, they were as angry, and as cold, as I'd ever seen them. "I think Siobhan has a vicious tongue, and I have no doubt that she provoked you deliberately."

"And that's it? She insulted me and I threw her out of a window? Does that really add up to you?"

His eyes narrowed. "Why don't you speak plainly? If that isn't what happened, tell me what did. I'm all ears."

I was a breath away from telling him the whole story when I stopped myself. If this was last time I would see him, what was the point in alienating him from one of his staunchest allies? And wasting our last precious hours talking about *that bitch*. That thought made the decision simple. I remained silent, and shrugged. "It doesn't matter."

He raised a brow at me. "That's all you have to say for yourself? It doesn't matter? How about your hostility toward my Arch? I left you alone for *two minutes* at a social function, and you slapped him across the face in a room full of druids. Everyone there says he never laid a finger on you."

"And did any of these witnesses happen to overhear what he was saying to me?"

His nostrils flared, as though sensing a threat. "No. Enlighten me, please. You keep telling me he's a danger to me, but you never elaborate. What has he been saying to you that would elicit such a reaction?"

I debated what to tell him. It all seemed so pointless, with only a few hours left between us. I tried one last time. "You need to challenge him. You can beat him in a fair fight. But if you leave it to him to try to assassinate you-"

He made a slashing motion with his hand. "We've been over this too many times to count. I don't believe in killing my way to the top. I'm not afraid of him. If he wants to kill me, let him try his best-"

"He won't be challenging you to a fair fight! This won't be a test of your strength or his! He's feeling out all of the people close to you, looking for a weak link. It would only take one to get you a knife in the back!" I hadn't meant to, but I was almost yelling at the end.

He raised his brows in a question. "And this is what he's been saying to you? He's trying to solicit your help to kill me?"

I inclined my head. "He wants your head on a platter, and he has no scruples about how he gets it. You can't fight someone who's fully armed, with your hands tied behind your back. You think because your'e stronger than him, that you can take him lightly, but he didn't get that position by being a pushover. What he lacks in power, he makes up for with deception and cunning. He's pulling strings that you aren't even aware of. You need to wake up and realize that the world is not going to follow your set of rules for decency. It's pure ignorance to believe that Declan will!"

He ran a hand through his dark hair, his face showing his obvious weariness for a subject we had beaten to death. "It's becoming clear that we aren't going to settle any of this in the short time I have before I need to leave. And I don't want to spend our last hours together arguing. Can you just promise me that you will at least try to stay clear of Declan and Siobhan while I'm gone? You don't need any more bad press with my people, especially if I'm not here for damage control."

I nodded, my jaw clenching. I wanted to argue with almost everything he'd just said, but I knew none of it would matter soon.

I stood, walking to the kitchen and placing my teacup in the sink. My head fell forward as I leaned heavily against the sink, feeling impossibly tired.

He pressed his full length in behind me, as I'd longed for

him to do. His arms folded around me. He buried his face in my neck, breathing in deeply. Strands of our long hair mingled together in my line of vision. Just the sight of of it, his blue-black, and mine pale gold, touched something deep within me. There wasn't a thing about him that I wouldn't miss all the way to my core. "I'll miss you," he said into my skin, his voice thick.

I arched back against him, feeling the fever take me. "Now," I said hoarsely, and as always, he obliged.

Later, we lay entwined, lingering together until the last possible moment. He cupped my face in his hands, looking intently into my eyes. "I know things have been bad lately, but I need you to trust me. And I want you to swear to me that you won't run." He knew me so well, knew that would be my first and strongest instinct. Years ago, when we'd reconnected after decades apart, I'd sworn him a blood-oath that I would never run again. Those things were a bitch to break.

It was because he knew me too well that I made sure to respond quickly and convincingly, looking straight into those beloved eyes. "I swear it."

He stroked my cheek. "You know you're the world to me, don't you? There's nothing I wouldn't do for you." His voice held a tenderness that was rare for him, a softness in his character that only I had ever been witness to, because it was a softness for *me*.

I never looked away from his beautiful eyes as I responded. "I feel the same."

CHAPTER FOURTEEN

The Sun's Orbit

BACK TO PRESENT DAY

"Hey there, Darlin'," I said into the phone. It just kind of slipped out.

"Hand Amy the phone," he bit out. I felt the geas that had bound me slip from my wrist. It turned to dust as it hit the floor. Apparently, speaking to him had been enough to break it. The realization started a debate in my head. Perhaps I could just slip away. I was a pro at running. I quickly decided against it. In for a penny, in for a pound. And he was so close. He was the sun, and I was in his orbit now.

I handed Amy the phone and she listened for a minute before saying, "Yes, sir," and hanging up. She turned and spoke to the nearest guard. "Rufus, Dom has asked that you escort Jillian to his office immediately."

The guard didn't say a word to me as the elevator sailed its way to the top floor of the hotel. Vaguely, I felt his power and hostility at my back, but it was an abstract sort of observation. I didn't even get a clear look at his face. I couldn't have picked him out of a lineup. Usually I tried to take in details, but I was too distracted just then to care.

It was one of those elevators that faced a spectacular view of the city. I tried to enjoy the beautiful skyline on the long ride to the top, grasping at anything so as not to let my nerves get the best of me.

I was led to his office right away. I was more than a little surprised that he hadn't made me wait.

My first sight of him in seven years nearly stopped me in my tracks. He was so familiar, yet so changed. His raven hair was cropped much shorter than before, shaved very close to his head, as though he cut it often. The last time I'd seen him, it had been a black waterfall down his back. It broke my heart a little to see that he had cut it.

The first time we'd been together, I'd run reverent fingers through it. It had hung longish then, just past his jaw. "I love your hair," I'd told him at the time, "I can't get enough of it. If you love me, you'll never cut it again." I'd been joking at the time, but he'd taken me very seriously, only trimming the ends of it for the decade that we were together. I'd grown my own hair down to my knees, because he'd loved it so much. It only reached my mid-back now. I'd cut it very short in a temper, after we had ended.

His pale, mismatched eyes had changed, gotten colder and harder, but they were still just as beautiful. They seemed to be lit with some inner fire that the years hadn't dimmed. He had always been an intense and dangerous man, but there was a harder edge to him now. I could read clearly a bitterness, and perhaps even a touch of cruelty, that the last years had given him. Or maybe it had been me.

His handsome, aristocratic face seemed harder as well, looking like it could have been carved from stone.

His jaw was clenched, a pulse beating below his right eye. The yellow one. The wolf eye. This was nothing new. I'd seen him angry plenty of times, and I knew the signs well.

I offered him a tentative smile as I walked into his office. He didn't rise, just watched me as I entered. The door clicked shut behind me.

He'd removed his dark gray suit jacket and tie, his crisp white shirt unbuttoned enough to show his tan throat clearly. I could see the pulse beating there. His hands were clenched tightly together on top of his black desk.

"Mind if I have a seat?" I asked him, gesturing at the chair directly in front of his desk.

His nostrils flared and his eyes studied every inch of me. He didn't answer me, so I sat. We studied each other for long moments before he broke the silence. "Is that a wig?" he asked.

I glanced around his office, asking. "Any cameras in here?"

"No."

"Yeah, it's a wig. You like it?"

He had been reaching for the glass of water on his desk. When I spoke, he crushed it in his hand, glass and blood flying. He shook his hand, brushing the glass away without so much as blinking. He leaned towards me, baring his teeth. "You should know better than to bait an enraged bear, Jillian."

Even with him bitter and looking at me like he hated me, it felt too good just to look at him. I drank in the sight of him, despite my better judgement. Gods, he was beautiful. His astonishing eyes held me captive, as they always had.

He was studying the diamond collar at my throat, gimlet eyed. He had given it to me on our two year anniversary. Probably not my wisest move to wear it here. I fingered it, and his angry eyes flew to my face. "What are you doing here, Jillian?" he asked me through clenched teeth.

I gave him a sad smile. He was not even a little bit happy to see me. I should not have been so hurt by that realization. "Actually, I came to ask you a favor."

I had handed him the upper hand on a silver platter. He seemed to relax a little, sitting back in his chair and stapling his already healed hands. "Really?" he asked, plenty of rage still in his voice. Okay, maybe he hadn't relaxed much.

"Yes. Your people contacted me recently. They want my information for your registry. I was wondering if you could just convince them to leave me alone completely."

His brows drew together menacingly. "Why on earth would I do that?" he asked softly.

"A few reasons, actually. I know how you always hated that I kept so many secrets. I'm willing to reveal a few of them to you, if in exchange, you can help keep me and Lynn off the radar." It was a paltry offering, and I knew it. Also, it was a lie. I had no intention of telling him the things he *really* wanted to know.

"Your secrets don't interest me anymore."

"I thought you might say that." I stood and removed my jacket, draping it on the back of my chair. This left my arms and shoulders bare. I walked the few steps to the front of his desk slowly, cautiously. He tensed up visibly at my movements, as though my moving closer was something he had to brace for. I held my wrists out to him. I laid them on the top of his desk, palms up. I closed my eyes, concentrating hard on just that part of my body. It took me longer to remove Lynn's shielding than it would have my own. When I heard his sharply indrawn breath, I knew I had succeeded. I opened my eyes to see his pinned to the bruises that made ugly cuffs on my wrists. They looked much worse than they actually were against my alabaster skin. "Two of yours did this. If you help me, I can tell you who directly defied your orders."

He was breathing hard, and I hoped this was a good sign. "Why aren't they healed?" he breathed.

"A spell was performed to prevent me from healing." Well, it was true. I certainly wasn't going to tell him that I had performed the spell.

I went in for the kill. "Would you like to see the rest of what they did?" I asked softly.

Sweat had broken out on his forehead. Dominant druid males had an almost obsessively possessive nature. I'd left him in such a way that I knew he hated me. But I also knew that his hate wouldn't cancel out his wrath for a deed that directly defied his orders. He had made it clear long ago that none of his people were ever to touch me. I knew I was kind of a bastard for manipulating that part of him, but it was the only leverage I had at my disposal. "One of them held me while the other beat me. I didn't harm one hair on either of their heads."

When he started to visibly shake, I knew I had gone a tad too far. His eyes went pale with the Beastcall, and his voice was huskier when he ordered, "Show me the rest of what they did."

I shook my head. "I won't show or tell you one more thing until you agree to help me."

His fists were clenching and unclenching. He was trying hard to control his rage. "I'll do what I can, but you will tell me what I want to know before you leave here."

I inclined my head at him. "I'll tell you all I can."

"Show me," he ordered.

Knowing it was a bad idea, I let my shields down completely. It took me several minutes. I looked down at my hands the whole time.. "Did they rape you?" he asked, low growls escaping from his throat between each word.

I shook my head, not meeting his eyes. Submissiveness was the only thing that could hope to calm him in this state. It wasn't something that came naturally to me, but I could fake it in emergencies.

"Who was it?" He uttered the question as though it pained him.

"I will tell you. When you're calmer."

He literally roared. Like a bear. I could feel the druids that burst into the door behind me.

"Leave us," he roared at them, and they beat a hasty retreat.

I had an idea. Better than any I'd had lately. Though I was

willing to acknowledge that *that* wasn't saying much. "Could you heal me, Dom?" I asked him quietly. It was something I could do myself, if in a more painful manner, but I knew this would shift his attention, perhaps even enough to calm him down.

"Come here," he commanded.

I came around his desk and gave him my hands. His touch was light, but I felt a shock go through my body, and my skin burned where he touched me. I felt the tingly, pleasant sensation of a druid's healing move through my body. Their magic was earthy and raw, and I had always loved the feel of it. It was like cool water running through me, so different from my own magic. I shivered visibly from head to toe. Only Dom's touch had ever given me this addictive feeling. I tried not to think about how much I'd missed it.

His powerful healing spell plowed right through the barrier I'd put on my own regeneration, which was a troubling thought, really. No druid should be able to slice through a dragon-kin's spell like butter. Arch's were different, though, which I had almost forgotten. And Dom in particular had always been unbelievably strong. I'd felt it even when he'd been just a teenager whom I'd had occasional, and very limited, contact with.

He let go of me quickly when he finished. I was standing so close to him, almost between his legs. Maybe this *wasn't* such a great idea. *Gods,* I wanted him. It was like a switch that had been in the OFF position for seven long years of total abstinence. All it took was proximity to this man and suddenly it was ON, and all of my self-control was gone. I was known for my self-control. I was practically famous for it. But how much could I possibly have if I couldn't go five minutes in this man's presence without giving in to my hunger? The answer was obvious.

I was on him, almost against my will, a second later. I was

still fighting with myself even as my body took action. I was straddling him in his chair, pulling his head back with both hands, and pressing my mouth against his roughly. He ripped off my wig, and grabbed a handful of my hair, hard. He pulled my head back slowly, looking into my eyes. His own were positively electrifying. "What. Are. You. Doing?" he growled.

"I don't know," I answered truthfully. I ruined it a second later when I whispered, "Please, Dom," and moved against him.

"I hate you," he growled at me, right before he caved.

"I know, baby. I think there's a club you can join for that now," I replied, trying to hide the catch in my voice.

He reached up into my micro-mini latex skirt and tore off my thong with one vicious motion. It took a few beats longer for me to release his hard length. I gripped him tightly, moaning. He was already impossibly hard and ready.

He shoved my hand away quickly, grabbing my hips and impaling me onto his length in one savage thrust. It was, perhaps, a punishment of sorts. But whatever he intended, it was exactly what my body craved. I screamed, coming instantly. He didn't miss a heartbeat, setting a punishing pace that had me quickly building toward the pinnacle again. I put my hands on his broad, hard-muscled shoulders, stroking, and he stood, still impaling me, until I was shoved roughly against the heavy wooden blinds that covered the huge windows of his office. Only his erection held me upright as he wrenched my hands above my head, gripping my wrists tightly, then started thrusting again, hard and fast and angry. I wrapped my legs around his hips, arching into his thrusts.

I felt the blinds give behind me as something broke above our heads. Dom didn't miss a beat. Turning, he cleared the surface of his desk in one quick swipe, the sound of breaking things surrounding us as it all hit the floor. He lowered me to the surface, and continued to thrust.

I felt another orgasm coming, and tried to slow it down,

wanting to wait for him this time. He gripped my chin hard, never slowing. "Look at me," he said. I'd been avoiding the intimacy of eye contact before that, not wanting to be reminded of all that we'd lost, but I did as he said. His hand moved from my chin to my neck, squeezing, exerting just the right amount of pressure.

His beautiful, other-worldly eyes were angry as he commanded,"Come."

I did almost instantly. His voice was a trigger. "Domhnall," I cried hoarsely.

"No one calls me that," he said without stopping.

We came together with the desperation of seven hard years of separation.

We tore up his office. Papers flew, priceless sculptures were knocked over without a second thought. We split his beautiful black desk right down the middle near the finish. I knew it was in spite of himself that his hard eyes turned tender at the end. My eyes had been there the whole time, I knew. He fingered my now magenta hair, bringing a lock to his mouth. We cried each others names when we came. Tears ran down my cheeks, and I turned my face away to hide it.

I ran my hands over his shortly cropped black hair. "Oh, Dom, your hair," I whispered to him, a break in my voice. He had been lying on top of me for a while. He stood when I spoke, wrenching out of my embrace. He started righting his clothes. I lay as I was, letting him eye me up in my sprawled, undignified position. "You told Mav that my hair changed color during sex. I never figured you to kiss and tell." He went completely still, and I was perfectly aware of what I'd revealed.

"I didn't reign in much of what I said or did, the first few months after you left. My uncle kept me tranq-ed at the beginning, after what I did to Declan. His killing was perfectly legal in the arena, but they were still a little alarmed about my state of mind...due to the- viciousness of it. It is a fact that we can ascend to the Arch position through right of combat. But my Uncle knows, better than most, that I could not have kept the position without support. And nothing will lose the druid people's trust faster than a lack of control. There has already been too many civil wars. A clear head means peace. What I did to Declan was not controlled. My Uncle did his utmost to salvage my political aspirations. He wanted to prevent a repeat performance, and so kept me sedated. I can't even say what I must have revealed, when I was so impaired." He was much calmer now. I'm sure his release had helped. "So was this to convince me to help you?" he asked coldly. It hurt, but I knew a good opening when I heard it. I told myself it was better for both of us that he hated me. When he had loved me, and I had left, people had bled. A lot of people.

I shrugged. "Did it convince you?" I asked. I stretched slowly, arching my back. He had yanked down the front of my corset earlier, and I was well aware of the view he was getting. I cupped my breasts in my hands, caressing myself firmly in the way I knew he loved. I pinched my nipples roughly, never looking away from his hungry gaze.

His nostrils flared when he said. "I could use more convincing," he snarled, and was on me. Well, that had backfired. We were at it again.

"So it was Mav and Michael," he panted into my ear after we finished.

"Yes," I answered, though he already knew the answer.

He climbed off of me and found his phone amid the mess his desk now made on the floor. He dialed a number and spoke quickly. "Cam, I want Mav and Michael in custody immediately. No, don't tell them anything. They know what they've done." He set the phone down and just stared at me for awhile. I stared back.

"So tell me who you're hiding from," he ordered me calmly.

"My family," I answered.

"Why?"

"Well, primarily, because if they find us, Lynn will be executed. And me, well, I suspect they'll rape me until I'm either pregnant, dead, insane, or maybe two out of the three," I answered. It was an almost sugar-coated version of the truth.

His gaze was shuttered, but the tick had started up under his glowing yellow eye again. "Your family would do this?"

"Yes. That and worse."

"They're the ones you've been running from all this time?"

"Yes."

"Why didn't you just tell me this seven years ago?" A pleading note had entered his voice. I knew he was unaware of it. "There is no force stronger than the druids. I could have protected you."

I shook my head at him sadly. "Not every race is in your registry. And they certainly don't follow any of your laws. Our kind could raze this city to the ground. Too many of your people would have died for me to start a war just for myself."

"What are you?"

"I can't say."

"You said you'd tell me any-"

"I said I'd tell you what I could. I can't tell you this because I know you. You'll rip the world apart looking for answers to questions too dangerous to ask. You're kind isn't mortal, it's true. You'll never die of old age. But a clean beheading will kill you. I don't know how to kill the things that hunt us. Even a clean beheading won't do the trick, just on its own." His phone rang and he answered it, never taking his eyes off of me. "Yes, Amy," he said into the phone. "Cancel everything scheduled tonight. Yes, everything is fine." He hung up.

"She wasn't too pleased to meet me. She seems possessive of you," I said. "Are you seeing her?" I could have sworn that my mouth formed the words completely independently from my brain. I didn't want to speak of this, didn't want to know anything about his love life, really. I told this to myself firmly, over and over again.

He just stared at me malevolently, his jaw clenching and unclenching. "You lost the right to ask me that question a very long time ago. Don't you think it's a little hypocritical of *you* to be keeping tabs on *me*, all things considered?"

I nodded, making my face into a careful mask. He was right, and I had nothing to say for myself.

"And how many conquests can you account for since we parted?" he asked, surprising me.

"Do you really want to know?" I asked softly, fully prepared to tell him the truth, no matter how stupid that would be. And it would be oh so stupid.

He shut his eyes tightly, and it was like the sun setting. I wanted to look at his perfect eyes forever, I always had, and all of the years apart had only made that craving worse. "No, I suppose I don't." He stood like that for awhile, eyes closed, and I knew that he was battling for control. "Please get dressed," he told me.

I disobeyed the order completely, instead stepping close to him again. "I don't want to," I whispered in his ear.

"Vixen," he growled at me, when we finished this time. It wasn't an endearment. He hadn't looked at me once that time, keeping his eyes shut tight. It hurt worse than I wanted to admit to myself. But he didn't budge, just lay against me, as if it were old times.

A moment later my skin began to burn, and I knew the attacks were starting again. "Get off me," I grunted at him. He misunderstood me, and jerked off of me in a flash, eyes sparkling in anger.

The anger faded when he saw that I was panting uncontrollably. The strangest sensation had begun in my stomach and chest, not pain really, but alarming all the same. It felt as though my insides were shifting around.

"What's happening to you?" he asked, brows drawn together in concern.

"I don't know, but it seems to be happening more and more."

He knelt down to touch me, but I stopped him. "Don't. My skin will burn you." As though to prove my words, everything touching me began to sizzle. I clutched my stomach as the feelings intensified. Something big knocked against my mind, but I beat it back. Now was NOT the time for that. To my dismay, I fainted dead away.

CHAPTER FIFTEEN

Last Word

I awoke in an unfamiliar bed that carried a very familiar scent. I breathed it in, closing my eyes. I was not so subtly sniffing a pillow when Dom walked into the room. I set it down nonchalantly. I would deny to my deathbed what I'd been doing.

Dom stopped in his tracks. He was dressed down now, in a simple black V-neck T-shirt and dark gray slacks. The effect was just as devastating as the three-piece suit look that he usually sported. His short hair caught me off-guard all over again.

He was staring at me strangely. "What?" I asked.

"What's up with your hair?" he asked. He was almost smiling.

I felt it and started swearing. The curls were back "It's just been doing this." I cursed some more. "Don't ask."

I looked around the huge bedroom. "Do you live in this casino?" I asked him

He shrugged. "More or less. I travel between here and Denver quite a bit." He moved and sat in a dark-brown leather armchair. It was set a good distance away from the bed, pretty much as far away from me as he could get while still in the same room. "So have you been in Vegas this whole time?" he asked abruptly.

I so did not want to go here, but I had promised him answers. "We've moved around a lot, but mostly, yes," I said. I could have given an explanation, something, but nothing would make it less hurtful, so I didn't bother.

"And all of the fake leads we had of you going halfway around the world? Were those meant for your family, or for me?"

"Both," I answered brutally. I could tell by his grip on the chair arms that he was getting angry again. "They had discovered us in Colorado. We made some fake trails, and cut all of our ties there. Then we relocated in Vegas."

His eyes were glowing in the room's dim lighting. I didn't think it was a good sign. "So all I needed to do to find you was follow the fucking dragonslayer? He followed you here, didn't he?"

I sighed. He'd latched onto that rather quickly. It was unfortunate. "Eventually, yes."

He cursed. "Right under my fucking nose this entire time." His agonized voice hurt my ears. Hell, it hurt my chest.

"My family found us from your registry. You should be aware that someone is leaking that information to outside sources."

"I'll ask my uncle about it."

"Please don't. Every inquiry you make just brings us closer to discovery. I was told that it was your family that had looked into our past seven years ago, and that they had tipped off the ones chasing us. Certainly someone had delved into our past and found enough about us to have us blackmailed. I wasn't told who-"

"You were told? Care to elaborate?" His voice was harsh. He had put the pieces together. I had been hoping I could just gloss over that part.

"Declan-"

"You dare say his name to me like that? You mention him like some kind of confidante?" His voice was a roar, and waves of power lapped at me. I knew that every druid in the building must have felt those tempestuous waves of his power. He was a fearsome being now, even more so than before.

I swallowed nervously. This was very dangerous ground for us. "I apologize. But there is a leak within the druids. It is not something I care to repeat," I finally settled on saying. I looked down. The less said about Declan, the better.

He was silent for a time, which was a vast improvement over questions about Declan.

All of my charred things had been laid beside the bed. They weren't in top shape, but still covered the essentials. It was enough. I began to get dressed, my back to him.

"So, what happened back there?" he asked finally

I assumed he was referring to my passing out. "I honestly have no idea. It's been happening to me a lot lately. Perhaps there's a mortal in my bloodline somewhere, and my number's up." I was joking, but hell, it was as good a guess as anything, at that point.

"How old are you then?" he asked. The subject had never come up between us before. I knew he had always suspected that I was immortal, considering how long ago we'd met, but I'd never confirmed or denied his suspicions.

I smiled at him, and his jaw clenched hard. "A lady never tells, darling."

He swallowed. "Don't toy with my, Jillian. Ever again. I'm immune to your charms now." I knew he was telling the truth, and it made me sad.

"What's going to happen to Mav and Michael?" I changed the subject.

He started rubbing his temples. "I'm undecided. I'm thinking about ripping their heads off. That's the only idea I've come up with. You're the wronged party. Tell me what you think their punishment should be."

Oh boy. A part of me thought the world would be a better place without those two thugs. But most of me thought that was too harsh a punishment. Perhaps I sympathized with them, just a little, because I knew their hatred for me was rooted in their love of Dom, and how I had hurt him. "I guess you shouldn't kill them," I said grudgingly. "Maybe just some torture and imprisonment?"

"Perhaps," was his answer. Frustrating man.

"So are we square then? I'm off your roster, and you're done with your questions?" I asked, not nearly ready to leave, but knowing that I had to.

"I'll have to enter something in the books. I'll make sure it's something unexceptional, and that you're not listed as sisters," he told me.

"I guess it shouldn't matter, as long as you don't enter the address of our house or shop." I got up and headed for the door.

He stopped me with a question. "Was it only ever a game to you?" His voice was barely more than a whisper.

I froze, my hand on the doorknob. "You know it wasn't," I told him softly

I could feel his rage building in the air. He stood several feet behind me now. He was like a violent storm being held at bay through sheer willpower. It was hard to keep my back to such a presence. "I know that you told me more lies than truth. I know that you jumped from my bed to *his*. Or were you sharing both the whole time?" His fist punched a hole into the wall, not a foot from my head, but he kept talking. I studied that gaping hole with wide eyes. "I know that you never would have looked back if Mav and Michael hadn't found you." I sure as hell wasn't going to mention that Collin had actually found me, too, geas in hand, and that *that* was the only reason I had come to him. He continued, "I know that you'll walk out that door with no regrets. I know a lot of things about you, but not that."

I lifted my shoulder in a jerky shrug, turning to look at him. I deserved all of his doubt, I'd practically courted it, but it was hurting me. "And what do you want me to say? I know all about your love life. There's probably someone waiting right now for me to leave your bed." He wasn't meeting my eyes, for once, and I knew it was the truth. "You can act the wronged lover all you want, but it's not love for me that makes you fuck all those other women. It's your pride. I have to suspect that's the only part of you that was really hurt when I left." I was walking out the door as I finished. I always seemed to get the last word with him, but I always wanted to take it back.

Sure enough, there was a lovely young blond waiting on the posh sofa by the elevator. I had the strong urge to scratch her eyes out, or maybe chop her head off, but I just nodded politely. I was wearing my wig, shades, and black getup again. Strangely enough, it didn't make me feel real cute anymore.

As I waited for the elevator, I felt his presence behind me. I turned around to see him standing in the doorway, arms crossed, fuming at me. The blond stood up obediently when she saw him. I looked between him and the blond, her waiting eagerly, him not even seeing her, and my vision just went sort of red and fuzzy.

I stepped up beside her, studying her closely, having to look down to do so. I looked pointedly at Dom. "Nowhere near tall enough," I told him. "Not blond enough either. Oh, and too tan." Steam might have been rising out of his ears, but he didn't move a muscle. "Her tits are way too small. And her face and eyes are all wrong. Is this the closest imitation of me you could come up with tonight? " The elevator arrived, and I stepped into it, smoothly finishing, "But I suppose, in the dark, lying down, it's all the same to you." I blew him a kiss before the door closed.

I might have indulged in a minor sobbing fit on the ride down.....I don't want to talk about it. But yeah, I always got the last word, and I always felt like a royal bitch for it.

I called Lynn on my way back to our house. She, of course, thought it was a terrible idea for me to go back there, after the day we'd had. It was, in fact, a horrendous idea, but I was too exhausted to care. The thought of searching the desert for some hidden retreat in the dark was just too daunting at that moment. I promised to head to the retreat first thing in the morning, then hung up wearily. She didn't ask me how it had gone with Dom. She knew me well enough, and was familiar enough with our sordid history, to know that I wouldn't want to talk about it anytime soon.

A black SUV followed me from a distance, and I wasn't even slightly surprised. Of course Dom was having me followed. I was too tired and heartsick to care just then. I'd try to get pissed off enough to lose them in the morning.

I had a strong urge to burn some mixed tapes that night. Dom and I had been broken up for seven years and counting, but it suddenly felt so fresh that I could barely stand it. So yeah, we'd fucked, and it had been beyond mind-blowing, but I knew it didn't mean a damn thing. Knowing someone that you'd once loved hated you, and seeing it firsthand, were two very different things. *He hated me*, I thought, for the thousandth time. It was finally real to me, and I was devastated. He had loved me for so long. Some part of me must have been taking it for granted that, if he ever caught up to me again, he could forgive me. But those staggering eyes hadn't had an ounce of mercy, not for me. And, perhaps even more devastatingly, they'd held no longing for me, either.

He had adored the ground I walked on since he was fourteen years old. I had been considerably older than that when we first met, so I had most definitely *not* returned those feelings. And, of course, I had not encouraged him to have those feelings for *me*. But it hadn't mattered. His obsession with me had been a long and enduring one.

He'd been an exceptionally beautiful boy, and my heart had broken as I'd seen him go through the tragedy of losing both of his parents three years after I'd met him. I had comforted him, and sympathized with him. He had taken my comfort, and brazenly confessed his love for me, when he was still just seventeen. I had rebuffed him, of course. He had been unfazed, and vowed to change my mind when he came of age.

Lynn and I had fled not long after that, shedding those long ago lives and identities for new ones. It was nearly fifty years before he found me again. He had more than fulfilled the promise of the man he would become. He had been impossible to resist, then. I had known at a glance that it was useless to try. And astonishingly, his feelings and plans hadn't been changed by time or distance. He had pledged his eternal, immortal love to me within hours of seeing me again. He had been right all along. His intuition had been dead-on all those years before. The realization had floored me, and I had fallen for him, giving him more of myself than I'd even known I possessed. Romantic love had never even been a consideration for me, before Dom. And now he despised me.

I felt almost paralyzed with the pain of it all that night. I lay on the sofa in our uncharacteristically deserted living room, unmoving for hours, reliving the horrors of what I'd done as though it had just happened. And I felt regret, such regret, for the first time letting myself consider that what I had done had not been my only option. I could have stayed and fought, risking both of our lives, but keeping our relationship intact. I had chosen to run and hide, and it had cost me his love. *Yes*, I felt regret, as my dense mind seemed to have just realized the lasting ramifications. And it didn't help that I had a clear picture in my mind of the woman he was probably fucking even as I suffered. I hated her. I hated him. Most of all, I hated the visuals that kept flashing through my masochistic mind of them together, while I was alone, and feeling lonelier than I had in my entire life.

I brooded on the couch for long hours before drifting off into a restless sleep. I tossed and turned, my sleep clouded by shifting, familiar nightmares.

CHAPTER SIXTEEN

Familiar Nightmares

Tears pricked my eyelids as my father grabbed my chin in a punishing grip, turning my head to look directly at the bloody figure lying limp on the floor of the dank stone cell. My older sister was naked, but I could see no actual naked skin, so much of it had been flayed off of her, leaving only so much red meat. "Learn from this, Sveinhild. Defy me and you will suffer the same fate." The stink of insanity radiated off of him in waves as he spoke. I had only seen eleven summers, but I smelled it clearly. A sickening sweet stench of decay coming from deep within his brain. I wondered, as I had countless times, how no one else of our kind saw it. But then again, most of them had it too.

They told me that we were immortal, and that the men of our clan were gods, but I often thought god-hood must be useless if your mind was lost to insanity. I kept these thoughts to myself, as I did most of my thoughts, because we learned very young in our mountain clan that what our elders called 'heretic beliefs' would get us swift punishment. And what they called heretic was anything that contradicted their demented teachings.

I thought of the humans that lived in the quiet village nestled in the valley below our mountain fortress. I escaped there whenever I could, feeling a vast relief whenever I was free of the cloying decay that permeated almost all of our kind. The humans seemed to be completely free of this sickness, and being amongst them made me almost forget it myself. The humans were wary of me, a child of the ones they worshipped as gods, and rarer still, a female one. Nonetheless, I sought out that village, time and again.

"When she heals, she will be chained with your mother, and spelled to sleep for as long as I wish. For eternity, perhaps. It is too late for Hedda, Sveinhild, but you can learn from her transgressions. Do you understand?"

I nodded against his painful grip. I got these kinds of lectures a lot. The scared child inside of me quaked, but I remained stoic. I was an old soul, and only thought of myself as a child when I was castigating myself. I knew why I got such special attention. It was because, though I usually kept my own council and stayed quiet, he sensed my rebellious thoughts. I told myself, as I did constantly, it becoming a mantra in my head of late, that he couldn't possibly know my plans. Unlike my brother Sven, he could not read our thoughts. And Sven must not have picked them up, either. If he had even an inkling, I would already be in a cage, or worse, chained beside my be-spelled mother. I had seen her once, deep within the mountain. She was in draak form, beautiful and golden, and terrifyingly huge. She did not stir when I touched her. She was be-spelled into a deep, unconscious state. There were thick metal manacles around her neck and ankles. Her sin, my father told me, was disobedience, and would say no more.

I had been whipped for visiting her, a fairly light punishment considering how clear my father had made it that I was never to go to her. This told me that he wasn't completely displeased that I had seen her. He wanted me to know what was in store for those who disobeyed. As though the notable lack of other females in our clan wasn't enough of a deterrent for misbehaving. I knew what had happened to them all. I knew what it meant that my father kept a pet slayer by his side almost constantly. I could feel his dark presence in the corner behind me even now, the blood of all of our fallen females on his hands. He was death, the only thing on this earth that could kill us.

They called it The Purging. It had happened at least a century before my birth. The women of our clan had been named unclean by the men. I suspected it was because they questioned the authority of the men. A bloody battle ensued. The deciding factor, I'd gathered, was the slayer. A ritual he performed when we were weakened was the only thing that could kill us. And so, at my fathers order, he performed that ritual on all of the females of the clan, save one. My mother was a child at the time, and so was spared. Even now, with the men grossly outnumbering the women, and one of those now lost to the sleep of time, my father still couldn't see that he'd been overzealous in his rage.

I was the only what they called 'breeder' left, which was why I got so many of these lessons. I was their one last chance for a biddable female. The thought chilled me, as ever. I would bleed my woman's blood in one more season, maybe two if I was lucky, and then be at the mercy of these depraved, demented monsters, as my sister had been before me. And he was showing me her fate yet again. As if I needed to be reminded. At least they hadn't had the slayer kill her. She and my mother had been spared true death, and given the sleep of time. Even in their insanity, the men could see that they couldn't afford to kill more of the women of our kind. Their need to avoid extinction apparently outweighed their need to be obeyed. It was a close thing, though.

He continued to force me to look at the pathetic creature in the cell. He was beating a dead horse at this point, since I knew explicitly what had been done to her before my father had beaten her with a barbed whip until she ended up here, unconscious to the world, for more than a fortnight now. Frankly, what had been done before the whipping seemed worse to me. In my young mind, a beating made sense, was common place, whereas the other things, they were confusing and horrifying. Not the least of which was marrying her to my uncle. And what my uncle Villi had done to her had not even been a punishment, but merely what he called his rights.

What she had done in return for him taking those rights almost made me smile now, in spite of the dire circumstances that had followed.   My hideous uncle Villi, the one they called Villi the Bestial, was in far worse shape than my sister, who at least still had a head. Her brave rebellion had incited my own, though I would have preferred more time to put it into effect. There was still so much I didn't know about my powers, things I couldn't learn from anyone but my demented elders, as much as I may despise them.

Is she healing? I wondered to myself. If she was, I couldn't see it yet, and that worried me more than any of my father's threats. If she couldn't walk, then she couldn't run. And we needed to run from this place and never look back.

I awoke, gasping, my body damp with sweat. I hadn't had that nightmare in years. It was a memory from my childhood, that, for some strange reason, my subconscious liked to recall in vivid detail when I was troubled.

It took me a long time to fall back to sleep, and when I did, it was to more nightmares.

I was back in Dom's bedroom, my back to the wall. The sight on the bed made me sick. Dom pleasured the vacant-eyed blond endlessly. Every touch, every kiss, was a stab of betrayal through my heart. Finally, I approached the writhing couple.

I gripped a hand in the blond woman's hair, dragging her roughly from his bed. He didn't stop me, merely sat up, giving me a wicked smile. She struggled, but it took no effort at all to throw her bodily from his room. I kicked her once, twice, before slamming the door on her crumpled figure. I turned back to the man on the bed.

He just smiled, a cheshire cat smile, and watched me, leaning back on his elbows. His arousal was hard, and still slick with that other woman's body. I straddled him, mounting his thick length without a second thought. I rode him hard, but he never touched me. He just watched, gazing at me with gimlet-eyed disinterest. I brought myself to completion regardless, falling against him when I finished. I kissed him, but he was unresponsive under my lips. Only his cock responded, hard as ever.

I sat back up, and that was when my hair trailed down onto his chest. It was all wrong. It was flame red, instead of blond, and I hated it with a passion. I recalled something I'd heard. I glared at him. His expression never changed. "Siobhan?" I asked him, feeling ripped apart inside. "You bastard," I sobbed, falling off of him.

He was a statue. No response to my hurt was shown in either his regard or his actions.

I stumbled into the bathroom, desperate to see my reflection, to make sure it wasn't wrong. Green eyes looked back at me in the mirror. My face was ravishingly beautiful, and one that I bitterly despised. I screamed my rage.

I awoke still screaming, and engulfed in flames. Everything was on fire. The couch I lay on, the walls, the ceiling, *the house.* I lay there for the longest time, thinking that I had stumbled into yet another nightmare. But I felt the heat licking my skin. My bare skin. My clothing had burned off.

When my mind finally started to operate again, I shot up, running quickly through the inferno. I couldn't burn. Fire lived inside of me. It certainly couldn't harm my person. But we had a lot of worldly possessions that it could harm. Things I didn't want to lose.

I went for the weapons first, filling my arms before rushing outside. I spilled them on the lawn before running back inside. It was some consolation when I realized that many of our weapons and valuables had already been moved, most likely to one of Christian's safe houses. Lynn had begun to move our things, obviously in preparation for a permanent move. Gods bless her. Still, I grabbed what I could of what was left, finding some of our horde of treasure, and even an armful of clothes that hadn't yet been touched.

When I dumped my precious items on the lawn that time, I wasn't alone. *Fucking Druids*, I thought, as suit clad men surrounded me in the harsh dawn light. One was on his cel phone.

"Yes, Arch, she seems fine. She's naked, but unharmed."

I grabbed the phone out of his hand. "I'm flame-retardant. Please go back to fucking whats-her-name. Nothing exciting here."

The bastard laughed. "Jealous?"

I handed the phone back to one of the druids. I wasn't even sure it was the one I had grabbed it from. I didn't care. I headed resolutely back into the engulfed building, intending to salvage what I could. I heard the druids shouting in panic behind me, but I knew they wouldn't follow me in. Druids occasionally sprouted fur in their beastskin. It seemed to be a rule that things with fur hated fire. And they had absolutely no immunity to it. It wouldn't kill them, but it would hurt like all hell. Not one of them would go through that kind of pain to save a woman that was infamous for breaking the heart of their beloved leader.

I was gratified to find a stash of jewels that I had missed on the first two runs, making my efforts worthwhile. I did a once over of the entire place, until I was satisfied that I had saved all that was salvageable.

The druids were still in a panic when I came back outside. One was still on the phone, giving a blow by blow account of my 'insane' actions.'

I ignored them all, loading my remaining possessions into Christian's tiny car. I had parked it at the curb, instead of in the garage, one of the few clever things I'd done lately. I had salvaged so little that it all actually fit into the limited space. I shrugged into a skintight Hello Kitty T-shirt, and slipped on some tiny pink cheer shorts. They were my most embarrassing PJ's, but they were better than running around naked. I knew I could find something more suitable at Christian's retreat, where much of our things had been moved the day before. Someone had even been forward-thinking enough to move our cars out of our garage, and to some other property. I was glad that I was the only one who seemed to be a step behind lately.

The druid on the phone waved at me rather frantically as I slipped into my car.

"The Arch is on his way. You aren't permitted to leave-"

I laughed, peeling out. I got out of there like, well, like it was on fire.

I had soundly lost my druid tail by the time I left the city.

I arrived at the retreat bright and early. I seriously considered blaming the fire on one of our many enemies, but eventually decided against it. Needless to say, Lynn wasn't thrilled with the news, though the loss of key pieces in her extensive wardrobe seemed to be her major concern.

I crashed for a few hours, woke up, and ate. I quickly noticed that Christian's retreat was missing a Christian. Lynn informed me that he'd gone back to his place for a few of his

'toys'. It wasn't long before I got dressed, taking off to join him.
It was not a day where I could sit around, idle. I needed action.

CHAPTER SEVENTEEN

Blood-Oath

DAY 4

I knocked on Christian's door yet again, waited another minute, then used my key. This was becoming a habit. I was grumbling as I walked in the door. At least I didn't see any hooker shoes in his entryway this time.

"Honey, I'm home!" I shouted in the direction of his bedroom. "Time to work off your flab, Candy Ass!" I removed my shoes, carrying them to the gym. When I reached his pristine living room, I froze. My shoes dropped with a soft thunk onto the carpet

Christian faced me, tied to a chair and gagged with a generous amount of silver duct tape. Six druids surrounded him, but I only had eyes for one of them. Dom lounged in a chair set beside Christian's, his arm propped casually along the back of the other man's chair in a deceptively relaxed pose. He eyed me coldly. I studied Christian. He seemed largely unhurt, with only a few bumps and bruises. So far.

I held my hands up to show I wanted peace. I addressed Dom. "Please, let him go. Whatever you might think, you have no reason to quarrel with him." Christian started trying to talk through his gag, making incoherent noises. I had a pretty good idea, though, that he was contesting the no reason to quarrel comment. One of the druids calmly punched him in the stomach, effectively winding him.

I glared at them all. "How very brave. Six of you to take on one?" I was speaking to Dom, and he knew it. He fumed at me.

"I'll gladly fight him one on one. In fact, I can think of nothing I'd prefer more."

"Then fight me." My temper was starting to surface. "I'm the one you want to lash out at. I'm the one that wronged you. All Christian ever did to piss you off was to associate with me, and be born male."

"Swear on your blood you've never fucked him." Well, that shocked me. Of all the conversations I never thought I'd be having with my psycho Ex. His tone was chilling. I sooo did not want to go here, but lately, everything important seemed to be out of my control.

I strode to him, holding out my bare arm. "Cut it," I bit out. He pulled out a knife and cut me carefully. It was barely a nick. I knelt in front of him, ripping open his shirt and jacket. If he wanted to make a scene, I'd give him one. I pressed my wrist to his chest, over his heart. I glared into those exceptional eyes. "I've never fucked him. I swear it. Feel better?" My tone was sarcastic.

He leaned back a little. "Not really. You've broken blood-oaths to me before. Why are you coming to his house dressed like that?" I was wearing my usual workout uniform of a black sports bra and bike shorts.

"I came here to work out. This is how I dress when I work out. Will you let him go now?"

"Actually, he's been accused of attacking some druids. It happened yesterday, at the ren fair. Going by the description of his companions, I don't think I have to tell you what their story is."

I groaned inwardly. "So that's why you're here?"

"Not quite. The specific reason for my presence here involves some foreign royalty that I met with earlier today, and some interesting things I learned at that meeting. We had no other address connected to you. What luck that we coincided with your weekly appointment." I wasn't going to correct him that our appointments were usually at least four times a week, and that this hadn't been one of them. Why fuel that fire?

"What's any of that got to do with me?" I asked him. His precise, disinterested tone was really starting to piss me off.

"These royals were looking for something that matched a particular description. Two somethings, actually." I got a sick feeling in my stomach, not wanting this subject to be going where I thought it was.

"Can we speak about this privately?" I asked suddenly, not looking at Christian.

Dom looked between me and Christian, a certain malice in his eyes that I was a stranger to. He smiled at me, and it was not a pleasant smile. "Is it be possible he doesn't know?" he asked softly, adding a disturbing amount of relish to the question.

"Please," I begged him softly, willing him not to say another incriminating word.

"Why would I listen to your plea?"

"Is there something you want from me? Is that what you're getting at?"

His jaw clenched hard. "Many of the answers I wanted from you I found on my own this morning. What else could you give me?" He was being more of a bastard than I'd ever seen him. At least in regards to me. Even knowing he despised me, the thought of him showing no mercy towards me just wasn't registering. And I'd thought I was far too old for naiveté.

I glared at him. "I don't know. I can't pretend to know you that well anymore. For instance, you never used to insist on conducting personal business in front of your men. Is that one of the ways you get your kicks these days?"

I could see the moment the nerve under his golden eye started to tick. "Don't flatter yourself that this is personal," he spoke menacingly, each word threatening me to contradict him.

I swallowed, and took a deep breath. His gaze stayed mercilessly on my face. I just wasn't sure how to get through to this new Dom. "I'll answer any question you ask, if we can do this in private."

His cold gaze ran down my body insinuatingly. "Answers. Is that all you're offering?"

Man, I wanted to punch him. It took me a minute to stifle the urge. "Aren't answers what you want? Is there something else that you're asking for?"

He took exception to the wording. "I ask for *nothing*." His voice raised only slightly, but a chill ran down my spine at his obvious rage. The other druids bowed their heads low as they felt the punch of his power.

I spread my hands in defeat. "Fine. You want nothing. This isn't personal. If you couldn't care less about any of this, why are you here?"

His right hand shot out, gripping my neck lightly. His hands were large enough, his fingers long enough, that he could span a great deal of it with just the one hand. "You tread too carelessly here, Jillian," he rasped. "Don't presume to know me after all these years. You far overestimate my care for your welfare." It occurred to me suddenly what he was doing. Was this all just a matter of his pride? I supposed that the only way to find out was to test him. Fuck his pride.

I pressed my neck harder into his hand. "Are you rescinding your protection of me, then? Am I fair game now, to all of the druids that hate me? Just say the word and they'll have me taken care of within a month. A year maybe, if I run fast enough. Is that what you came here to tell me?" I threw my trump card at the bastard with no expression on my face.

He shut his eyes tightly, and I knew I'd won. He turned his rage-filled eyes on the men who'd stood silently and watched our tableau. "I do not rescind protection. If anyone touches her, I'll make them pay, and pay dearly. Leave us!" His voice built into a roar at the end.

When we were alone, he moved his snarling face against mine, until we were nose to nose. "I met with the dragons this morning, as I can see you've guessed. They've proposed to ally with us, to lend their support to our numbers. They would be a formidable weapon to add to our army. They had only a few, peculiar requests. If those requests aren't met, they've sworn to go actively rogue."

A knot formed in my throat, despair trying to choke me. "What were the requests?" I asked, though I had a good idea already. My mind began to work furiously. If he took me into custody, I had to find a way to warn Lynn. She could still get away.

He pushed away from me, beginning to pace. "Both requests are deal-breakers for them. We must agree categorically, or find ourselves at odds with their wishes. We adjourned the meeting long enough for me to deliberate with the council. I give them my answer first thing in the morning."

"What were the requests?" I asked again.

"The first is that we help them retrieve two of their own. Apparently two of their daughters left the clan a long time ago. One was a prisoner, the other a runaway who helped her escape. Both brought grave dishonor to the dragons. They have been named heretic, an apparently grave charge to the draak. They are to face the justice of their people. They will show no mercy."

My body was shaking, but I was proud my voice came out steady. "What was the other request?"

"The other request was not so unexpected. As you know very

well, the dragonslayers have long been on our rosters. They have, for the most part, been abiding by our laws for centuries. The draak request that they be named rogue and given into the dragon's custody. Understandably, there's some animosity between those two enemies."

It shed a whole new light on Dom's interest in Christian's involvement in our skirmish at the fair. It could be named a rogue act, and help to justify the changing of alliances.

I was silent for awhile, eyes clenched tightly shut. Me and Christian were caught. But Lynn still had a chance to get cleanly away. I needed to get to a phone. "So that's why you came here? To take us both into custody?" I tried to keep the fear out of my voice.

CHAPTER EIGHTEEN

The Element of Fire

He was suddenly back in my face, angrier than ever. "Is that the only logical conclusion to you?" His wolf eye had succumbed to the beastcall, but his blue eye was shining with emotion, and his gravelly voice was all human. All pain. "No, actually, that is far from the reason I came here. I came here to tell you that I know what you are now, and that I didn't have to learn this way. I'm going to refuse their offer tomorrow. We would never turn on our allies. And we hardly make a habit of handing over innocent women to the grisly justice of any clan. There was never a time that the druids would have considered accepting such a treaty. Not fifty years ago. Not even seven. I came here because I wanted you to know that. You killed anything we had when you betrayed me, and broke your oath. There's no going back from that. But I wanted you to know that you-" he swallowed hard, visibly trying to calm himself, "you were an idiot if you thought I wouldn't have protected you."

I laid my hand on his shoulder, but he wrenched away, pacing. The relief I'd felt just a second before, when I'd realized he wasn't here to take us, left as quickly as it had come. Now I felt fresh a pain that should have been more dulled by the years.

"It wasn't just that, Dom, and we both know it. You were assumed heir to one of the Arch positions, and your people hated me. The demons of my past were just one thing in a very long list of reasons why it never could have worked. Your people mate with humans, or other druids. I'm neither. You wanted Arch. You lived for it, more than anything. You've been preparing for it since you were a child. Your uncle would never have held elections while I was around. And your people never would have elected you to Arch with a mysterious Other as consort. And you refused to take it through combat." Who was I trying to convince? I wondered. Him, or myself? I didn't like the answer, so I made my mind ignore the question.

"You're a fool. Don't pretend you did what you did as a favor to me," he said bitterly.

I swallowed hard. "We're both fools. But I want you to tell me that you could have made Arch with an unknown Other on your arm." He was silent. "Exactly. I get it. I handled the break-up badly. You have every right to hate me for that. But I didn't exactly have to return a ring when I left you."

"What the fuck does that mean?" His voice was a shout. He was back in my face in a flash.

"It means that you weren't going to give up Arch, and I wasn't going to make you. So maybe we aren't such fools, after all."

"Bullshit. That's all bullshit. The only problem we had that couldn't be worked out was your propensity for fucking other men." I kept my expression blank, but my nails dug into my palms hard enough to draw blood. "At least have the decency to take credit for a decision you made alone."

I inclined my head towards him. "I take it. I always have."

He stared at me for awhile. "How was I with you for so many years and I never saw how cold you are? Your element must be ice." He'd done some research. Not many knew much about the dragon elements.

Each dragon adopted a different element. It was the gnosis to our power. And the focus. The element colored every magic we had. In my clan, fire was believed to be the most powerful element, but I had always been skeptical. Every element could wield equal power in the right hands. Fire simply put on the biggest show.

"Is that a question?" I finally asked.

He just shook his head at me. "I can't believe you've trusted the dragonslayer all this time. But perhaps trust is the wrong word. You know what he'd do if he found out what you are. He couldn't help himself. An unfulfilled destiny is a powerful thing to come between friends."

I smiled at him sadly. "Indeed. It's a problem without a solution. The story of my life."

"Maybe you like your life like that. I mean, how perverse do you have to be, to be a dragon, with a slayer for a best friend?" He wasn't being funny, he was being mean, but strangely, it still made me want to laugh.

I smiled wryly. "Pretty perverse, I suppose. No more perverse than the druid King who lives in the desert." He glared at me for the jab, but was silent. "Are you bringing any charges against him?"

His mouth hardened. "I don't see the point. He won't learn anything, and he's too stupid to be humbled."

"Thank you."

"Don't thank me."

We were silent for awhile, and I thought we were done. We didn't look at each other. "The dragons won't stop hunting you. None have been born to your clan since you left. I got the impression that your clan was very short on females."

I shrugged. I always assumed I was being hunted. And I didn't want to talk about The Purging. "Are you having them followed?"

"Of course. They wait patiently at the hotel for my answer.

You should wear more clothing," he commented, changing the subject suddenly. "You never used to dress like that."

I rolled my eyes, still not looking at him. "I always dressed like this to work out. I didn't come here expecting a meeting."

"Does it work, not looking at me?"

I shrugged, still not looking. "It helps some. I haven't jumped you, so that's a good sign."

"So much has changed, but the wanting hasn't gone away. Do you suppose it was only ever lust?" he asked. Ouch, that one hurt. I tried to shake it off. His shot had hit its mark squarely, though. I only wished it had been aimed to take out my libido.

Finally, I met his stare. It hurt my chest just to look at him. The pain was sharp and enduring. He was the only thing in my life I'd ever wanted badly enough that it made me shake like an addict.

I had never been like him. His absolute faith in our love, in our ability to be together, in spite of the odds, had floored me. And I had stolen it from him. And from myself. In the cruelest way that I could think of.

I'd never just been with him, thinking it would last forever. I'd always known the clock was ticking on our affair. My sense of borrowed time had always been acute. But it still made me ache to know I'd never have him like that again. A brief taste of his body only made it harder to bear the permanent loss of his love. Still, I couldn't seem to stop myself from coming back for more.

"Maybe," I said vaguely. "We can always just blame our libidos."

"I've grown rather accustomed to blaming you," he said with a rare combination of bitterness and humor.

A corner of my mouth lifted slightly. I shrugged. "Join the club."

He moved toward me, and that was all it took to sweep me

back in.

He backed me deliberately into the wall, pressing hard against me until I gasped from the sheer, solid contact. "Ask me for it," Dom growled at me, and it was clearly an order. He was trying to get a reaction, I thought. I wasn't in the mood to balk at his methods, though.

I ripped his shirt open. My hand slid down his chest and directly to his heavy erection. I gripped him with just the right amount of pressure that I knew he would love. "Please, Arch, may I have this?" I asked without a hint of mirth.

He answered by gripping my hair and pulling down until I went to my knees. I freed him from his pants and he buried both hands in my hair, pulling me towards his length. I obliged eagerly, taking him into my mouth with wet lips pulled taut over my teeth. I sucked him hard, drawing a groan out of him that I knew he was reluctant to give. I began the familiar rhythm that I knew he wanted, and that I myself relished. I used my hands at his base in a wet, twisting motion, and took him deep into my throat. He held my head and pushed into me. I felt the very air around us changing when he was close to release. He climaxed deep in my throat with a muffled groan, and I swallowed. I pulled back to look up at him, licking my lips. He put a hand on the wall, leaning heavily against it for a moment, but he'd always been quick to recover.

He lifted me back up to stand not even a minute later. And this time it was him that knelt, pulling down my tiny lycra boy shorts and my lacy thong in one efficient movement. He buried his face against my core, throwing one of my legs over his shoulder, and his clever tongue had me screaming in seconds. "Please," I said, even after I came. I loved what he could do to me with his mouth, but it never felt complete until I had him buried deep inside of me.

He rose fluidly, burying himself to the hilt in the smoothest motion. He kissed me while he thrust, and I ate at his mouth, missing that intimate contact amidst all of the rest. He pulled back to watch my eyes near the end. Their changing depths had always mesmerized him, I knew. I wondered, not for the first time, if I had inadvertently cast some sort of spell on him. There was so much I didn't know about my own power. But if it was a spell, why would I myself be just as caught up? I lost myself just as completely in his extraordinary gaze.

"Come," he commanded harshly, and it did the trick. We climaxed together, our eyes staying locked.

"What do you look like as a dragon? I've never seen one before. Is it similar to the legends?" he asked unexpectedly. We were both getting dressed. I finished first. My few scraps of lycra were much quicker to get in and out of than his tailored gray Armani suit. I kept my back to him as he finished getting dressed. Why did it sometimes seem so much more intimate getting into clothes than it did getting out of them?

"All of the dragon-kin are different. Different sizes, different shapes and proportions, different colors. But yes, we're much like the legends. I have to imagine that most of those renderings came from real encounters with dragon-kin. My family does love to be worshipped."

"What color is your dragon?"

"It's unusual actually. My dragon never chose a color. She's just like my hair, she changes on some whim, against my will."

"Does that happen to dragons often?"

"Never that I've heard of. But I left the clan before I knew much. I'm flying blind on most of that type of information. Why do you ask?"

"So other dragons' hair doesn't do that?"

"I don't think so. I'm horrible at changing my appearance on purpose though, which would be far more useful. I think the shifting colors might just be a sign of my lack of control over my magic."

"What is your element?"

I looked at him now. He was just finishing his tie. It was a solid, vibrant blue that set off his left eye to perfection. "Fire. A lot of our kind are a mix of elements, which can be useful, but I'm almost completely fire. It's the least subtle magic."

"So no ice at all?"

"No. Are you surprised?"

"Only a little. I guess I always saw the fire. Though I have seen you practice subtle magics."

I shrugged. "I was taught that we are the Firstborn. The gods gave us many magics to work with. I can use some of the subtler stuff, but it's always been my weakness. Even simple glamour gives me a headache. I have no patience for it. Fire is great for an all-out battle, but outside of that, the other stuff is far more useful." I studied him for a long time. It was so strange, talking to him about this, about what I was, after all of the years of secrecy. It made me want to tell him more, now that I was free to. "I don't know if they believe it now, but draak used to believe that every kind of Other race after us was a sort of bastard version, stealing just pieces of our lesser magics. They believed that we were the perfect prototype that couldn't be improved on, only copied poorly."

"Did you believe that?"

I smiled ruefully. "I left them when I was barely more than a child. But no, I believed little that they tried to teach me. You won't be surprised to know that I was always obstinate. I despised my father and his ways. He and his brothers believed themselves to be gods. You and your druids struggle to be fair and just. The dragon-kin are the opposite. They are so deluded about their own godhood, they believe that any horrible thought in their heads is divine. Power has driven them mad."

"I do recall that Lynn doesn't mind playing goddess."

I smiled at that. "It's different. She doesn't mind being worshipped, I'm sure. It is more her dark sense of humor though, than any belief in her divinity, that makes her collect lost souls to follow her. Sometimes you have to laugh in the face of the things that scare you about yourself, or the fear alone will drive you mad."

"Both of you always did have a dark sense of humor."

"In our family, you either go insane from the horror, or learn to laugh at it."

He handed me two business cards that were blank but for two phone numbers. "Keep one, put your contact information on the other. Don't worry, I won't be calling you. My people will simply keep you updated on the draak's activities if it seems pertinent."

I nodded, jotting it all down. "Thank you."

"I hear you've been invited to the necro assault."

"Yes. I'm rusty, but I should still be useful against a race that can burn."

"I'm having them put you in my unit. You're less likely to get any trouble from my people that way." He left the room. I watched him leave. Neither of us said goodbye.

I followed him out no more than a minute later. The druids were gone, leaving Christian still bound and gagged. I couldn't really blame them. There was murder in his eyes as I approached him. I ripped the tape off his mouth, and he started cursing fluently. "You should have let him fight me when he mentioned it, Jillian. You don't know how much I'd like to take a shot at him."

I raised my brows at him. I should have known that would be the only thing he focused on. "Are you ok?" I asked him.

"Yeah. You?"

I nodded. "Just the usual Druid politics bullshit," I lied, adding to the already huge pile. "Let's head back to the retreat."

"Those wankers," he said darkly..

"Your British is showing."

"Bloody wankers," he elaborated, making me smile.   He smiled back, always quick to shake things off.   It was by far his best quality.

CHAPTER NINETEEN

Too Much Dough For A Super-Nerd

Christian took the condition of his slightly charred porsche better than I would have expected, considering how much he always waxed poetic about it. He was more teasing than mad about it as we drove to his retreat.

Christian's mountain retreat was an impressive compound set up with Christian's keen eye for both security and style. It consisted of several small buildings, and one much larger building. The entire compound was tucked into the mountains, almost completely hidden from the small dirt road that took us the last few miles from the interstate. The exterior of the buildings were stones that matched the desert mountains like camouflage.

I had no idea what was in the smaller buildings. I knew that the larger building was all of the housing, with enough rooms to comfortably house us and even most of Lynn's followers comfortably. If I had to guess, I'd say the smaller buildings were probably bunkers stockpiling weapons. I knew I wouldn't have to wonder long to find out. Christian would give me the grand tour.

"Does it make your skin crawl to have all of the goth humans in your safe house?"

He shrugged, seeming unaffected. He probably loved the thought of showing off his pride and joy to more people. "I'd rather not be bored up here. And anyways, they're all humans. What's the worst they could do? Lynn even made them all leave their phones behind."

It still made me antsy. An overcrowded safe house… so much was wrong with that.

Christian sped into the oversized garage that opened before us with surprising swiftness. The concrete ground below the porsche began to lower immediately. It was a surprisingly smooth ride, and went down a shockingly far distance. I gave Christian wide eyes. "How far underground does this thing go?"

He grinned. It was such a smug, toothy grin. It made me want to either smile or punch him, depending on why he was wearing it. "You'll see."

Something occurred to me. I smirked at him. "Did you make yourself a bat cave?"

He wiggled his brows at me, shameless. "A slayer cave, to be exact."

I shook my head, grinning. "You have way too much dough for a super-nerd. The combination is a danger to society at large."

He threw his head back and laughed. It was infectious, especially after such a tense, volatile morning. "Wait 'til I give you the grand tour."

We got out of the car. The room could have almost passed for an oversized version of a normal garage, all smooth gray concrete. A small elevator took us back up to the main floor of the house.

As we stepped out of the elevator and onto the main floor, a goth kid handed me a note and a flower, darting off without a word. I shared a confused look with Christian before looking at the note. I handed Christian the flower, muttering, "candy ass," when he took it. He just smelled the flower, smiling pleasantly, unfazed.

The letter was on old parchment, wax seal and all. "What the hell," I said, ripping it open. I felt my whole face turn red as I began to read it.

Christian whistled softly from behind my shoulder. He had read it shamelessly from over my shoulder. "Oh boy," he said, and I could hear the laughter in his voice.

I turned sharply, jabbing a finger hard into his chest. "Don't even think of breathing a word of this to anyone."

He shrugged, grinning. "I won't, if that's what you want. But, damn, Jilli-"

"And don't breath a word about it to me, either," I growled. I was shocked that he actually listened.

Lynn approached me next, looking strange, and worried. Christian gave us a moment of privacy to speak to each other, and I caught her up quickly on all of the messes I'd been making, and attempting to clean up.

She seemed distracted at all of my news, which worried me. Some messy stuff must have been going on with her life if she didn't so much as blink at the the catastrophe of mine. "What's going on, Lynn?" I asked her finally. "Are you okay?"

She nodded. That was all. I got a real bad feeling, deep down in my gut.

My guided tour of the palatial retreat ended at the full-sized bar. It was an impressive room, complete with an actual bartender manning the fully stocked bar. "Is that one of Lynn's followers, or did you really hire a bartender?" I asked him, running a hand along the grainy pattern on the sandy toned granite that topped every surface in the place.

Christian laughed. "That is a goth, making himself very

useful." He raised his voice so it carried to the bar. "Fix me whiskey straight up, my good man. The stuff in the fancy crystal decanter will do. And the lady will have a glass of room temperature water with a lime. Thank you."

The kid nodded happily, humming to himself as he followed Christian's instructions. "He makes a terrible goth," I whispered in an aside to Christian. "He's downright chipper."

We thanked the boy for our drinks and took them to a seating area that could have passed for VIP seating at a club. "Well, what do you think of the place?" Christian asked. I could tell by his eager expression that he wanted me to be impressed with his desert palace. He was so like a kid in some ways.

I smiled at him indulgently. "It's perfect," I finally answered him. He beamed at me.

"You gonna share some of your weapon's stash with us for the necro roast?" I asked him, even though I knew I didn't have to.

"You know it, girl." His usual endearment with his faint british accent almost always made me smile. "And Caleb brought us all some nifty gifts. He says I can't see mine until the necro roast. He seems to think I would waste it before it's needed. That makes me think it's some sort of flame thrower. It feels like waiting for christmas."

I shook my head at him, laughing.

We stayed in the bar room, chatting, and I was surprised to have a packed house before long. Apparently this was the popular hangout spot of the house. I shouldn't have been surprised. It *was* a bar.

I was even more surprised about a half an hour later. Two goth girls had just introduced themselves to Christian and I. Mostly to Christian. They both had black hair and brown eyes, with about a pound of black eyeliner on. They were like different sized versions of the same person. It was bizarre. One of them was a short, heavy girl. The other one was of medium height, and was stacked like a playboy model. The pinup girl was named Cherry, and I knew by the way they flirted that Christian had found his bed partner for the night. I rolled my eyes. He was about to take a walk on the goth side. Whatever. And by the looks the other girl, Juliet, was casting at him, he could get a twofer tonight. *Barf.* I tried to erase the mental image from my head.

"I'm hungry," I said suddenly, to no one in particular. I didn't think anyone would pay me any mind. Seemingly out of nowhere, a bag of food from my favorite mexican joint appeared on the table in front of me. Two more bags joined it. Slowly, I looked up and to my left in to black-lined, dark blue eyes half hidden behind curly dark hair that fell into a handsome face as though it had been arranged that way. Luke was staring at me with an intensity that made me feel immediately uncomfortable and embarrassed. "Mistress, I drove back into town and got you your favorite barbacoa bowl for lunch. It has brown rice and all four kinds of salsa, just how you prefer." In a fluid motion, he sank to sit in a classic submissive pose, his eyes downcast. "Please, Mistress, may I watch you eat your lunch?"

I nearly choked on the water I'd been sipping. Christian started laughing hard. I glared at him. He just laughed harder. He didn't stop even when tears started running down his face. He was clutching his stomach like he couldn't keep it in. I kicked my foot sideways, catching him viciously in the shin. His knee bent into his chest, and he clutched his hurt shin, but didn't stopped laughing.

I turned my glare on Luke. "You may not. Thank you for the lunch, Luke, but please stop this silly game. I'm not your dominant. And while I'm on the subject, what kind of a submissive pursues a dom? Doesn't that seem a little off to you?" I tried to keep my voice quiet, but I knew the whole room was listening to this mortifying exchange. "I read your letter, and I can say with no hesitation at all that that is never going to happen. So just drop it." My words fell on deaf ears. All he heard was the unconscious authority I had used.

"Yes, Mistress. Shall I remove myself from your presence? Where would Mistress have me go?"

I shook my head at him in exasperation. I pointed at the opposite wall, a good distance away. "Somewhere that way. And don't cast me any more of those mournful looks, either."

Christian, who had finally fallen silent, started laughing all over again. Dammit.

"And how will my Mistress punish me if I disobey?" Luke asked. He cast me his most mournful look yet.

Christian clutched his sides. "Oh, God, I can't take it. This is too good. I'm taking this kid everywhere with me from now on."

I pointed at him threateningly. "Don't. You. Dare."

He pointed back at me. At my hair, rather. "Oh, God, your hair is lavender again. I think it does it every time you get pissed off now. This really is like Christmas. Will you move in with me, Jillian? I want life to be like this everyday. You complete me. And I have room for Luke."

That was it. I'd had it. I simply got up and moved to a different part of the room. I sat down in a cushy light-brown leather chair. I glared at the goth's who had taken up residence in the chairs around it. They beat it. Good. I was officially unfit for company.

CHAPTER TWENTY

Spiked Drink

Lynn shocked me a few minutes later by walking into the room with the strange asian man we'd seen at the renaissance fair. *Was that the man who'd put a love charm on her?* Shit, that was bad. He was bad news, I just knew it. She was giggling and holding his hand, and just acting very un-Lynn like in general. I stared, mystified. He was some kind of foreign dragon-kin, and she had just brought him into our sanctuary. It wasn't a safe house anymore. What the hell was she thinking?

The strange dragon sat down in a chair by the door, pulling her into his lap with an ardent look in his eyes.

I glanced at Christian to see how he would be taking the entrance of the strange intruder into his home.

He was completely oblivious, making a kissy face at Cherry while she and Juliet decked him out with goth makeup. I couldn't keep the disgust off of my face. Way to stay focused on the problem at hand, Douche, I thought at him childishly. And he looked way more pretty than any man should in black eyeliner.

Luke had a cow-eyed stare fixed on me. I sent him a quick glare. That was a mistake. He liked that. I looked away.

I caught Lynn's eye, and glared. She and I needed to talk,

but she just giggled and looked up at the strange dragon as though they were old lovers. His heated eyes on her showed a certain knowing intent, as though they'd slept together, and he was confident it would happen again very soon.

Caleb strode into the room, all business, and I was relieved. He wouldn't like this strange development any more than I did. Caleb motioned with his head for Lynn to join him at the bar, and I was appeased somewhat when she got out of the strange man's lap and joined him there. They spoke quietly for a few minutes, and I couldn't make out what they were saying.

Suddenly, Lynn looked at me, glaring. She was swaying a little, and her eyes were glassy. If I didn't know better, I'd say she almost seemed drunk, but there was no way she'd do something that irresponsible. *Was there?*

"What?" I asked her, glaring back. Why was Miss Basket-case mad at me?

"Nothing," she said, her words slurring alarmingly. "Just talking about some stuff I lost recently. Good thing some of my favorite comfy clothes were already here." She lifted a foot and wiggled a fluffy black kitty slipper at me. She swayed precariously.

I flipped her off. Like that was our main concern at the moment. Caleb and I seemed to be the only ones here without a ticket on the crazy train.

"At least she's sorry," Lynn raised her voice dramatically. I smirked, just to taunt her.

Lynn turned back to Caleb. They spoke quietly for several minutes. I went back to eating and brooding.

Suddenly, out of the corner of my eye, I saw the bar top go up in flames. My head whipped around. *Shit.* The flames had come out of Lynn's throat. And it was going to happen again, going by the way she was taking a deep breath. All of the air in the room seemed to be going into her lungs for the next breath of fire.

I looked in panic at Christian, whose head was just starting to turn toward the commotion. There would be no explaining away breathing fire. Even fire sorcerer's couldn't do that. Shit. Shit. Shit.

I was across the room in a flash, punching Christian square in the jaw before he could get a good look across the room. It was an instinctual, knee-jerk, retarded reaction to the inevitable threat of discovery. I didn't think it through enough to work out why it would help the situation. I just knew that I had to get his attention away from Lynn, and fast.

Christian stood up slowly, rubbing his jaw. "What on earth, Jillian?" he asked me, sounding wounded.

I covered up quickly. "Any guy wearing makeup deserves to get punched," I told him with a smirk. There were gasps from goth boys in makeup all around the room. They were all looking at me, expressions of either fear or anger on their faces. Except for Luke. I noticed he was sending me even more smitten looks from beneath his mascara coated lashes. I heard Lynn fail to stifle a giggle across the room, where I saw the strange dragon had joined her and Caleb at the bar.

Suddenly the strange dragon-kin got everyone's attention as he pointed at one of the goth boys. "It's him." The stranger's voice was deep and certain. He walked towards the terrified goth kid. "Everyone else in the room had a proper response to what was going on. They all looked surprised or scared. This one showed no emotion until I pointed him out just now." His accent was faint and asian. His english was very fluent, but still not his first language.

"Adam," Lynn identified the goth kid.

Adam didn't even try to run away when the strange dragon approached him. He just held up his hands, saying, "Ok, ok, you got me." He was addressing Lynn. "I work for your Uncle Villi. He sent me here to spy on you. What are you gonna do about it? I know you don't hurt humans." His tone was belligerent. Stupid kid.

I beat the strange dragon to the kid. I slapped Adam hard across the face. Okay, it was a bitch slap. They seemed to be going around. But it floored him. Beating up humans was no fun. They were just too soft. But I was never one to balk at what had to be done. And any human who was unfortunate enough to be mixed up with my uncle had far worse things coming to him. "I'll tell you what we'll do. We will torture you until you tell us everything you know. Sound fun?" As I spoke, I hauled him to his feet. I dragged him across the room by his hair. He whimpered. I threw him roughly into a chair.

"K, what the hell is going on, guys?" Christian asked, confused. "Everyone is acting crazy. Anyone gonna tell me why?"

I ignored him, focusing on Lynn's traitor. Caleb came up quietly beside me, speaking softly. "I'll do this, if you don't mind. I think we can all agree that torture is more my specialty than yours."

I just raised my brows at him, but I was secretly relieved. I waved a hand at Adam, taking several steps back. "By all means, have at it." I started to pace. I stopped mid-pace, addressing Adam again. "How old are you?"

Adam looked puzzled, but answered automatically. "Twenty."

I nodded. "Good. Twenty, and too stupid to live long. I'm not too comfortable torturing anyone younger than that. Congratulations, you are of torturing age." My tone was off-hand, even casual, but I felt none of it. You couldn't look sick to your stomach, or scared out of your mind, when you were trying to intimidate someone into telling what you needed to know. I wasn't nonchalant about torturing some dumb kid. I wasn't even okay with it. But the thought that Villi might be moving to ambush us at any moment quickly dispelled me of any notion to take it easy on our one available source of information.

Caleb gave me a slight, chilling smile. His eyes were scary

right then. He was going to enjoy this way too much.

"I'm over twenty," Luke said quietly, but his voice reached us all. He was still giving me that cow-eyed stare.

I just frowned at him, and for some reason I felt myself blush. I pointed at him. "You just keep quiet," I ordered him. He looked down submissively, a faint smile on his lips. Dammit, it was impossible to discourage someone who liked to be mistreated.

Lynn giggled. It was a stark contrast to the rest of the room. Most of the goths around the room were sobbing. Guess they didn't see the humor. This was probably the most horrifying thing they'd ever seen. Lucky them. This little scene was more civilized than even the most tame family dinners of my childhood. At least I never had to wonder why I was so fucked up. It would have been a miracle if I wasn't.

"Have you considered torturing him in a different room, perhaps?" the strange dragon was asking Caleb. "Or do you prefer the crying audience?"

Caleb eyed him coldly. "I prefer it, actually. Let all of them see what happens to traitors." Caleb addressed the room at large. "If anyone speaks of anything they've seen tonight, far worse will happen to them. And if I'm really put out, to their families as well."

I shook off that sobering picture. The scariest thing about that speech was that Caleb always meant what he said. It chilled me that I couldn't have stopped him from doing what he'd just said if I tried.

I addressed Adam, wanting to get on with it. "Have you spoken to Villi since you arrived here?"

Lynn giggled at me. "Her hair looks like purple cotton candy," I heard her say to someone.

I glowered at her.

Adam just smirked at me. Stupid, stupid kid. I guess he would have to be, to be a human mixed up with Villi. "Um, I'm gonna have to say no."

The strange dragon casually gripped Adam's shoulders, effectively holding him in place.

With no expression on his face, Caleb reached over, casually snapping Adam's right index finger completely back. It made a sick popping noise. It sat at that horrible angle for a moment before anyone reacted. One of the sobbing kids sounded like they were throwing up. Adam held up his finger in horror, screaming.

"Okay, same question, but without the attitude," Caleb him told him, deadpan.

Adam shook his head vehemently. "No, no. I swear I haven't. Remember, you searched me and took my phone before we came out here."

"What have you told Villi about us?" Lynn asked, her words slurred. That strange little broken finger seemed to have cured her of the giggles. Torture was a major buzz-kill, to be sure.

He just kept shaking his head. "Just the location of your shop, and your house." Caleb snapped his thumb this time. More screaming and sobbing rocked through the room.

"Try again?" I prompted in a bored tone.

"I-I told them about Lynn's following. How I thought most of them were loyal. I told them who her lieutenants were." He paused for too long, and Caleb snapped his pinky this time.

"More," Caleb said curtly.

"I-I told them about you, though I don't know what the fuck you are." He addressed Caleb. His panicked gaze swung toward Christian. He nodded in his direction. "I told them about him, though I don't think they believed me."

"How many does my Uncle have with him?" Lynn asked. I understood her concern. His 'them' answers were alarming, to say the least.

He shook his head over and over. "Dude, I have no idea. I can't tell one of those things from another. They don't tell me stuff like that."

"What things?" Christian spoke up suddenly.

Adam just laughed at him like a lunatic. "You don't even get it, do you, dude? You're even more in the dark than I am. How can you not see that you're surrounded by-" Suddenly, surreally, his head just disappeared, pieces of it decorating the wall behind him. It hadn't even been a conscious action, my hand had just found the gun in my ankle holster, aimed and shot on pure instinct. He had said enough incriminating things in front of Christian. The sound in the echoing room was deafening for a moment.

I bent down, calmly re-holstering my gun. The entire room was staring at me, mouths hanging open, jaws slack. Understandable, I supposed. I swear a few of the goths started putting curses on me.

Christian was the most shocked of the four of us, of course, since he couldn't know the reason I'd needed to silence Adam so immediately, and so permanently. "What the hell, Jillian?" he was shouting over my ringing ears. "I can't believe you shot him when he was giving us information. Was that really necessary?"

I just shrugged, acting nonchalant. "He was just wasting our time."

Christian threw his hands up in the air. "And here I thought Caleb was our resident sociopath."

I looked at Caleb. "Yeah, Caleb. Where were you on that one?" I asked him, an edge to my voice. What was his angle? Usually he was the fastest draw. I was good with guns, but they weren't even my best weapon. I needed a blade to show my real talent. And guns, well, they were Caleb's passion. Caleb looked at a solid piece like most men would look at a lover. *Was he messing with us?*

But he was studying me thoughtfully. He seemed to be as surprised as the rest of us that I'd beat him to the punch.

"That was impressive speed, considering that you were drawing from your ankle. You may actually be faster than me," Caleb's tone was speculative, making my trigger finger start itching. Knowing Caleb, he was considering drawing on me just to find out...

"He was full of lies from our uncle, Christian," I said, turning away from Caleb, effectively ending the tense standoff. "Villi was using him to try to hurt Lynn, and I told you only the nice parts of what that monster did to my sister. We could have never let him go. He would have led them to us."

"Ok, ok, just someone needs to explain to me a little more of what's going on here. I hate being kept in the dark." As Christian spoke, his phone started ringing, along with Caleb's. I found this to be an odd coincidence.

The connection made sense a moment later, when I realized that it was a call from the druids. Tonight was the night. Time for a Necro roast.

"Maybe it wasn't such a bad night for Lynn to get sloshed," I muttered under my breath.

"I will take care of cleanup, and watch over Lynn's children," the strange dragon spoke into the charged silence. We had been absorbed in thoughts of prep and battle.

"Who the fuck are you?" I asked him, finally.

He gave me a little mysterious smile. "I'm Drake. And you are Lynn's sister, Jillian. You have a very strange choice of lovers. Where I'm from, your affair with the druid King would be considered quite taboo."

I just blinked at him. I really, really didn't like Drake. The feeling was instant and almost blinding. He knew way too much about me, about us, and I didn't care to hear anyone's observations about my love life, not even someone whom I didn't hate on sight. I didn't trust him, but if he was staying and we were leaving, I decided to deal with the problem later. One thing was for certain; We wouldn't be coming back here until I knew more about the bastard.

I smiled at him rather unpleasantly. It was no coincidence that he had rolled into town at the same time as my family. It simply couldn't be.

I addressed Lynn, knowing even as I did so that she was in no condition to help me just then. "What were you thinking, bringing him here?"

Her eyes seemed clear enough as she stared me down. "You need to trust me on this, sister. He's on our side. I don't have time to explain it now, but I will tomorrow. Can you wait until then to question my judgement?"

I sighed. She'd gotten way too defensive way too fast. I knew my sister. When she got defensive, she got stubborn, and a stubborn Lynn was nothing I wanted to deal with. "Fine. Tomorrow will work, I suppose, if it all doesn't blow up in our faces before that."

CHAPTER TWENTY-ONE

That's Siobhan

The meeting place we'd been assigned was a large warehouse in a seedy part of town. Cars nearly filled the parking lot. Anyone driving by the place probably thought a rave was going on.

The first person I noticed when we walked into the room full of druids did not set the evening off to a good start.

Siobhan was tall and voluptuous and every bit as beautiful as I remembered. And the moment her bright green eyes met mine across the room, I knew that she hated me every bit as much as she had seven years ago. The feeling was very much mutual. She started whipping her deep red hair back repeatedly as she stared at me. I made a note to tell her that horses did the same thing when they got agitated. That might sound a little catty, but Siobhan brought me to catty in seconds flat. She and I did not have a friendly past. Ok, that's putting it very lightly. She'd hated me from the moment she'd heard of me. I hadn't really cared one way or the other. Until she'd poisoned me. The poison didn't kill me, of course. It did make me throw-up my dinner. Oh yeah, and it pissed me off royally. I'd returned the favor by throwing her headfirst out of a twelve story window. It's safe to say that didn't help us to patch things up.

Siobhan was childhood friends with Dom and his cousins. They had also dated some years before he and I became an item. According to her, I was all that stood between them reconciling and living happily ever after. According to everyone else, they'd always just been friends and occasional bedmates. I was the only woman Dom had ever dated exclusively. I'd also heard from other sources that Dom had flat-out told her he was planning to marry me. So, all of her jilted lover angst always fell to me. Go figure.

Christian, who had entered the room right behind me, whistled softly. "This should be an interesting evening." His whistling suddenly turned into the tune for the theme from 'Rocky'.

I shot him a glare over my shoulder. "For you, maybe."

"Hell yeah, for me. I'd say I have your back, but if I touch that prissy druid princess, they'll gut me outright."

I nodded. "Yes. You definitely need to stay out of it. It's fine. I'm going to ignore her anyways. It's all ancient history. If she has half a brain, she'll pretend she didn't see me."

"She always had more tits than brains," Christian muttered. Sure enough, she was striding across the room to us as he spoke. Several druids paced after her, talking rapidly. Trying to talk her out of doing anything stupid, I was sure. The room was full, mostly of men. Not surprising. Most of them wore black, with various armored vests. Christian and I were decked out the same. Not Siobhan. She wore a slinky red dress that barely covered her crotch. Oh, and it clashed with her hair.

She stopped a few feet from me, her hands clenched. "Whore," she spat. Not a good start.

I calmed myself before speaking. "Siobhan. It's pointless for us to still be fighting each other for a man that doesn't belong to either one of us. Let's just leave it at that." I really was trying to defuse the situation. Honest.

If anything, it worked her up even more. "Don't you tell me where to leave it, you dumb bitch! I'll leave you buried in the fucking desert!" I just blinked at her for a minute. She wasn't alone with that sentiment. Apparently my desert burial was a popular fantasy amongst the druids.

"I'd love to see you try," I told her softly. I couldn't help it. Seriously. When someone threatened me, and I was ninety-nine percent sure they couldn't kill me, I had to call them on it. And I would sincerely love to see her try.

"One of these days I will." Her voice was a purr. I'd forgotten how much I hated that venomous drawl.

I shrugged. "I'll be waiting. Has it ever occurred to you that your problems with Dom have nothing to do with me? I left for over seven years, and it looks like all you managed to get out of him were some pity fucks." Okay, even I thought that jab was on the bitchy side. But it felt so fucking good to say it.

She was literally quivering in rage. She was showing considerable restraint though, for her. Years ago, whenever we'd had a confrontation, half the room had had to hold her down. "They have everything to do with you. You fucked with his head. If he had never met you-"

"Um, sorry to correct you, but he's known you all your life."

"Luckily I was there to comfort him when you left. You were exactly what I'd always told him you were. Guess whose bed he crawled into to lick his wounds?"

The revelation stung more than a little, but I shrugged, my face serene. "Hmmm, let me think. Probably whoever was clinging closest? I'm assuming that was you? He'll fuck anything these days, I've heard. Seems like he's getting your kind of comfort from a lot of girls."

"Even you now. Rumors are you two tore up his office. You think you're reconciled? He'll never care about you again. I hope you know that. He's on to you now. I always told him you were screwing around on him. He denied it, but I knew he always suspect-"

I'm not even completely sure how it happened, but before she finished her sentence, my fist was flying through her face. Not into her face, but right through it, as though I'd been aiming at a spot a foot behind her, and her face just sorta, I don't know, got in the way? I'd be lying if I said I wasn't gratified to see her fly back twenty feet, slamming into the wall. Though I have to admit, it wasn't quite as fun as that time I threw her out a window.

She lay there, stunned. Every eye in the room was staring at me in shock. I wasn't sure whether they were shocked that I'd punched her, or that I'd punched her hard enough to throw her that far. Suddenly every eye was centered behind me, on the open doorway. I didn't turn. No way was I giving my back to the bitch after what I'd just done.

"I swear you show up just to cause trouble." I recognized the gravelly voice instantly. Cam strode past me, going to help Siobhan to her feet, I assumed. I assumed wrong. He restrained her arms as soon as he reached her. "This ends now." His authoritative voice commanded the room.

"You had sex with Dom?!" Christian's voice whispered loudly behind me.

"Shut up," I whispered, just as loudly.

"Oh my God! You really did!"

"Shut. Up."

"You sneaky little tramp." Christian was laughing at me.

"I'm going to rip your head off!" Siobhan was screaming from across the room. I stuck my tongue out at her. It's entirely possible that I was actually losing maturity as the years went by. Likely, even.

Suddenly she ripped free of Cam, rushing across the room. I braced for her, but Cam caught her again. Christian grabbed both of my arms from behind, pulling me farther into the room. I struggled against him, though I held back. She'd almost made it to me. I wished she had.

"If you touch her, and Dom finds out about it, he'll punish you. As unfair as it is, none of us can harm her," Cam was murmuring softly to Siobhan, but I heard him clearly.

"You all act so scared about that," Siobhan responded. She sounded more calm than she looked. Then again, she wasn't talking to me. "I poisoned her once, and he didn't do a damned thing about it."

"He never knew about it," I spoke up. A room full of angry eyes turned to me. I shrugged at them. "I didn't tell him. Unless someone else did?" I knew no one had.

"I won't tell you this again," Siobhan was screeching again, in my direction. "Stay away from him. If you ever touch him again, I'll fucking kill you!"

I couldn't help it. I smirked at her. She went crazy for a few minutes, but couldn't get loose of the growing group of men restraining her. Christian was still the only one restraining me. I knew he was really just trying to help. He knew that if he didn't restrain me, one of the druids would try, and things would get quickly out of hand, then. I let him get away with it, though I didn't make it too easy.

Siobhan stilled as two figures filled the doorway. Her tantrums had brought her within arms length of it.

Lynn and Caleb studied the scene in front of them rather indifferently.

"Good," Cam panted at Lynn when he recognized her. "Go get your sister under control, and tell her to shut her fucking mouth." I had the urge to tell him I hadn't even spoken for several minutes, but bit my tongue.

She didn't obey, but she looked at me, raising a brow in question. She looked remarkably recovered from her drunken ordeal. Caleb had obviously succeeded at sobering her up. I nodded at Siobhan, who was carrying on like a maniac again.

"That's Siobhan," I told Lynn.

Lynn's fist met Siobhan's face before anyone saw it coming. Siobhan finally stopped running her mouth. She was out cold. Adding insult to injury, I swear Lynn muttered, "Cunt," at her loudly enough for all of the druids to hear. The druids wouldn't appreciate having the C-bomb dropped on their favorite princess.

Lynn totally ignored all of the shocked looks aimed her way. Even Caleb was looking at her strangely. She just grinned at me across the room. "Man, I've been wanting to pop that bitch in the face for years." Oddly enough, we were the only two in the room that laughed.

None of us were surprised when Cam ushered the four of us into another room. We'd been separated from the rest of the group like naughty children, though I'd be the first to admit that we kind of deserved it. But only kind of. Siobhan had more than kind of deserved a few punches to the face.

CHAPTER TWENTY-TWO

Wouldn't Know Functional

Christian started instigating the moment the door closed. "Jillian did the wild thing with Dom. Word is, they tore up his office." He grinned at me while he spoke.

Caleb looked at me, disbelieving. Lynn merely raised a brow at me, though she didn't look like she believed him, either.

I looked pointedly at the ceiling, refusing to respond.

It was the wrong approach to take. All three of them started laughing and talking at once.

"That didn't take long," Caleb noted.

"Wow, so you lasted a whole five minutes before you jumped him, huh?" Lynn smirked at me.

I curled my lip at them all. Bastards. "I don't want to talk about it."

"Apparently they can't be in the same room with each other and not bang. I'm surprised you managed to keep your hands off each other at my house." His eyes widened in realization. "Shit, did you screw him in my living room?"

I glared at him. "Bite me."

Lynn and Christian hooted with laughter. Even Caleb was grinning.

"Sounds like someone has been," Lynn chortled.

"Dirty girl," Caleb said with a small smile.

"Goddammit, girl, that's just rude. That room will never be the same now. I might need new furniture."

"And new carpet," I added just to torment him. He winced. "And new walls."

"So you reconciled?" Caleb's tone was dubious.

I shook my head. "Far from it. In fact, he hates me."

"Well, that's not at all dysfunctional," Christian quipped, his tone sarcastic but annoyingly lighthearted.

I gave him that look reserved for when members of your family say something particularly dense. "Ya think? The people in this room wouldn't know functional if it gave us all a roundhouse kick to the face."

"Amen, Sista," Lynn said, snapping her fingers.

"Dom and I just need to stay away from each other. I've known that for a long time. He's a stick of dynamite, and I'm a blow-torch. Dysfunctional is putting it lightly."

That depressing conclusion was enough to move them on to a new topic rather quickly.

About an hour later Christian and Caleb were comparing the sizes of their guns while Christian braided my hair. No, that's not a joke. They did it all the time. It was the number one topic the two of them liked to talk to each other about. It was definitely a man thing.

And yes, Christian loved braiding hair. He carried hair ties and bobby pins in his pocket on the way to any fight, doing my hair on the way. We always gave him shit, but it never fazed him. His favorite style was tight braided buns on each side of my head. He actually executed the style perfectly, and I let him get away with it. No, I hadn't lost a bet. The buns actually worked well for fighters with long hair. Seriously. "It's just a tinge purple at the moment," Christian tried to comfort me as he finished up. I gave him a dirty look for even mentioning it.

Caleb was carefully adjusting the heavy shoulder harness for my battle axe. It had felt a little tight. I barely had to mention the issue before Caleb made me take it off, and started fixing it. He wouldn't tolerate backup who didn't have their equipment up to par, was what he always muttered right before he repaired whatever problems we were having.

Lynn and I were just getting warmed up, making men and their gun sizes jokes, when the door slammed open. Cam loomed in the doorway, his eyes settling on me with their usual loathing.

"Jillian, may I have a word with you out in the hallway?" The words were civil enough, but his tone was far from it.

I got up, curious more than anything. "Holler if you need us," Lynn said quietly when I passed her. I nodded slightly as I left the room. I really didn't want to leave my axe behind in that room, but I did it. I was trying to play nice, goddammit.

Cam led me down the hallway, stopping when we were out of earshot of the others. He faced me, trying to make his face blank. I could still see his contempt. I gave him my own blank look. I pulled it off much better than he did.

Cam was a bear of a man. He was Dom's height almost exactly, but he was just...massive. His shoulders were broad and bulky with bulging muscles. There wasn't an ounce of fat on him, but he had none of Dom's lean elegance. He was built too much like a pro wrestler, or a bulked up football player. He had the raven blue-black hair and stunning eyes that were a stamp of his bloodline. Side by side with his own brother, and even his cousin, no one could have failed to note that they were related. They were good-looking sons of bitches, I'd give them that. He loomed over me, and if anyone could have intimidated me with menacing size alone, it would have been Cam. Luckily, I was too stubborn to be intimidated. I met his gaze head-on, my stance as aggressive as his own.

"What do you want, Cam?" I'd always found it best to just be direct with Cam. He was a mean son of a bitch, but he had always been plain-spoken as a rule.

He continued to study me for a moment. Finally, he spoke, "What I've always wanted. You, gone. Mav and Michael have been taken into custody for some fiasco that I know you were involved in. Siobhan had to be escorted away. You can thank yourself for losing us a valuable soldier tonight. I hope that little scene back there was worth it for you."

I just gave him a level stare. No way was he going to make me feel bad about Siobhan leaving. "If you think she would have let it end any other way, you're kidding yourself."

"I didn't see the whole altercation, but I do know that she didn't get a shot at you. If you're going to throw the first and only punch, you can't exactly blame her." I didn't point out that Lynn had gotten a punch in too. That would hardly help my case.

He may have had a point, but frankly, I had no intention of admitting it to him. I just gave him a blank stare. "Your point?"

"My point," he said softly, "is that you bring nothing but trouble, and I want to know if you intend to screw with Dom's life again. He's only seen you twice and he's already more distracted and volatile than he's been in years. He sent away his 3rd Lieutenant tonight, rather than you. Do you know how fucked up that is? Siobhan would *die* for him, it's her job, and he sent *her* away after you punched her. He can't be reasonable about you. You need to stay the fuck out of his life. Is that too much to hope for? I'd rather know up front."

I stared at Cam for awhile, debating whether to give him a straight answer or not. We had never gotten along. He'd always been a bastard to me, even before he had a reason to be. I felt no particular obligation to put his mind at ease. Finally I did, but only to avoid more drama. "Don't get your panties in a twist. I mean to stay as far away from him as possible."

"I wish I could trust that. You know, don't you, that he never would have made Arch if you had stayed together. Having anything to do with you at this point would discredit his leadership. If you have any care at all for him, you'll stay the hell away."

I curled my lip at him. "I've always been able to read the writing on the wall crystal clear. We done here?"

He shook his head at me. "You may have the obsession of our leader, but you also have the hatred of our people. You walk a dangerous path. Siobhan is much admired among the druids. What you did here tonight is only going to add to your infamy. You had best watch your back."

"Is that a threat?" I asked softly, my eyes going very cold as I studied him closely.

He shook his head. "As much as I'd love to punish you for the things you've done, I would never disobey my Arch."

"That is reassuring, Cousin." An all too familiar voice spoke from behind me. I shivered involuntarily.

Cam started visibly. He bowed his head briefly to his leader. "Cousin." His tone was respectful.

I turned to look at him in spite of my better judgement. He was dressed in a black armored vest and cargo pants, his arms bare. The same as most of the fighters here. The same as me. Why was it so much more distracting on him? His arms were crossed over his chest, upper arms bulging. I nodded at him in greeting, then pointedly looked away.

"I hope you have a good reason, Cam, for interrogating Jillian in the hallway. Alone."

Cam's jaw clenched. He sent a quick glare in my direction. "I do, actually. Jillian here knocked Siobhan across the room. She wasn't here five minutes before she started some shit. I thought someone should address the issue."

Dom looked more surprised then mad, which made Cam even angrier. I could tell Cam wanted to speak, but with great effort, held his tongue. "Leave us, Cam. I'll speak with her."

Cam bowed his head briefly, then strode past Dom. The two huge men barely fit by each other in the narrow hallway. I wasn't sorry to see Cam go, though being alone with Dom was not a good idea for me.

He studied me for a moment. I made a point of not meeting his eyes. "It's never a healthy idea to go around hitting druids, Jillian. Anything in particular that set you off? A jealous fit, perhaps?"

The bastard actually sounded a little smug. "For her, maybe. She called me a whore, and I decked her. She threatened to kill me if I ever touched you again. Same old shit as always. You need to keep that bitch on a leash."

He sighed. "You two never should have been in the same room together. It won't happen again. It's a pity, really. Siobhan is one of our strongest fighters. She would have been useful tonight."

He studied me silently for the longest time. I could hear my own pulse as I waited for him to say or do something, but I at least had the self-control not to look at him.

It all felt so surreal, going from years of separation and back to being allies, fighting together almost like old times.

"What kind of weapons are you carrying?" he asked. "Where is your axe? You can't be thinking of fighting without it. This is not going to be a small raid, Jillian. We are going against a very large horde of the necros. You don't even have a long sword?"

I smiled wryly, watching my feet. It had been years, but still, he should have known better. "My axe is back in the room with Caleb. He's making some adjustments to my harness. It was a little tight, with my gun harness. And I didn't trust myself to be in a small space with Cam, holding my favorite weapon bare in my hands."

He made a deep sound in the back of his throat. It made things low in my stomach clench.

"Show me what else you're carrying."

I complied, showing him my guns first. I wore a shoulder holster that carried matching pistols. They were modified by Caleb, as almost all of my goodies were. Specialized weapons were the biggest perk of staying close friends with a sociopath chameleon alien. Ok, I didn't actually think he was an alien, but I wouldn't have been all that shocked if I ever found out that he was. He was just so profoundly *off* from everyone else that tried to pass for human.

The pistols were clearly visible, mounted just below my armor covered breasts, but Dom checked them anyways. He even removed them from the holsters to check the rounds.

"Explosive rounds," I told him. "They only carry ten. I have more of the good rounds packed, and some normal clips."

He re-holstered them. I watched his hands as he did it. I had thought that it was his eyes that seemed to be-spell me, but the sight of his hands had a very similar effect. I shook myself, looking resolutely at my feet.

"They're placed a little low. Let me see you draw."

I had already checked this myself, but I humored him. He was the man in charge, and I didn't want to argue with him. If we started fighting, gods only knew what would happen. I just couldn't trust myself with him.

I drew the guns swiftly and smoothly, their mounted position just below my breasts perfect. I aimed them at the ground. "See? Good to go." I re-holstered them just as smoothly.

He made a low sound of approval in his throat. I could see my chest rising and falling with my harsh breaths. Hadn't we fucked just that morning? How had that not assuaged even an ounce of the wanting?

"Show me the rest."

I showed him my pockets of extra ammo. "I'm carrying a duffle with additional ammo. I figure we'll move forward in waves. I'll just drag it along when I'm not actively fighting."

I showed him my knives next. I had only the two guns on me,

the larger ones would go in the duffle, but I had a shit-ton of knives. I showed him the longest one. It was mounted on my thigh, and ran nearly the entire length of it. That made it closer to a short sword than a knife, since I had a very long thigh. It had been a bitch to find pants with a thirty-six inch inseam before online shopping came along.

Torturously, he knelt down and examined the sheath, running his fingers over the buckled straps. I crossed my arms, suddenly baffled about what to do with my hands. I knew what I wanted to do, but that was *not* what I *would* do.

"I have an ankle sheath as well, with a bowie knife with a serrated edge." He checked that as well.

I showed him all of the smaller knives I had along my arms and torso, detailing all the additional equipment that I had packed. He studied it all personally, even checking my vest with his hands. I should have told him that any gear that had already passed Caleb's inspection was above reproach, but I remained silent. I stood perfectly still for his appraisal. I was determined to get through this encounter without laying a finger on him.

Finally he stepped back. I breathed a sigh of relief. See, I could be in the same room with him without jumping him. It was a close thing, though.

He smiled briefly. It was a sad smile. I wondered if his smiles ever looked happy anymore. All of the brief glimpses I'd seen of them had been bittersweet at best. "I like your hair." His expression quickly went serious again. "Be careful out there," he told me softly, before walking away.

"You too," I told his back.

CHAPTER TWENTY-THREE
Battle Charge

The nightmare voice drifted out to us as if by accident. Like we were overhearing a conversation that grew in volume as we listened.

That voice inspired a fear in me that was reserved almost exclusively for my bloodthirsty family, oh yeah, and the occasional demon from hell. It was that, oh shit I wanna run and hide somewhere until life goes back to what it should be, kind of fear. And it wasn't just the glamour in that voice that inspired it. It was also a fear of what the necros represented, what they could do. If left unchecked, they could turn the world into ravening monsters like themselves. Perhaps thats why I took particular joy in butchering them in bulk.

The huge necro settlement had been a military base at one time, and was surrounded completely by a tall, barbed-wire fence. The druids were making short work of the fence, using cutters to make a large opening for our large force to slip through. They were almost done when we realized that our presence had been detected by the nightmare creatures inside. It was far from ideal timing.

I could hate the druids for a lot of things. In fact, I did. But I did have to give them some serious credit where the necros were concerned. They were the major force that kept the things from running completely amok. If not for their considerable efforts, and constant vigilance, the world could quite possibly turn into something from a zombie apocalypse film. And for that, even I was a little bit grateful to them.

After what was called 'The Great Druid Wars' had ended nearly fifty years ago, the 'cleansed druids' had fought and eventually abolished the 'blood druids'. The cleansed druids were what we knew today, a law-enforcing people who had turned their back on a dark past riddled with human sacrifice and other atrocities. Blood druids sought the old ways, and refused to give up the practice of human sacrifice to gain powers. From what I had heard, the blood druids were more powerful, but a great majority had sided with the cleansed. It had involved centuries of battles, the last years of it dwindling down to routing out the enemy in hidden keeps, caves, and groves. I had learned all of this, and nearly everything I knew of druids, and that I shouldn't know, from Dom. His parents had, tragically, died just before the very last battle in the war. Their heads had decorated spikes on the walls of the fortress that the cleansed had stormed to take out that last malevolent pocket of bloods druids. They had been captured just days before the entire war had ended.

Dom had been just a teenager when it happened. I had comforted him in his grief. He had run to me when he learned the devastating news, and it had broken my heart to see his anguish. I had wept for him, the first time I had wept since I was a small child. It had been too much, to see a perfect boy who deserved his perfect parents, lose everything in a senseless act of brutality.

We'd had to run again shortly after that, as a too young Dom had started to become too attached to me. He had been impossible to deter or resist almost the second he'd turned eighteen. The only way to deal with his relentless pursuit had been to leave. He hadn't found me again for decades.

After that horrible war, the bulk of the druids' attention turned to the growing threat of the necros, whose sickness spread like wildfire. I'd assisted with many of their raids, but this was one of the biggest druid forces I'd seen gathered for such an attack.

"Druids!" Its voice was like a mix of dead tortured things sewn together, some screeching, some singing discordantly. The core of the voice sounded almost human, deep and menacing, with a strong punch of power that raised the hair on the back of my neck. "You trespass here. You thought to burn us in our sleep? Well, we are ready for you!" He screamed at the end. A legion of unearthly screams cheered his words. If all of those voices were more than illusion, we were vastly outnumbered.

In spite of myself, I felt a tremor of terror move through my body. I willed it away, knowing fear was one of their greatest weapons.

"Sounds like we won't have to fight over kills," Christian's voice rumbled into my ear. He was directly behind me, almost hugging my back. I couldn't imagine it was comfortable for him, since I had a massive double-bladed battle-axe strapped there. We were surrounded by druids in various animal forms, using the magic of their beastcall. Many were over-sized wolves, cougars, and other cats. The more powerful druids were mostly bears or tigers. They were the strongest and most coveted forms. Some were armored, others preferred to fight unencumbered, covered only in their fur. More still kept to human form, either by preference or necessity. All of those ones were heavily armed and armored.

We were one of three units flanking the settlement. Our unit was assigned to the west side. Dom led us, poised at the front line. It seemed foolhardy to place your leader at the front, but I knew from experience that Dom would allow nothing else. The druid leader's battle prowess was a matter of greatest pride to them all. Sloan, Dom's 1st Lieutenant, led the group to the north, poised to charge the front gate, and Cam, as 2nd lieutenant, led a large force that would be taking the east. A much smaller force was stationed on the outskirts of the complex, in position to catch any runaway necros. Lynn and Caleb had been roped into joining that crew, which was led by Collin, Dom's 4th Lieutenant. I hadn't liked the separation, but we cooperated, since we all figured we'd raised enough hell already that evening. They might not invite us to any more of these parties if we were more trouble than we were worth.

"You think because you are Born Other it gives you the right to rule the Created?" The chilling voice wailed again into the night. It seemed to be slithering around us now. There was no way to tell which direction it came from. "Tonight we will show you who has the strength to rule! Necros, tonight we will feast on druid blood!" A chorus of unearthly cheers rent the air.

"Who speaks?" Dom's voice bled into the night. His voice held all of the power of the necro leader's, but was so much more compelling. Where the necro leader's voice made terror race down your spine, Dom's inspired submission. Every druid around us knelt on the ground when he spoke. The few of us who weren't druids were the only ones still on our feet. I could see that he retained his human form, but his voice had gone beast.

"I am the necro King!" the thing screamed.

"I recognize no necro King!" Dom roared back. "The necros have named no King! If you want to be king, you will fight! No King sneaks off in the dark after the fight begins. I am the druid King, and I will lead the charge! I will burn this city of abominations to the ground! Fight me now if you want to call yourself a King!"

"I think not." The voice slithered around us again. "But you will die tonight, Arch. My people will make a banquet of your flesh!"

"Take your best shot. Coward!" Dom roared. I shivered watching him, a little awed. Power literally poured off of him in visible waves. I'd never seen him quite like this, at his full potential for power. He was like a beacon to the other druids, his power a thing to behold. I doubted another druid, alive or in the past, could touch his powerful command. Not even his Uncle, the European Arch, who had ruled for centuries, was his match.

I wondered if all the blood I'd given him was responsible for any of it. I still didn't know the full effects of what our blood did for the drinker. Could it be responsible for a permanent increase in power? I wondered about this, not for the first time.

I had put my blood into his drink many times over the years we'd been together. I had felt an almost uncontrollable urge to feed him my blood. Lynn and I had discussed it before, this urge to give our blood to the ones we wanted to protect. Though, unlike Lynn, I had no urge to give mine to anyone but the closest of friends. So far, that had only ever been Christian, and Dom.

Dom had even caught me at it once.

I had been in the kitchen of our shared apartment. Just thinking of that place in passing made me sigh with longing and regret. I still dreamed of it, our apartment in Denver. It had been ours, the place we shared with so much freedom. It was small, a downtown pad, with only two bedrooms. But it had been perfect. Many of the best memories of my long life had happened there. I would have stayed there forever if I'd thought it was possible.

I had been fixing us drinks. Hot tea, I recalled. Dom had been waiting in bed for me. It was almost a habit to prick my finger, and place a few drops into his. As I rinsed the pairing knife in the sink, I felt his presence behind me in the modest kitchen. I turned, startled, my hand to my heart, wondering what all he'd seen.

He had watched me for a long moment, his gaze enigmatic. He strode to me, unhurried, and unruffled, it seemed. He circled my wrist softly, then brought my pricked finger to his mouth, sucking on the tiny wound until it closed, using just a touch of that wonderful magic of his. I gasped. He ignored me, reaching for his doctored drink behind me. He downed the scorching hot liquid as though the full-sized glass were a shot. He set the glass in the sink, then stepped close to me again. He cupped my cheeks, touching our foreheads, his eyes intense but unreadable. I knew, just knew, that he'd seen what I had done.

"It's not what you think," I had told him tremulously. I hated how guilty my strange actions made me look. What must he be thinking?

He just stared at me for an endless moment. "It doesn't matter. If you were trying to harm me, I'd want to be harmed. Whatever it is you think your blood will do to me, I want it done. My life and my heart are in your hands, to do with as you please."

I shook my head at him slowly, thinking he was an impossibly hopeless man. An impossibly crazy man. An impossibly wonderful man. "It's to protect you. All I want is to protect you," I had whispered.

Finally, he had smiled, a heartbreaking smile. It had devastated me. Even the memory of it devastated me. "Then I'll live forever."

Back in the present time, moments from the bloody battle, Dom raised his fist into the air, and in the dark I could see the outline of one giant bear claw, his other arm still human and gripping a flame-thrower, the weapon of choice against these creatures. I hadn't even known it was possible to partial shift. And it wasn't as though I hadn't spent years among the druids. In the years we'd been together, I'd seen many, including the previous Arch, shift for battle.   I made a note to ask around about this strange ability.

"Charge!" Dom's voice boomed into the night like a gunshot. The battle was on.

CHAPTER TWENTY-FOUR

Battle Dance

The first wave of necros went directly for the Arch, since he had already charged recklessly through the opening in the fence. I watched, a little stunned, as he dispatched one after another brutally. The ones that were able to rush past the druids around him were met with his flame-thrower. The ones that avoided the flames had their heads ripped clean off. He was a wild-thing fighting, and I freely admit to being mesmerized. A wave of druids quickly separated us from him, but I caught glimpses of him fighting as I was pulled in another direction. "Quit ogling your boyfriend, Jillian. We've got things to do," Christian shouted as he pulled me along by my left arm. I glared at him, but followed.

"Make that showy axe useful, girl," Christian said as we approached a still intact section of fencing. He had Dragonsbane bare in his hand, and it was growing as I watched. He held it in one hand, but it grew massive in seconds, glowing like blue fire. It was impressive. He used both hands to bring it down on the fence.

I shook myself, drawing my axe. It wasn't like me to get distracted so easily when there were things to kill. My familiar axe was heavy but well balanced in my hands. The double edged metal of the blade was shinning in the moonlight. It sang in my hands as I swung it at the fence. Christian was using his sword to carefully cut the links on the fence, but I hacked at it with gusto. It was just how I fought. I was controlled, but you wouldn't know it by looking at me. I had cleaved the fence in front of me nearly to the ground with the force of my blow. I swung again, loving the feel of the axe even when it was still only a fence that I attacked. I couldn't wait to kill things that *bled.*

Christian's line of fence fell just moments after mine. We had cut it from top to bottom, so it fell forward with nothing left to support it. Druids around us were trying similar techniques to reach the action faster, but ours had been the most effective. Several druids saw our success, rushing in directly behind us. You might have thought we were leading a group of them, if you didn't know a thing about druids and their disdain for other races. Oh, yeah, and that every last one of them hated my ass with an enduring passion.

I saw that we were maybe forty yards from where Dom was fighting, but it was close enough to get instant attention from the writhing mass of necros. A section of them broke off, rushing right at us like the rabid flesh-eaters they were. Christian got into a familiar stance, readying to fight at my back. We both needed space to fight, using such long handled weapons, but we had fought side by side too many times to count, so we positioned ourselves naturally. We waited for a wave of them to hit us, the druids behind us passing us with a few scathing comments about getting our asses into the fight. They were on us in seconds either way.

My battle-axe sang as I swung it high, bringing it down on the first unlucky undead to get within my reach. Its skin was graying, it's eyes blood red. It looked like a walking corpse that had been through hell. And that about summed up the life of a necro. They were dead humans who just refused to recognize the fact, feeding on other humans just to buy themselves a little time. Its head went splat, and I sliced him in half in an almost smooth motion, the noise wet and loud even amidst the loud sounds of battle. Necros were squishy. They were diseased and decaying, rotting from the inside out. They had to feast constantly on human flesh to keep from rotting until they had fallen to pieces. This group seemed particularly squishy, I noted, as I swung hard, decapitating a second monster in a flash.

The trick to fighting with a big-ass weapon in the crowded battleground was to turn every strike into the next attack. I didn't draw back to hack at the enemy, but just kept pushing, hacking through one undead body, and into the next. It was an effective tactic, considering my strength and my huge weapon, though the technique wouldn't have worked for many.

Something bit my back, and I screamed, more in anger than pain. I turned, blade sweeping at everything in reach, but the necro was already down, Christian's sword being drawn from its body.

I gave him a nod, then turned back to the chaos. In a blurringly fast movement, I raised the axe above my head, cleaving it down into the thick swarm of Necros. I began to turn my body with the motion, chopping into flesh as I spun. I had never been swarmed by so many before. It was both terrifying and exhilarating. We would take heavy losses in this crush of a battle, but on the other hand, I didn't need to hold back. I could just let go, becoming the dangerous thing that I was born to be. I let my body and mind go into the trancelike state that lived for battle. I was a berserker, and this was my rage. Things would bleed, and I would glory in it.

Some of the necros held weapons, knives and machetes, or something similar, mostly. But they were a largely untrained fighting force, teeth snapping and arms swinging wildly as I cut down one after another, or even several at a time. A few held guns, but that was uncommon. Guns were just harder to come by, and Necro's didn't have a long lifespan, thanks to the druids.

I wasn't a dancer, except for in battle. Here, I danced, spinning and lunging, swinging and slashing. I even had a song in my head, and I moved to the beat as I killed, and killed.

We had cleared a break in the mob when I paused to take a breath. "Fuck, you're scary," Christian said behind me, his voice quiet. "Let's stay friends, k?"

It broke me a little out of my trance, and I laughed, a rich sound.

I saw Dom maybe thirty yards away. He too, had cleared the first wave, and paused to appraise the carnage. I caught his glance for one endless moment. The look he gave me was... enigmatic. It was hard to say what he meant to tell me with his intense regard. I did learn one thing with that shared look. He still loved to watch me fight.

We moved towards the compound's spartan buildings, taking the fight into smaller spaces. The force had to split up to accommodate the change.

Christian and I found ourselves leading a small group of non-druid Others. I'm not sure how it happened, but we took the new company in stride, breaking away from the main wave of druid fighters. Druids were an extremely exclusive group, so it wasn't really a surprise that the leftover Others had banded together.

Christian had a small arsenal of explosives that he was way too excited to use, so our first order of business was to scout from house to house, basically blowing shit up. It was a simple plan. Christian threw the explosive in the door, and I lit it midair. The rest of our group helped us finish off whatever ran screaming out of the building. As far as demo-ing the whole necro settlement went, our plan worked well. We were doing more than our share of destruction. Oh, and as another plus, it gave Christian his blow-up-shit fix for awhile. Win, win.

I swung my two-handed battle-axe in a circle, beheading two escaping necros at once. Yeah, I was showing off. Or rather, showing up Christian. He just gave me a disgruntled look. "Quit hogging," he muttered, sending an explosive shotgun round into a running Necro as he spoke. Its head exploded, spraying black liquid everywhere.

I sent Christian a warning look. "Don't even think about shooting one of those bullets anywhere near me. Those things are a mess. I don't want any Necro gunk on me."

He snorted, eyeing me up and down. "You are already covered, you prissy b-"

"Show a little respect," one of the non-druid Others who'd been following us, spoke. "These things used to be human."

I turned my head slowly toward the new voice, glaring.

"Uh-oh," Christian said in a loud whisper when he saw the look on my face.

"Respect? Have you fought these things before?" I asked the man, speaking slowly.

He was a small man with thick black glasses. His nearly gray hair put him past forty. He looked more than a little out of his element in his armored vest, carrying his handgun awkwardly. He glared right back at me, answering. "No, but anything that once had a soul should be shown respect on its passing."

I raised my brows at him. "Is that so? Well, Mr.?"

"Allen."

"Well, Allen, any soul these things possessed left them a long time ago. Me and Christian here have had more than a modest number of encounters with the necros. It's been a few years since I've been on a necro raid, but let me tell you a little story about the last one we went on. It was at an orphanage the necros had ravaged in the middle of the night. They drank from the bodies of over sixty children. Killed all of the little ones in their beds. Not one of them rose from the dead. Not one. Do you know why that is, Allen?"

He swallowed hard. He looked a little sick as he shook his head.

"Because children don't turn. In fact, many who're bitten never turn. You have to make a choice to take another's life to survive. And the taking of that blood creates another talking zombie. If you never feed, you never turn, you just die. The action that makes them a necro is murder, and most, given the choice, choose to abstain. So I don't feel too guilty about not showing proper respect to the ones that choose to spread disease and death wherever they go. You wanna show respect, you take the safety off of that thing and take out some of the monsters that demolished an entire human city just weeks ago."

CHAPTER TWENTY-FIVE

Death Spell

"Watch this," I told Christian as a growling necro came rushing from the building we'd just blown up. As he got closer, I stomped my left foot hard on the ground. A five inch blade switched out of the front of my navy running shoe. I kicked my foot straight up in the air, catching the creature dead-on with my blade in the bottom of his chin. I pushed forward hard with my right foot, taking him to the ground, his wind-pipe collapsing on impact. I pulled the blade out quickly, swiping my foot sideways and taking his head, just to be safe.

I clicked the blade back into place as I turned back to Christian. He grinned, nodding in approval. I grinned back.

"Badass," one of the Other soldiers muttered.

"Those look like your normal shoes. You wear that thing all the time?" Christian asked, bending down to get a closer look.

"Naw, it's a little trigger happy. I save these for special occasions. Having a blade pop out of my shoe in the middle of grocery shopping isn't my idea of a good time."

Christian laughed. "You get these from Caleb?"

I nodded.

"He's so getting me a pair."

I shrugged. "If you want to owe him a favor-" I stopped, going completely still.

I heard it again, the faintest voice calling out, "Help." It was somehow separate from the sounds of battle, as though the voice was echoing from inside some small, quiet space.

I looked around at the crowd of soldiers. "Anyone hear that?" Several of them, including Christian, looked at me strangely.

"Hear what?" he asked.

I held up a finger for silence again. No one moved. "Hurry!" the voice prompted. It was more clear this time.

"No one heard that voice?" I asked them, glaring.

Several of them shook their heads at me.

"How can you guys not hear that?"

"They're killing Dom!" the voice yelled this time, and the words got me moving.

"Follow me, you deaf bastards," I told them as I broke into a run. I made a beeline through the compound, toward the loudest sounds of fighting. I knew Dom would be at the center of the battle.

I stopped when we came in sight of the fighting. We were on a grassy incline overlooking the carnage, and I searched frantically for Dom.

"They're right in front of you! They're casting his death spell!" the voice yelled, and I looked around, confused.

"Where are you?" I screamed at the voice.

"Don't look for me, look for them. They've formed a circle. Find the circle!"

"Jillian, what's up?" Christian asked me carefully. I didn't address the fact that it was his, 'I'm dealing with a crazy woman,' careful tone. There wasn't time.

"Everyone look for some kind of circle. It's close, I think. Just cover every inch of this clearing." Everyone started looking carefully at the grass. In the near-dark of the clearing, it was almost impossible to make out anything on the ground, so all of the soldiers without nocturnal vision quickly broke out flashlights.

As I searched, my attention was drawn to the battle below us. Piercing animal screams filled the night as my gaze finally found Dom. He was in the middle of it all, of course, the light from a street lamp falling directly onto him as he ripped out a necro's throat with his teeth. It was clear the druids well known bloodlust had a firm grip on him. I was staring at him, fascinated, when I saw it.

It was just a break in the air that caught my notice at first. The voice had been right. It was literally right in front of me. I took deep breaths as I studied it, preparing for the pain I would feel upon breaking a powerful ward.

I began to chant as I walked towards the circle determinedly. I stopped when my shoe touched a strange spot in the grass. The wind wasn't strong, just strong enough to sway the grass gently. Or some of it, anyway. Where the grass stayed still was where I focused. "Christian," I said softly. He appeared at my shoulder.

"What's going on?" he asked.

"I need you to swing Dragonsbane at the ground exactly when I say. Ok?"

He looked at me like I was crazy, but nodded slowly. He clutched the ancient sword in his hands, waiting for me.

I pointed at the spot in the grass. "Watch that spot carefully. Swing with all your strength the instant I say 'break.'"

I began chanting again, holding my palms out to the circle. It was no comfort to stand empty-handed before such a circle, but a necessary evil. "Prepare yourselves to fight," I told the soldiers who'd come to gather around us.

I felt the spot weakening. "Break," I screamed with every fiber of my being. Christian swung.

It was like shattering glass as the circle broke. Within lay a large gathering of necros. They formed a circle, their King kneeling at its center. I identified him by the crown on his head. He held an unconscious druid in his arms, cutting deep symbols into the skin of its wrists. I didn't recognize the druid it held at first, he was covered in so much blood.

The necro King snarled at me, ordering his minions. "Kill them. We still have time to remake the circle."

The necros rushed our small group, and we met them head-on. I ran straight for their king. He stood, roaring at me, "You wish to die?"

I pulled the huge axe from my back, hacking it down at him with one fluid motion. His own blade met mine, the druid tumbling from his arms. My eyes swung down to the unconscious man, and I sucked in a sharp gasp. It was Collin, and if he was breathing, I couldn't see it.

I sent a bolt of red fire straight into the air. It was a make-shift warning flare, accompanied by my scream, "Dom!"

I couldn't tell at first if it worked, occupied as I was with the necro King. I hacked at him relentlessly, cursing him every time our weapons clashed. Finally I sent him sprawling. I wasted no time, sending a wave of flames crashing into him. He screamed, rolling away, frantically beating out the flames.

He flew at me, sharpened teeth sinking into my neck. "That doesn't work on me, you zombie bastard," I muttered, ripping him off my neck. I threw him hard across the clearing.

He rolled to a stop and lay still, but his eyes were open wide. "What are you?" His discordant voice filled my ears.

I approached his still body, my foot stepping hard on his neck. "Haven't you ever watched a zombie movie? You guys aren't supposed to speak. So shut the fuck up." I punctuated this with a hard stomp of my heal to his throat.

I took a quick glance around at the rest of the fight. More necro bodies littered the ground than not, but it still looked grim.

I looked west at the sound of approaching howls. Dom and crew were bearing down on us at full speed. I braced myself for the onslaught.

The rest of the circle's necros perished with one viscous wave of fighting.

Cam reached his brother first, frantically feeling for the pulse in his neck. He was nude, obviously newly changed from beast form. I got way more of a show than I wanted as he sprinted to his fallen brother's side.

"He lives," Cam finally spoke. Dom loomed over his shoulder. Their eyes turned to me. "Why was he carving these symbols into his arms?" Cam asked me. His tone was cold. He didn't seem to properly understand that I had just saved both his brother and his Arch.

"He," I indicated the necro I spoke of by bouncing my heal on his neck, "was using him to cast some sort of death spell against your Arch. I'm not familiar with his magic. Don't ask me to interpret those symbols." My tone was just as cold. "They were practicing their magic within a very powerful circle. It was almost completely invisible. I wasn't even aware that necros could do this kind of magic."

Dom looked grim. "That's because it's druid magic. Apparently the necros have been learning a few things."

I tapped the neck beneath my foot again. "Want this one for questioning? Or should I finish him?"

"We'll take him." At his words, the unconscious necro was bound, bagged, and dragged away. I tried to be subtle as I knelt down and quickly grabbed his fallen crown, clipping it to my belt. I had a slight problem with hoarding treasure. So what? Name me a dragon who didn't.

I looked back at the two brothers, healers now descending on the unconscious one. Cam met my eyes. "How did you know about the circle if it wasn't visible?" His voice held accusation.

I looked at him coldly. Leave it to Cam to turn it around on me. He'd always been an asshole like that. "There was a voice calling for help, actually. It was loud enough that I caught the sound from across camp."

"Collin's voice?" Dom asked.

"No."

"Whose voice was it, then?" Cam asked, standing.

"I have no idea. It sounded like a child. A little boy, maybe." My tone was flat.

Cam looked back at the soldiers who'd accompanied me. His gaze settled on Christian. "Did anyone else hear this voice?"

They all answered with a no. Christian glared at Cam. "So she has better hearing than the rest of us. What are you getting at?"

Cam looked at Dom, jaw clenched, eyes defiant. "I ask that she be taken in for questioning. You know how hard these circles are to detect. It makes no sense that she could find and break one. I charge that she was involved in this plot."

Dom stared back at him for long moments. I saw that familiar tick in his jaw. "This woman just saved your brother and your Arch from possible death. You can guess very well what he was doing with those marks on Collin's arms. Your reaction is to accuse her of a crime? Your hatred blinds you-"

"Your obsession blinds you!" Cam interrupted with a roar. Dom silenced his outburst with a look.

"Your request is denied. You have much to learn about showing gratitude."

Cam sent me a murderous look. I mouthed, "you're welcome," at him. He visibly reigned himself in from reacting violently. I smirked at him, pretending to scratch my nose as I flipped him off. He had to turn away, shaking with rage.

"These things had help learning about our magic," Cam was saying to his Arch again. He just wouldn't quit. He paced back and forth in front of Dom as he set up his case. "No druid would betray such things. It's unheard of. She was in close proximity to our kind for over thirteen years. She picked up enough information about our magic to detect a circle of power. It's obvious she picked up more than that! You can't think it's a coincidence she shows up days before this fight, and everything goes to hell. Would you rather accuse one of our own of betrayal than see this whore for what she is?"

That was it, I was done. I braced myself to give the bastard the beating he deserved, but Dom beat me to it. His back was to me as he backhanded his cousin, hard. "I said *enough*. You do not question me in the midst of battle! I've heard your argument. We will settle this after the fight. The longer we stand here, the more of them we're allowing to escape."

Cam sent me a scathing look as he stood, touching his bloodied lip as though I'd done it. I only wished. "Asshole," I mouthed at him. Both of his hands clenched. Yes, I kind of enjoyed baiting enraged bears. It was one of my hobbies, and clearly I excelled at it... Just ask anybody.

"Nice crown," Christian said quietly as he came up beside me. "But why nab it? You have the urge to play dress up? You like to pretend to be Queen Jillian?"

I bit my lip, embarrassed. "It was shiny." He stifled a loud laugh that got us some dirty looks. "It has rubies on it. It's hard to pass up rubies." He laughed harder and I elbowed him in the ribs.

Dom sent us a stormy look. "Back to battle!" he roared at any soldiers still milling.

"We're running low on explosives," Christian told me as we set off.

"I'm sure we'll have no trouble improvising," I told him with a grin.

CHAPTER TWENTY-SIX
Badass Supermodels

Our ragtag crew was advancing carefully into the next bank of houses, when a voice from the back of the ranks spoke up. "Far be it from me to slow down two badass supermodels on a mission, but we have a problem," a male voice said wryly.

I could see Christian out of the corner of my eye as we turned, his stance and movements almost synchronized to my own. We shared a look, our expressions almost identically similar, with arched brows and half-smiles. "What's the problem?" I called out, scanning the faces to see who had spoken.

"You're a badass supermodel," Christian muttered under his breath at the same time, taking the mature approach, as usual.

A tall, thin man stepped forward. He wore a long, high-collared trench coat over the standard body armor. He looked more like a scholar than a fighter, with unkempt, long dark hair, and thick glasses, a keen intelligence clear in his eyes. His appearance was deceptive, though, as I saw that his hands on his impressively modified crossbow were steady and sure. In fact, just about everything about him that I could see was a contradiction. His shoulders were slumped, but his body was tensed and alert. His smile was sheepish, but his tone when he spoke was clearly wry and sarcastic, his look sardonic as he met my eyes steadily. "You're really pretty and all-"

I shot Christian a look. "He's talking to you," I told him.

He spoke at the same time, smirking, "He's talking to you." Christian stifled a laugh. "Jinx," he said, under his breath, just like a ten-year-old. I turned my attention back to the strange man as he continued, as though we hadn't rudely interrupted him.

"And I've seen that you have a particular talent for finding and killing things, but you might want to let me take point for this next bit." He tipped an imaginary hat at us. "Corbin, vampire hunter, at your service."

"Fuck," I said succinctly.

"Shit on bloody shingles," Christian swore.

We weren't the only ones cursing. Soft and not so soft cursing could be heard from our strange little crew for several moments while we processed the information. If a vampire hunter wanted to take point, that could only mean one thing. He sensed vampires. I hated vampires. Everyone did. Everybody hated necros, too, but necros were easy, clean kills, for the most part. Vampire kills were never easy, and never clean. They rested in nests, and swarmed like insects the second any of the others in their Kiss were threatened. If it was a small Kiss, and you had a hunter with you, it was still usually a messy business, but larger groups of them just sucked, no matter how you planned it. Yes, I used the word sucked to describe vampires. So?

What was almost worse than the messy kills was the fact that you couldn't just kill them on sight, like necros. The damned fair-minded druids, always wanting to give everyone a shot before they named them rogue, actually required the hunters to have a warrant that justified killing any of the monsters.

Innocent until proven guilty, blah, blah, blah. Of course, that meant that humans died, usually a lot of them, before a vampire got the stake it deserved.

Vampires were a lot like witch-hags, in my mind, when it came to going rogue. It was always only a matter of time.

Corbin ignored all of the cursing, used to it, I was sure. He spoke into the tiny radio clipped to his chest. The radios had been issued to all of us, back at the meet-up point. They'd been silent since before the battle started, which was a good sign. You only used the radio during a fight like this when the shit hit the fan.

"We've got a vampire Kiss. Need permission to take it out."

The response was quick and succinct. "You are cleared to take out any damned thing you find in there."

Corbin's eyebrows shot up into his messy bangs. "Is it my birthday or something?" he asked the crowd at large.

Christian shot me a smirk. "I like this one. He speaks our language."

I had to agree. "He does seem like our kind of people."

Corbin heard us. "Now, now, I'm not pretty enough for all that, but I'll do my best to keep up."

I smiled at him. He was quickly growing on me. "Give us the head count, and the plan, Mr. Personality."

He sighed, growing slightly more serious and less sarcastic. "It's not good." He pointed to one of the larger buildings. It looked like a large house with a lot of windows. It was very out of place in the spartan compound. "They're all in there. And there are too many of them for me to place."

Another round of quiet cursing rocked the crowd. He waited patiently before continuing. "I would say we need backup, but I'm pretty sure that most of them are newborns, because every single one of the bastards is sleeping. And here's the kicker."

He paused for a dramatic moment, smiling a very grim smile. I knew he was good at his job, just by that smile. You earned a smile like that. It was a little scary. We were right about him. He was our kind of people.

"The Master is sleeping. I don't understand it, given that it's the middle of the night, but he is definitely dead asleep at the moment. That leaves us with two very unpleasant choices. We can try to stealth in there, quick and quiet, and take the master before slaughtering his flock. If they're newborns, as I suspect, they'll go down real easy, with their master dead. That's option A."

He let us process that, studying the crowd intently. "Option B is an almost guaranteed bloodbath, but with more favorable numbers for us. We risk losing our advantage to wait for some heavy druid backup, which will take god only knows how long. I'll put it up for vote, but I'll tell you now, I strongly favor option A, though I'll need a few bloodthirsty volunteers for that one." He looked at Christian and I as he said this. I wasn't surprised that he'd meant us. We were more experienced, by far, than the rest of our little company.

"A sleeping Master is the best-case scenario when it comes to killing vamps, I can attest, but let's vote on it. Raise your hand for option A."

All but one raised their hand. The one was me. Ah, hell, I raised mine, too. Everyone looked at us as they voted, knowing that they were all as good as volunteering us. I sighed. I supposed I'd rather go get messy than watch the rest of them get sucked dry in a bloodbath later. Most of them were just humans, really, with a little supernatural talent thrown in. Christian and I were, at least, born pure Other, and hard as all hell to kill. Vampire hunters were born Other, as well, with blood no more human than Christian's, and would be just as hard to take out.

"We'll do it," Christian told Corbin, without consulting me. He sounded way too chipper about it, too. I liked a good fight as much as he did, but hated messes more. Christian didn't mind the messy so much. It had been awhile, but I could remember clearly the last time we'd gotten mixed up with vampires, and I sure as hell didn't want a repeat performance. Of course, we hadn't had a vampire hunter with us that time. It had just been Christian and I with some unfortunate humans, in the wrong place at the wrong time. We'd emerged from battle victorious, but we'd been bitten and stabbed and none of the humans had survived it, despite our best efforts, and that had been a *small* Kiss of the blood-suckers. The memory still pissed me off royally.

I sighed. There was really nothing else to be done. At least we wouldn't be trying futilely to protect mortals, this time. I hoped. "Yeah, we will," I finally agreed. "Let's get to it, then. What's the plan?"

Corbin gave me an almost fond smile. "You're not at all what I expected. Guess I should know better than to listen to the rumors."

That soured my mood. Of course he'd heard of me. I shouldn't have been surprised, but the reminder of my spotty reputation was, as always, a mood killer.

Except to Christian, of course. The punk actually laughed. "You want to stay on her good side, my good man, and that's not the way to do it."

Corbin grimaced, smacking his hand to his forehead. "My bad. Didn't think before I spoke."

I waved a hand at him, brushing it off, since that was the only productive thing to do. "It's old news. Druids think I'm the anti-christ, and they like to spread that opinion around. I don't have to wonder what you've heard about me, and I don't have the time or the patience to disprove any of it, so let's just move right along. The plan. Please."

His face got real serious. "The three of us will move in together, real quiet like. I'm assuming, from what I've seen from you both so far, that you guys can each handle a room full of newborns, once the master is dead."

We both just nodded.

"You'll scout the house with me, and I'll put you where you need to be when the master goes down. You guys can use those fancy weapons of yours to behead the bloodsuckers, which will put them out of commission long enough for me to come and do my whole stake thing."

I didn't bother to mention that we'd dealt with vamps before, and that we knew the hunter staking routine. He wasn't exactly long-winded. And his quick, to the point, explanations might be helpful to the crew waiting outside, if the shit really hit the fan, and the mess spilled out to them.

"What happens if the master wakes up?" I asked. I didn't want to ask. It wasn't my fault I only saw in worse-case scenario vision. I was born that way, honest.

Corbin gave me his grim smile. "We start swinging, and hope we win."

I smiled back at him, my own grim, scary smile. His answer was only what I had expected.

Christian rubbed his hands together, giving me a toothy grin. "Let's do this."

I smacked him in the back of the head. I swear it was barely a tap.

He sent me a disgruntled look.

"Don't *wish* for it all to go to hell. That makes you crazy. And crazy gets you smacked."

He gave a half-shrug. "I am what I am," he said with a smirk.

I rolled my eyes at him.

"Right this way, Barbie and Ken," Corbin said, heading resolutely towards the house.

"Okay, Buffy," I murmured to his back. He'd started the name calling, after all.

He stifled a laugh. "Guess I asked for that," he said, his voice pitched-low.

"That round went to Barbie," Christian added, helpful as always.

CHAPTER TWENTY-SEVEN

Barbie And Buffy

We fell silent, wise-cracks and all, as we got close to the eerily silent house. It had a bad feel to it, which was understandable, but I thought I would have felt a chill up my spine even without a vampire hunter there to tell me what was inside.

Corbin opened the front door without a sound, easing it open agonizingly slowly. He disappeared inside, and I followed next. Christian brought up the rear, closing the door as quietly as it'd been opened.

There were street lights on outside, but they were dimmed, and we had been fighting in negligible light for most of the night. That didn't bother me. My eyes had adjusted just fine. It took just a second for my eyes to adjust to the even darker interior of the house, but when I did, I froze, my eyes going wide in dismay as I looked up.

The ceiling was covered in the creatures, this one room alone holding more vampires than I'd ever seen in one place before. Their bat-like wings were wrapped around them, hiding their hairless, slimy bodies from view. It was a mercy, that. Vampires were hideous looking creatures, when they weren't using glamour, and only the strong master's even had that ability. How the monsters had turned into modern day sex symbols, I would never understand. The depictions of hideous nosferatu were much closer to the real thing than brooding teenagers with over-styled hair.

Corbin moved forward silently, and I followed closely behind, Christian a steady presence at my back.

The house was bigger than I would have guessed, and we made slow progress, through room after room, most of them empty, thank the gods. Corbin finally stopped at the bottom of a set of narrow stairs. He addressed Christian. "Fall back to the first room. Jillian and I will head upstairs."

Christian nodded, disappearing without a word. Corbin didn't have to mention that the master had to be upstairs. We had combed every inch of the first floor, so it was a given.

I followed Corbin very carefully up the stairs, trying hard not to make the old steps creak. We had just reached the top when Corbin froze, his entire body going stiff. I moved around him to see his face, rather than making a noise. I wasn't reassured by what I saw.

His eyes glowed red, his face suddenly all harsh bones and angles. His mouth hung open, sharp fangs now protruding, dripping saliva. He took off his glasses and sniffed the air. He looked vaguely like a human version of a bloodhound on a scent. This was bad. He hadn't gone all scary on me just for the hell of it. This was a vampire hunter's reaction to being near a vampire. A vampire that *wasn't* sleeping.

A deep voice called out from somewhere down the long hallway. "Helsing. I feel you. You cannot hide from me."

"Fuck," Corbin said around all of those sharp teeth, and broke into a blindingly fast sprint, heading for that voice.

I followed, pulling my axe from its shoulder holster as I moved.

All hint of the harmless scholar was gone as Corbin rushed

into a room down the hall, so fast I couldn't keep up. That was what I hated most about vampires. They were so freaking fast. I was fast, but they moved in a blur, even to me, finding a place to sink their fangs before you knew what hit you. And if they were real hungry, the place they found was usually your throat, right before they ripped it out. I'd be real salty if I got my throat ripped out tonight.

Corbin was moving vampire fast as he charged at the master, who met him in a loud clash, halfway into the room. I had barely rounded the doorway when they collided, snarling, into a furious brawl.

"The room down the hall," Corbin barked at me. "Hurry, we don't want any newborns escaping."

I tore out of there, searching each room I passed, his description of my destination leaving something to be desired. In his defense, he had been a little preoccupied at the time.

I had passed three empty rooms before I found a nest of new vamps rising from the ground, blinking away their deep sleep. The master had arisen, and his whole nasty flock had just joined him. I cursed. The last few stragglers dropped from the ceiling, climbing slowly to their feet, confused and disgruntled at being disturbed. There were fourteen of them in the spacious room, and they were obviously disoriented from sleep. I struck.

I swung my axe in a large circle, using its weight as momentum to increase my speed. They scattered dizzyingly fast. Newborns were much weaker than the older ones, but unfortunately, they were just as fast. I only caught one on my first attack, clipping the hairless thing in the chin, then pushing forward to cut its head in half. Regrettably, it was the wrong half to cut, and I had to move into another broad swing to sever its head from its neck. All of this gave at least some of the vampires enough time to swarm me, pushing me onto my back.

I felt fangs sink into my wrist at the same time a pair ripped into my thigh, going right through my heavy cargo pants. I screamed, equal parts rage and pain. I was pissed.

My hand still gripped my axe even as another bloodsucker attacked that wrist with gusto. Hmm, hands useless. I tried to kick, but both legs were pinned, as yet another ugly bastard latched onto my other leg. Legs out, too. That effectively eliminated my options for both hand-to-hand and weapons. I was pissed enough not to even care. When all else failed, I always had fire. I took a deep breath.

Vampires, fortunately, had no immunity to fire. One latched onto my neck even as I breathed out, reigning blue fire onto all of the beasties directly in front of me. My hand let go of the axe even as I reached out, feeling for a grip of anything slimy. I gripped a slimy head in one hand, a cheek in the other. It wasn't even a thought so much as an instinct to burn everything I touched. All of the creatures near me began to scream in agony, and I knew that every part of the skin that they touched burned them. I *was* fire.

I only saw how many of them had had me pinned as they scattered back, rolling, slapping, beating, to try to stifle the flames. I smiled. Blue fire was harder to douse than normal fire. It was like fire on crack. They would burn in agony until Corbin came and put them out of their misery. Six of them were out of commission, for the moment. I turned my attention to the others. They had scattered to the corners, cowering rather than fighting, and I almost felt sorry for them.

I bent down and grabbed my axe. "I'll let you pick. Axe or fire. As you can see, fire hurts a lot more. But if you bite me, you get fire."

One vampire broke for the window, making a dive at the glass. My axe caught it in the back, pinning it to the wall near the window. I pulled back, and swung again, taking its head. Before the head had hit the floor, another one was on me, straddling my back, its teeth sinking into my neck from behind. I screamed, shifting my axe to one hand and reaching back. I felt its disgusting head, and pushed the fire out.   It fell off, screaming in agony.

Six vamps remained, darkening the corners. They hissed at me. I pointed to the headless vamp, and then to the one ones on fire, their tormented screams filling the room. They were writhing in pain, no longer a threat. "You pick. The easy way, or the hard way."

One scuttled forward awkwardly, its eyes sad and anguished. There was no way to tell if it had been a male or a female when it was human. Its slimy white body was smooth and sexless. "Please," it said around a mouth full of teeth. "End my suffering. I did not choose this." It bent until its head nearly touched the ground. I swung before it saw it coming, feeling like a real bastard, something I'd never felt for killing a vamp before. This was one weird fucking Kiss. Most newborns couldn't speak, let alone communicate clearly. I had been doubtful that they would even understand me when I spoke. I made a note to ask Corbin about talking newborns, first chance I got.

I waved my axe. "Anybody else wanna go the easy way?" I asked, almost wanting them to fight now. That last one had seemed too pathetic to be a threat, even though logically I knew better than to doubt that it was.

Another one scuttled forward.   Its forehead tilted to the ground, and it let out what sounded suspiciously like a sob right before I took its head. I felt one rush me from behind and I used the momentum of the swing to turn, catching it on the side of the jaw, then following through for a clean beheading. At least it hadn't bitten me.

Three more remained.   One scuttled forward, bending its head. I was swinging when it struck, going for my ankle, of all things. I chopped its head off right as its teeth made contact, before they had time to sink in. I decided to be nice, and let my axe take it, since it hadn't technically bitten me.

Predictably, one jumped on my back as I dealt with that one, and I used blue fire as it tore into my shoulder. Bastard took the hard way.

The last one never moved, just cowering in the corner, making me go to it. I felt oddly reluctant to strike. These were like no other vampires I'd ever seen, and I felt pity as I looked at the slimy thing. "I'm sorry," I told it, raising my axe.

It hid its face, but I heard its muffled words just before I struck. "Don't be sorry. I want death. Death is much better than this." I took its head.

I shook myself, moving to the doorway, sure there were more rooms to clear, though if Christian had faired as well as I, the two main nests had been eliminated.

Corbin Helsing met me in the doorway. His eyes widened as he saw the room's carnage, blue fire rampant. "The master is dead, the Kiss weakened, though it looks like you hardly needed the advantage, since I just barely killed him. What the fuck is that blue stuff?"

I blinked at him, shocked at myself for a moment. I usually avoided using the blue, particularly if Christian was near, and here I had almost just left it burning. "Don't speak of the blue flame. Just stake them, so I can get rid of it," I told him, sore, and pissed, and depressed about those pathetic creatures. I couldn't scrounge up an ounce of good manners just then, so I sounded as mean as I felt.

Corbin didn't even seem to notice, just nodding and setting to work, staking all fourteen of the creatures quickly and quietly, chanting softly over every crumpled vampire.

He stood as he finished, his chanting increasing in volume. All at once, every still body in the room turned to ash. Corbin nodded grimly.

I called off the flames, closing my eyes as it rushed back into my body, causing me to shiver. Corbin was giving me wide eyes. I shook my head at him. "Don't ask. Just lead."

We searched the rest of the floor, finding one, smaller pocket of vampires. They all fought hard, but they were weakened, and no teeth reached us as we dispatched the ugly creatures, one by one.

"Some of them begged me for death, back in the other room. I never knew the new ones could even speak," I told Corbin, as we made our way down the hallway.

Corbin shook his head, his jaw tightening. "They can't, normally. Something truly fucked-up was going on with this Kiss, though I can't say for sure just what. I'm determined to find out, though. If not tonight, then tomorrow."

He looked at me as he spoke, and I nodded at him. I believed him, and I wanted him to find those answers. Those vampires being something other than the mindless killing machines I was used to had been disconcerting, to say the least.

We made our way downstairs, taking out another five vamps in a closet of a room. They cowered all the while, one of them sobbing almost like a human as it begged for its end, and Corbin grimaced even as he turned them to dust. "Something is very wrong here," he said. I agreed wholeheartedly.

Christian was still fighting in the first room when we joined him. Ten lay headless on the ground, and he was actively fighting one, with two more cowering in the corner. He took its head as we entered the room, as though he'd just been toying with it. Perverse bastard probably had been.

Christian pointed to the two vamps cowering in the corner, looking almost angry. "Those things begged me not to hurt them, and didn't attack. Make fun of me all you want, but I don't have it in me to kill something that pathetic."

I raised my hands, giving him a look. I hadn't been about to make fun of him. Not for *that*, anyways.

Corbin just nodded, approaching the two vamps. "That's fine. I have it from here." He knelt down near them, holding out a hand. He whispered to them, sounding reassuring. "I'll end your suffering," he told them.

I watched, fascinated, as one of them actually reached out and clutched his hand. Corbin chanted softly, and the creature went slack. It didn't even twitch when he staked it. The other vamp didn't hesitate to take his hand when he reached out again.

The house was completely clean of vampires when we headed out.

Our misfit crew was waiting outside, looking anxious and tense, as though expecting ravenous vampires to break out of the house at any second. We got a lot of relieved looks when they saw that it was us.

"The house is cleared," Corbin told them, and that was all.

We didn't tell them about the strange, depressing vampires we'd encountered. I don't think any of us were anywhere near approaching proud of the slaughter.

I advanced silently to the next house, wanting to move on from that strange ordeal, Christian a silent presence at my back. Our ragtag crew followed.

CHAPTER TWENTY-EIGHT

Best Friend/Arch Nemesis

We were fortunate to have a necromancer with us. Their magic had almost no use against the living, but they had a special affinity for the dead. Gretchen was able to sense a necro presence from small distances. Which was particularly useful here since she could give us a sense of what we were walking into with each building we came to.

She froze as we approached one of the larger buildings. "This one is swarming with them." Her voice was hushed with fear. "We're going to need a lot more backup. This building must have many underground levels. I can feel *thousands* of them."

"All in this one building?" I asked her.

She nodded. "I sense heavy movement in there. I think it is some sort of escape route they're using."

Christian cursed. "We're almost out of TNT. And nothing I brought is big enough to take out that many of them."

"Back up a little. There's something I can try," I told our small group. Christian raised a brow at me, but they all backed away.

I approached the structure cautiously. I placed my hand on the wall, concentrating. I paced back to my group, speaking to the necromancer. "Can you bind the door against them? Keep them from getting out?" My knowledge of necromancy was negligible, but I could remember that they had some spells for binding the dead to a location.

She bit her lip, looking unsure. "For how long?"

"I only need a few minutes. But during those few minutes they will be wanting very badly to get out."

"I *can* bind them, but I've never tried with so many before. My spell will hold, but I can't guarantee more than a few minutes."

I nodded. "It should be enough." I turned to Christian. "I need the rest of you to go for backup. Tell them we've encountered a hive." Christian was shaking his head at me. He didn't like this idea. We usually stuck together in battle. It was an old habit.

"You'll be back in five minutes. Trust me, please." The thirteen soldiers who had taken to following us, obeyed. Christian followed them reluctantly, shooting glares back at me as he did. I would be getting hell for this later, I knew.

Gretchen began her ritual at the door of the deceptively small, windowless building. It was cinder block. There was no fuel to burn inside. Unless, of course, you counted the bodies.

I worked about five feet away, hand on the gray stone wall. I was no fire sorcerer. I didn't need to call the fire down from above or below. The fire was inside of me. I merely had to unleash it. It was even somewhat of a relief to unleash some of the furious inferno that resided inside of me. I pushed it out with less effort than I expected. It pushed through the walls and to the creatures within almost too easily. And once there, it blew out like a silent explosion to engulf the creatures inside, too quickly to track. It felt good to release the fire I kept so tightly reigned most of the time. I didn't hold back a bit of it, because for once I didn't have to. I felt the fire leave me, but it was *my* fire, so I also felt what it did, touching one flesh-eater after another as it engulfed the hive.

The sounds that escaped from the building were tortured and wretched. Anguished screams filled the air. I pushed the fire inside the building, burning. Burning them all where they stood. I stood braced against the building by one arm, my being centered on the destruction inside. For long minutes I stood that way, mercilessly trapping them in that all consuming inferno.

The building's flat roof suddenly burst into the air. It seemed to fly up and disappear. In fact, it disintegrated. A light rain of ash that peppered the battleground was all that remained of it. It was only seconds before necro hands began to emerge through the top of the building. They were making short work of climbing out.

In a flash I was hovering above them. Against my will, I had become flame personified. I looked down at my now glowing body. My power was shifting me against my will. Already I felt wings of flame unfurl from my shoulders. I halted the shift, but seemed unable to reverse the damage already done. I hung suspended in that in-between form, arms spread, back arched.

The climbing Necros froze at the sight of me. I shifted my gaze to them, and they began to scatter back into the building in terror. "Burn," I tried to tell them, but my in-between mouth would not form human words. I breathed fire down on them in a tidal wave, and they burned.

Within minutes all that remained of the building was a great gaping hole in the ground. I drifted gently down to the earth, kneeling slowly to touch the ground. That touch was all I needed to ground myself. I shifted slowly back to human form, my clothes now singed and tattered. Well, that was new, and I wasn't even winded. There was definitely something very wrong with my powers. I had never lost control like that before.

It was a moment before I noticed the crowd of fighters that stood frozen around me, mouths agape. I cringed as I realized the revealing show I'd just given them. It was then that I noticed

Christian standing only a few feet away, Dragonsbane unsheathed into a double blade in his trembling hands. He was shaking his head back and forth as dawning terror lit his face.

"Jillian." Christian's voice sounded panicked. "Tell me I'm wrong." Dragonsbane had unfurled into a bigger blade than I'd ever seen in his hands. Every fighter watching backed far away from him to stay out of its reach.

"You're wrong," I told him calmly. I had been lying for so very many years that I was more than good at it. I didn't just know how to lie, I knew the perfect timing of a lie, knew how to inflect my voice with just the right conviction. I was still hopeful I could talk my way out of this one. Apparently I had an unexpected optimistic streak. Who'd of thunk it?

"How come I don't believe you?" His voice broke.

"Nothing's changed, Christian. You're still a brother to me. What I am has nothing to do with-"

"Don't you get it?" He was shouting now. "It doesn't matter how I feel about you! My instinct is far stronger than my will. How could you? How could you be this abomination for all this time and I not see it?" Tears ran down his face, but he raised Dragonsbane to me threateningly.

I shook my head at him. He was my brother. He was one of a small handful of people I had ever allowed myself to get close to over the course of my wretched life. My strongest instinct had always been one of survival, but I didn't think I could bring myself to fight the brother that my heart had chosen, not even for my life. "I won't fight you. I love you, Christian. Nature won't dictate my actions. It doesn't have to dictate yours."

"My line was created to destroy yours, when your kind descended into madness. It is my sole purpose for being."

"I haven't gone mad. You know that. Lynn is perfectly sane, as well. I agree that many of the dragons have gone mad.

Most of them have, in fact.   Those ones do need to be put down. But not me, Christian. Nothing about me has changed."
   His eyes were wild. "I was always taught that enchantment was your strongest power over the slayers. My father told me not to engage your kind in conversation.   'They will try to deceive you, Son, into thinking they are benign creatures.   In this way, they can take your soul before they take your head.' But I couldn't have dreamed...I never imagined...."
   I just kept shaking my head at him, despair beginning to sink in. "I don't want your soul. Or your head. Just your friendship. I'm sorry for all the secrets and lies, but you have to see that they were necessary. Put down the sword, Christian." I began removing my own weapons, throwing them at his feet. Was I feeling suicidal? A little bit, apparently. "Would you attack me when I'm unarmed?" I blinked away the tears in my eyes as I waited for his answer.
   He stared at me unblinkingly. His body was shaking, but his hands were steady. Finally, he nodded. A great roar sobbed out of his throat as he lunged at me.   Dragonsbane was swinging straight at my neck. I braced myself to roll out of the way when he suddenly froze.   A large fist in his hair had stopped him. I followed the hand up to the great figure looming behind him.
   Dom brought his other hand to Christian's throat. It was still a great bear claw, dripping blood from the battle, and Christian swallowed hard just looking at it.
   "Take his arms and pin him down," Dom spoke through a mouthful of bloody fangs. I didn't recognize the animal they came from, but I knew it wasn't bear. Wolf, like his eye, I realized, as I studied him, trying to focus on anything other than the fact that my best friend had just tried to kill me.
   Druids swarmed the slayer, pinning Christian against his will. Sweat broke out on his forehead, but he was silent.
   Dom arched his back into the night, letting out an earth

shattering howl. It was a victory roar, and it was met by countless other animal calls. Despite heavy casualties, the druids were clearly victorious.

As he straightened, I noticed the dark blood seeping out of his torn vest and down his body. He was badly wounded and ignoring it.

"Dom, you're hurt. You need to call on your healers-" I started.

"Silence!" he roared. Now was not the time to be giving him orders, I saw. He turned back to the slayer. "Cam," he barked at his 2nd lieutenant. Cam stepped forward, completely nude and obviously newly changed from some beast form. He handed Dom a fist-sized object I couldn't make out. He gave me a hard look before stepping back.

Dom knelt beside Christian's struggling figure. "You will not seek to harm Jillian or Lynn. You cannot. On pain of death." It wasn't until he was snapping the bracelet of bones onto Christian's wrist that I realized he had been placing a Geas. The most powerful one I'd seen. The eleven druids touching Christian all lent their power to it. Dom had clearly planned ahead for this. Christian finally stopped struggling. He shut his eyes wearily, tears slipping down his cheeks. He said something to Dom, too softly for me to make out. It could have been, "thank you," but I wasn't sure.

"Take him away," he ordered. Several druids obeyed, carrying Christian away. I watched silently.

Dom stood, and a team of healers descended on him. He let them, staring straight ahead. They stripped off his body armor, and I could see clearly the damage he'd taken. His body was covered in countless, deeply gushing wounds.

His neck was the worst. I gasped when they revealed it. It looked like someone had literally taken an axe to it. It had several huge gashes, as though they'd wailed on it like a tree trunk. The joke was on them. Dom's neck was made of sterner stuff. Dom stood stoically while the healers worked away, mending it back to normal. It would be perfect again by morning.

As I watched them work, I realized that I was sitting on the ground, my knees clutched to my chest pathetically. No one came near me. Tears ran silently down my cheeks, and I felt utterly defeated. Having your best friend try to chop your head off will do that, I guess.

As the full extent of Dom's wounds became clear, my numb mind began to work. This hadn't been the clean ambush we'd been planning on. The necros had been fully prepared for battle. They had known Dom was coming, and made their best effort to kill him. They had clearly been warned.

Cam's mind was apparently on the same track. "They were expecting us," he was telling Dom. Dom merely nodded, his face a mask.

"Someone planned your assassination tonight. Half of their force came after you." Cam's voice was grim.

Dom smiled slowly. It was chilling. "That was no assassination. Let them come for me. All the better."

As the team of healers continued to work, a tiger plowed through them, knocking several of the white-clad druids over in its haste.

The tiger shifted in a heartbeat into the naked form of Siobhan. Apparently she had recovered quickly enough for the battle. She hugged Dom tightly, unmindful of both his injuries, and the now scattered healers. "Thank the gods you're alrig-," she stopped as Dom pushed her away.

"Let the healers do their work, Siobhan," Dom growled at her, not even bothering to look in her direction. "The battlefield is no place for that kind of behavior. For god's sake, show a little restraint."

She was visibly distraught at his put-down. I didn't even self-examine myself for sympathy. I knew I had none where she was concerned.

"What will you do with him?" I asked Dom. I was dismayed at my still tear-filled voice.

He turned his cold gaze to me. "Any regrets yet about the company you've preferred for all these years?"

I shook my head at him as more tears slipped down my cheeks. He just watched me for a moment, stone-faced. Finally, he relented. "The geas will be hard for his body to accept. Its nature goes against his most powerful instincts. We'll keep him safely in custody until he acclimates."

"Thank you," I told him softly, closing my eyes.

"Don't thank me for sparing him. It just makes me want to change my mind," he growled.

"Well, well, well," a hated voice purred at me. I'd known it was only a matter of time. The bitch had never been able to shut her mouth for long. "How the high and mighty have fallen. Was that fight too much for our poor little Jillian?" Siobhan asked, a snicker in her voice.

"Someone please put a muzzle on that bitch," was my diplomatic reply. I didn't even bother opening my tired eyes. There was a lot I couldn't predict about Dom anymore, but I knew he wouldn't let her near me.

"Nice hair." I could hear the smirk in her voice.

Goddammit, I thought. My hair seemed particularly partial to lavender lately. It would have been my last choice, so of course that's what I got stuck with. Typical.

I opened my eyes, curling my lip at her. "Just shut it before I find out if you're flame-retardant."

"I wouldn't say that too loud around here if I were you, Jillian. You're not exactly surrounded by friends. Oh yeah, and didn't your *best friend* just try to take your head? Imagine what the rest of us would like to do."

I raised rage-filled eyes to her. It was a simple thing to turn the rage I felt for circumstances beyond my control onto someone I already despised. "Keep talking, Bitch. I'm quickly forgetting why it's a bad idea for me to take *your* head." My voice was filled with menace.

"Please try it." Her voice had gone beast. "I'll hang your head on my wall like a fucking trophy!"

I was taken aback for a moment by her reference to the druids long buried habit of head-hunting. Usually it was a topic they refused to talk about, along with several of the less than peaceful aspects of their history. Apparently Siobhan wouldn't mind bringing at least one of those practices back.

"That's enough, Siobhan. Go help with cleanup," Dom ordered.

"Jillian, could you come with me real quick?" Caleb's voice called out from the dark. He stepped closer, and I wondered how long he'd been waiting, unseen, to speak. I supposed it couldn't have been long since he was slightly out of breath.

"Where's Lynn?" I asked, immediately noticing that he was alone.

"Um, she's ok," he answered, but something in his voice bothered me. He seemed way too ruffled, a characteristic that was usually anathema to Caleb. "Just a little tied up at the moment. Everything ok with you?"

I nodded, wiping at my wet cheeks. Caleb was the last person I wanted to see me crying. "Christian tried to chop my head off a few minutes ago, but I'm dealing with it."

He wasn't amused. His eyes swung to Dom, narrowing. "You kill him, Druid?" he asked softly.

Dom just bared his teeth, not bothering to answer.

"How'd he find out?" Caleb's gaze swung back to me.

"It was my fault. I started to shift in the fight. I couldn't control it. I didn't complete the shift, but it was enough."

His eyes widened. "I have to say, I'd have paid to see that. Next time we have one of these things, I might have to roll with you."

206

I curled my lip at him.

"So, um, could you come with me? I could use your help with something."

I stood, brushing off my tattered clothes as though they were still intact enough to even bother with. I nodded at him to lead the way as I started walking.

"Wait," Dom ordered from behind me. I looked back. "When you've finished there, I need to ask you some questions. Sloan here will go with you to help you find your way back."

At his words, a tall woman stepped out of the shadows. Apparently I was off my game tonight, with both her and Caleb approaching me, undetected. I knew Sloan well, she was one of the few druids I'd been friendly with back in the day. Our relationship had never been close, but we'd understood each other. She was a tall, lithely muscular woman, a fighter through and through, and I'd always felt a sort of kinship with her. She was no-nonsense, but always fair, and I'd long respected that.

Her long, straight, pitch-black hair was braided back tonight, so the expression on her even, eurasian features was hard to miss. She looked at me with loathing now, and I shouldn't have been surprised.

I looked back at Dom, trying to work up some righteous anger, but my mind was just too tired. "So you agree with Cam about this? You think I helped plan that fiasco earlier? I need to be put under guard for saving your life?" I asked wearily.

He shrugged his massive shoulders. "I didn't say that. I just have some questions about what happened. Don't be long." He dismissed me.

I walked away, knowing Sloan was on my tail. We moved briskly through the camp to match Caleb's pace. "How ya been?" I called back to Sloan as we moved. No reason not to be polite just because she hated me now.

"Fuck off," she answered. Ok, guess that was a reason. "I'm here to make sure you don't run off, so finish with your errand, but leave me the hell alone."

"Fair enough," I muttered.

Caleb led us briskly to his car, which was parked a good distance from the settlement. I had no idea how he'd gotten it there. Christian and I had been forced to travel in a huge truck, packed in like sardines with the druids. I made out what was inside before we reached the car. "Tied up, huh, Cal? What the hell?"

"It was for her own good," he said, opening the passenger door. "She is being summoned, and she was having a hard time resisting. She said you could help her."

Lynn had several chains wrapping her to the passenger seat. Her arms were even cuffed above her head. I gave Caleb a sardonic look. "Think you have enough chains there?"

"Better safe than sorry," Lynn spoke up.

"Ok, so someone is calling you to them against your will?"

Lynn nodded.

I looked at Cal. "We need to get her locked down someplace safe. No enchantment I put on her will last long. We need to take her straight to a safe house after I place it. And not the retreat. It's been compromised."

"Obviously," Caleb said, insulted. I must have forgotten for a second who I was talking to. I was a little shocky, I acknowledged.

"He'll have to take her alone. You're not to go anywhere until you've been questioned," Sloan spoke suddenly.

I rolled my eyes. "Ok, you'll have to take her after I've enchanted her, Cal. I'll meet up with you guys later."

"Fine." Cal's voice was curt.

I placed the enchantment on her quickly, using a relic I wore around my neck to draw power. "Feel better?" I asked her after I finished.

She nodded, closing her eyes. "His call is much fainter now. It still stings to resist it, though."

"Here, look at this." I held the relic in front of her eyes. She looked at it, brow furrowed in confusion. She didn't know about this spell, though it was one of my personal favorites.

I clocked her, hard, on the back of the head. She was out cold.

Cal gave me a questioning look. "Hurry," I told him. "Get her locked down someplace safe, pronto."

"That was jacked up," Cal muttered, but he waisted no time, getting in the car and taking off without further ado.

I turned back to Sloan, mouth twisted bitterly. I waved her ahead. "Lead on."

CHAPTER TWENTY-NINE

Old Buddies

"Is this really necessary?" I asked Sloan after a long period of silence. She gave me a hard look, which was answer enough. "We could go out and help with cleanup, while we wait. Sitting here seems a little pointless." We were in the back of the Arch's limo. We'd been doing nothing but sitting and waiting for at least an hour.

"My orders are to wait with you in this car. No one said I had to listen to you. And I certainly don't want to speak to you."

"You have to admit, it seems a little pointless for us to just be sitting around."

"Shut up," was her response.

"I have to say, I'm a little surprised you're acting like all the other druids. You of all people should be happy I left him, Sloan. You've been in support of Dom as Arch from the start."

She turned murderous eyes to me, opened her mouth to speak, then shut it abruptly. "No, I'm not gonna get into that with you. I promised myself I wouldn't give you the satisfaction. Just shut up."

"If I promise to stay out of his life as much as humanly possible, can we call a truce?"

"Bullshit. If you wanted to stay out of his life, then what the hell are you doing here?"

I raised my brows at her. "I didn't get discovered on purpose. I'd still be in hiding if I hadn't had a few too many bad luck run-ins with druids lately."

"Bullshit," she said again. "Word is you waltzed into his office yesterday. You sought him out. Why?"

"I went there under a geas, Sloan. Collin found me before that, and bound me to seek Dom out. I never would have gone to him if I'd had a choice in the matter."

She curled her lip at me. "Well, I guess that's something." She paused. "Not much, though. You know, when I first saw those pictures, I told Dom that they must be doctored. I was so sure you wouldn't have done that to him, I would have bet my life on it. I had him half convinced, at first, that it was a ploy of Siobhan's. He was even more crushed when he found out they were legit. I bet it makes you happy that I helped to dig your knife in deeper, huh?"

I made my face carefully blank. "No, that doesn't make me happy. Far from it. I was trying to make the break as clean as possible."

I didn't see the punch coming, but it sent me clear across the cabin of the limo. I slammed hard into the glass partition that separated the drivers side. I just lay there, stunned, trying to work up the desire to retaliate. It was very uncharacteristic for me, but I just couldn't find it.

"You wanted it fucking clean? That was the messiest-"

The door nearest Sloan slammed open. Cam shoved his snarling face inside the car, growling, "What's going on in here?" His glare was all for Sloan.

Sloan and I looked at each other, and shrugged. "Nothing," I said.

"I don't know. Why?" Sloan responded at the same time. It was somewhat reassuring that Sloan and Cam seemed to still be hostile to each other. They had always bumped heads, and neither were subtle enough to even try to hide it.

"Don't mess with me, Sloan. I heard fighting in here. What happened? Why does Jillian look like she just got punched in the face?"

Sloan shrugged. "Ask Jillian. I don't know what you're talking about."

He called her a bitch under his breath as he looked at me. "What was all the noise about?" he asked me. It was obvious it pained him to even have to speak to me.

I shrugged. "Ask Sloan," I told him.

He looked at Sloan. "What, you guys are old buddies again?" Every word dripped with disgust..

We both laughed, then stopped, glaring at each other.

"Hardly," Sloan told him. "We both just happen to hate you."

He gave her a murderous look. "Right back at you, you half-breed bitch." He slammed the door in her face. She shrugged.

"He's even meaner than he used to be," I noted.

Sloan's mouth turned up on one side in an unhappy smile. "So am I. But he's been impossible since Siobhan started dating Dom again. You see, before Dom started seeing her again, she'd been slumming with Cam for awhile. He's been on his period ever since she dumped him."

My eyes widened. "She dated Cam? Does Dom know?"

She shrugged. "Kinda. He knows that they dated. Don't think he knew they were dating so recently, or that it had gotten serious."

I curled my lip in distaste. "Dating two cousins? Creepy."

Sloan nodded. "It's worse than that, even. She's dated Collin, too."

I was more than a little surprised. "I never knew. I thought druids were way too possessive to pass around women like that. I always thought Siobhan was just waiting patiently for Dom to finally fall for her."

She snorted. "Hardly. She's certainly never waited for him at home, if you know what I mean." We fell silent.

I remembered something I'd heard. "Good job wiping the floor with her in the arena. When I heard about that, I wanted to cheer."

She smiled a little at the mention of her victory over Siobhan. I just don't think she could help her mouth turning up when she thought about the memory. "It felt good. And now I outrank her."

My brow furrowed. "You're 1st lieutenant now, right?"

She smirked. "Yes, this half-breed bitch is 2nd in command, and 1st lieutenant."

"So does that mean that you fought Cam for the spot? I never heard the details of that." When an Arch took his vows, he personally appointed seven lieutenants for himself. Their rank was then voted on by the people. Whatever was voted became the chain of command for the leadership. However, the vote was not the final decision. The lieutenants could all challenge each other to combat to move up in rank. If one was challenged, and refused to fight, the challenger then moved up in rank, pushing the challenged down one spot. You could only challenge the one directly above you, however, so no one could just skip to the top. Originally, when Dom had become Arch, Cam had been the 1st, Siobhan the 2nd, Sloan the 3rd, Collin the 4th, and so on. When Sloan had beaten Siobhan, she had moved up to second, putting her in a position to challenge Cam, if she wanted to be 1st. Since she was now 1st, I assumed that had happened, though I'd never heard anything about it. My sources weren't quite that good. All I'd heard was that it had been a private affair.

That wiped the smile right off of her face. "He refused to fight me, just handed me the spot like a little bitch. You can't know how much I wanted that fight. How much I still want it."

I blinked at her, surprised at her, surprised at them both. "Did he say why? He's so big on rank, I just can't picture him doing that."

She flushed, looking down at her fisted hands. "He said that he didn't want to hurt me, the bastard. I fucking hate that guy."

I thought that said a lot, but apparently it hadn't said anything that Sloan wanted to hear. We were both silent for a long time, lost in thoughts.

"I tried to talk to him before that, Sloan," I spoke after a while, going back to the exhausted subject of Dom and I. "The pictures were a last resort."

"You are such a stone-cold bitch," was her only response. I decided to stop trying for a truce, after that.

Eventually Cam got back into the car, rudely crowding Sloan to the opposite end of the bench seat they shared. "Asshole," she muttered loudly.

"Man-hater," he responded without sparing her a glance. "The Arch is on his way."

Dom finally slid into the car, forcing Sloan to take a seat beside me to avoid having to sit too close to Cam. Dom didn't spare anyone a glance as the car starting moving. He pulled a large bottle of whiskey out of the trench he wore over his tattered vest, taking a long swig. He passed the bottle to Cam without saying a word. Cam followed suit, passing the bottle to Sloan.

I'd asked them about this after battle habit years ago. I'd been told the hard liquor was the best way to get the taste of flesh off their tongues. I'd wondered out loud why, if the taste of flesh was so unpleasant to them, they couldn't just use claws instead of teeth for fighting. The answer I'd gotten was that a berserker couldn't hold back from using its teeth. And the whiskey wasn't really that much of a problem. It was very difficult to get a druid drunk. I, of course, had refrained from mentioning that my kind had invented berserker rage.

Dom stared moodily out the window, until Sloan spoke. "Was there any way to tell how many of them got away?"

He looked at her, shrugging. "Impossible to say, for sure. Their casualties number in the thousands. It seems we accomplished our goal tonight, though we lost far too many of our own in the process, far more than we anticipated, and I want to know why. Those things were expecting us tonight. They were prepared for us, prepared to fight druids."

Cam sent me an accusing glare. "It has to be her. None of our own would betray us."

Dom sighed. "Just because you want something to be true doesn't make it so." He looked at me. "It's easy enough to see if your story checks out. I'll just need your cooperation for a small spell."

I gave him a blank face, shrugging. "Whatever will get me out of here faster."

His mouth hardened. "Of course. Cam, switch places with her. I'll need to touch your forehead for a minor memory spell. That voice you spoke of. I should be able to get some clue as to its origins."

I moved onto the seat beside him, and he touched my forehead with just a finger. I closed my eyes. He began to chant, and I felt the moment when he delved into my recent memories, looking for the voice. His brow furrowed when he finally found what he was looking for.

He ripped his hand away suddenly. "She speaks the truth, a voice led her to the necro circle. It does sound like a small child's voice, but that must be some kind of illusion. The one that spoke to her was an unbelievably strong telepath. There's no way to know where it was contacting her from, or how it knew what was going on. Logic tells me it must have been someone from within the compound, but with that kind of telepathic power, it could have been picking up the circle's intent from god only knows what kind of distance."

"So I'm cleared then?" I asked.

Dom shrugged. "To some extent. Sloan will be escorting you around for awhile, just to be safe."

I felt my temper finally start to simmer. "You gotta be kidding me-"

"It's not negotiable," he said shortly.

"That's bull-" I felt a sharp pain pierce my abdomen, then my temples. "Shit, not again," I muttered, as my vision started to swim. Vaguely, I felt Dom grab both of my arms as I started to collapse. He called my name sharply. I blacked out.

CHAPTER THIRTY

The Grove

I came to again in the hotel section of the druid casino. A lobby of some sort, I thought groggily. I was lying on a plush, deep red couch facing a set of elevators. There were hallways on both sides of me. I immediately noticed the strange earrings I was wearing. I fingered them. They felt like large black pearls, but I knew instantly what they actually were. Dom had placed tracking devices disguised as jewelry into my ears as I slept. Typical Dom behavior. And did it even matter at this point? I was already found.

I sat up straighter and realized that I badly needed a restroom.

I picked a hallway, walking until I found a rather swank public restroom. The bathrooms in Vegas could be fancier than most people's living rooms. When I came back out I was all turned around again.

I headed back the way I thought I had come from, but something felt off. Nothing was quite the same. The wallpaper was upside down. That couldn't be right... It was such a silly detail. It was nondescript wallpaper to begin with, some aesthetically pleasing pattern that didn't mean anything. How would it do that, and why had I even noticed such a thing?

I shook my head dismissively, and continued walking. The carpet began to squish wetly under my shoes. I quickened my speed. The whole place was really starting to creep me out.

I passed a large open space that I hadn't noticed on my way to the bathroom. It was lovely. A pine oasis amidst the usual casino decor. We must have been on the top floor of the building, because the ceiling of the indoor forest was completely glass and streamed in sunlight, which was weird, since I had thought it was still dark out... I walked into the atrium, fascinated by this druid mark on their casino.

I hadn't taken more than a few steps into the room before I froze where I stood. The hair on the back of my neck stood on end, and my hands itched to reach for weapons that weren't there. Where the fuck were my weapons? I had woken up stripped of them, and promptly walked into a trap. The impressive but harmless forest scene I'd thought I'd seen was a figment of my imagination. Or rather, it was an illusion imagined by someone and planted into my own mind.

Even down to the smell, it had fooled me briefly. No fresh pine scent here. The space was saturated in the sickening sweet smell of earthy decay. And blood. It was as though a switch had been flipped, and I caught the real picture. The trees were suddenly darker, the deep brown bark of the trunks almost black, almost every hint of green in the foliage gone to darker shadows.

The pleasant brook had no hint of blue now, but a deep, crimson red. The reddish brown earth was suddenly dotted with stark white objects. The white dots near the water were bigger, and I swallowed hard as I realized that they were human bones.

The druids had turned their backs on a violent past, where their greatest powers were earned through human sacrifice. Or so I had thought. This was a place of power earned through blood, and it was apparently still in use.

A white object bobbed near the surface of the water. I assumed at first that it was a skull, like the many spread among the dirt throughout the grove. But a gasping sound pierced the air as it reached the surface. I didn't realize at first what I was seeing. The creature was palest white and hairless. Its every movement was slow and..wrong, but it moved towards me unerringly. It had no eyes or nose, not even dents or bumps where they should have been. Its mouth was a wide, toothless black hole, much too big for that strange white head. Wrong was the best word to describe everything about it. Its body was vaguely human, but again, it was all...wrong. Its body was emaciated and sexless, but I could see no bones moving beneath the slimy white skin of the too thin figure. It had ten fingers and ten toes, but all the digits were too long, and they were shaped with too many joints.

As I was studying the abomination I hadn't moved, and it was in arm's reach far too soon, considering how slowly it was moving. I wanted badly to back away, or better yet, turn and run, but I was literally frozen in place. It spoke, and its voice was gasping, like it was sucking the words in rather than letting them out. "First-born," it said to me.

I didn't respond. I couldn't. Apparently dragons weren't the only ones that called us the first-born. That was a revelation to me.

"First-born, I thirst," it said, lifting one of its awful hands to me. I tried to shake my head, but to no avail.

"Speak," it said, and I finally could.

"I can't move." Was all I could think to say.

"This place is a prison, and you our new prisoner. If you want to leave, you must pay us blood-price." The way it said this seemed almost obscene.

I cringed away. "What is blood-price?"

"I drink my fill of your blood. If you can walk away after I am done, you may."

I really did not like the sound of that. But I was frozen in place, and no other options were presenting themselves. Still, I needed to be clear about the limitations. "You may have blood, but only what you can take in one feeding. Then you must take this enchantment from me, and allow me to leave."

It gave me a grotesque parody of a smile. I flinched. "The first-born has spirit, yes. But not many choices here. Who are you to make terms, when you cannot even move?"

"Those are the terms. Obviously, you need my permission to take my blood, or you would have already done it." I was bluffing, and mentally crossing my fingers. "So, that is how you can acquire it."

Now its gaping mouth turned down. "I take these terms. I have never tasted a first-born." Its obscene mouth opened wide, and revealed the teeth hidden there. I gasped. It had only four of them, far apart, lined up side by side, top to bottom. The size was the terrifying part. They were closer to the size of tusks than teeth, but razor sharp.

It gripped my arm in its slimy hand, and slowly moved its head over the inside of my wrist and elbow. In a dizzying flash, it struck.

I screamed. The pain was agonizing, and I wasn't exactly a stranger to pain. It began drawing hard, and still I was frozen. It drew on my arm roughly, relishing every draw, until I felt the pull of unconsciousness.

I came to, lying near the bloody brook. I heard Dom's voice, as if at a distance. "How dare you?" He was speaking to the creature.

"Master, she offered blood freely. She is first-born, and she is more. If you offer me tribute, I'll tell you a secret. It is knowledge you will value."

Dom's voice was as icy as I'd ever heard it. "I'm not interested in your secrets. I will deal with you later."

"It is your secret, Master. Your's and the first-born's."

Without another word Dom turned, picked me up like a child, and strode out. It felt good just to breath outside of that nightmarish place. "What the hell was that thing?" I asked softly.

Dom sent me a cold look. "You think you're the only one with a fucked up family? There have always been skeletons in my closet, but not all of us just run away from everything that scares us." Ouch, that one hit home on several levels that I didn't even want to think about.

He strode quickly back to the lobby where I had first roused. This hotel had the most confusing floor plan I'd ever encountered. I thought it might be deliberate, to keep people away from that thing.

I shot him a wary glance, my good hand to my still pounding heart. My injured arm was cradled against my stomach carefully. "I have to say, it's not that easy to shock me, but I must admit you've done it."

Angry eyes bore into me silently for a moment before he spoke. "It's nothing like you're thinking."

I waved the hand of my un-injured arm in the direction of the abomination I'd just witnessed. I wasn't surprised to note that it was shaking. "How could I misunderstand a thing like that? Are you going to tell me that room wasn't a grove full of-"

He cut an impatient hand through the air, effectively stopping me mid-sentence. "Of course it is. But you misunderstand. We did stop all of those practices centuries ago, just as we've been saying, but we can never undo what's been done in the past. You can't get rid of a thing like that. You can only hope to contain it."

"I know you've always been avid with curiosity as to why we set up such a huge population in the desert. Well, that was your answer. We don't get to *choose* where that thing resides. It chooses, and we follow. The ancients used to sacrifice humans to gain power, and we pay the price for their

221

transgressions. We feed it power, to stop the bloodshed. As Arch, I am that abomination's guardian."

"Only druid eyes have ever witnessed the grove. You wanna tell me how the hell you found that place?" As he spoke, he set me down gently on a plush dark-brown leather chair in one of the hotels many sitting areas. Where the hell were we? I still had no idea. Damned annoying druid casino…

I shook my head. "I think it lured me in. I went to the bathroom, and when I came out, everything was wrong. It was subtle at first, so I have no idea exactly when the enchantment overtook me. It knew what I was, and it wanted to trap me. It called me first-born. I haven't heard that term from anyone in-I don't even want to think how long it's been. But I've only ever heard other dragon-kin refer to us that way."

Dom knelt down beside me as I spoke, gingerly taking my injured arm. He sucked in a harsh breath at the large holes piercing my arm, two near my elbow, two on my wrist. They were already starting to heal, but they looked gruesome and they hurt like a son of a bitch.

He began to heal me without a word, and I gasped in pleasure as soon as he began, biting my lip. To go from a persistent, deep pain, to that kind of pleasure made me suddenly weak. I tried hard not to recall all of the ways he could cause me pleasure with his magic. And his hands…. I tried not to moan a protest when he finished.

He cleared his throat, obviously trying to stay on the subject at hand. "As I said, that thing is meant only for druid eyes. It is one of our darkest secrets. I only hope that you finding that grove doesn't cost us both too dearly. You must never speak of it. Even thinking of it gives it more power. Let us hope it had its fill of your blood. We should get farther away. My rooms are warded against it."

He didn't ask, just carried me to his rooms without another word. With the pain in my arms gone, I became all too aware of who was holding me, who was touching me. He cradled me like a child, and I lay my cheek on his chest, inhaling that intoxicating scent of his. I fingered the material over his chest. He had changed since the battle. He wore a soft black T-shirt. I rubbed a hand over his hard chest, kneaded at the firm flesh of his pectoral.

"Stop it," he said, his tone expressionless.

I sighed. I had no clue where he and I stood, or even where I wanted us to, but it was a fact that I couldn't keep my hands off of him.

"Why was I lying on that couch, anyways? So close to that... thing?"

His chest rumbled against my cheek when he spoke. "I had some urgent business to tend to. I left you right outside of the office while I went to make a quick phone call. It should have been perfectly safe. The grove is hidden to all but the most powerful of druids. And that *thing* moves."

"I'm no druid, Dom," I told him.

"I'm well aware," he responded flatly. "This is a troubling development, to say the least." As he spoke, we reached his room.

I recognized it as the one he had taken me to the last time I'd been in the casino, but absolutely nothing leading to it was familiar. "What the hell is with this place? I remember this room, but nothing else about this floor. And where are all of your people?"

"I dismissed them. We have half of a floor to ourselves, for the moment. I wanted some semblance of privacy. News of our reconciliation is already running rampant among my ranks."

"Reconciliation?" I asked softly, shocked and...something that I didn't want to examine.

He sent me a hard look. "The very idea is absurd, I know, but the rumor mill that I'm sure you remember is still alive and well."

Absurd, yes. I let that sink in as he carried me to his bed, laying me down, a strange look on his face. "And if you notice anything strange about this hotel, I'd suggest you stick close to me, and speak of it as little as possible."

That only whet my curiosity, of course, but I dropped it, suddenly much more interested in the fact that he had lain me on his bed.

He stood at my side, studying me intently, an enigmatic look on his face. I didn't last long under that regard, much to my everlasting dismay. I shifted impatiently, watching his face as closely as he watched mine. "Please, Dom," I said softly.

He was suddenly over me, our lips touching. "Damn you," he said roughly, kissing me with all of his pent-up rage and anger.

"Damn me," I agreed, when he finally came up for air. The storm took us yet again.

CHAPTER THIRTY-ONE

The Pictures

I knew it was a touchy subject, but I asked anyways. "What did you think I was for all those years? Of course you didn't buy any of our covers. I never expected you to. It was always enough that you didn't press me for answers."

I could only see his profile. His mouth tilted up slightly in a bitter smile. "Actually, I thought you were an angel. I couldn't have been more wrong now, could I?" He didn't look at me as he walked into the bathroom, shutting the door hard behind him. Well, shit, it had been stupid of me to ask. But it hadn't occurred to me that the answer would hurt so much, reminding of all that we'd lost. Reminding me of how he had adored me once.

I was perched on the side of his bed, completely undressed. I had a fleeting urge to get dressed and get out of there before he came back out, but couldn't seem to make myself move. I just sat staring at my feet, listening to the shower run in the background. I was trying hard to talk myself out of following him in when my eyes fell on the drawer of his heavy-wooded black nightstand. It was slightly ajar. I vaguely recalled him closing it quickly when I woke up. I sent a quick glance at the bathroom door before I peaked inside the drawer. Yes, you can add nosy to my already impressive list of character flaws.

A large manilla envelope was the only thing inside. I hesitated briefly before plunging my hand inside. My hand trembled a little when I realized what was inside the envelope. I'd never actually seen the thick stack of photos before, but I was very familiar with their contents.

The man in the photos couldn't have looked less like Dom if I had gone in search of a man just for that purpose. He was pale, with long yellow-blond hair, lithely muscular rather than bulky, and almost exactly my height. There could have been no mistake that it was not Dom's naked back facing the camera in the first photo I looked at. My hands were gripped tightly in his curly golden hair. Our coloring had complemented well, two golden forms melded together. The pictures were even prettier than I'd thought. I'd angled myself in the first dozen shots so that the photographer would capture my angled face and naked torso perfectly. My naked hip just peaked out from behind his naked butt, which was practically plastered to the window where my hand-picked photographer was taking furtive shots with a trigger-happy speed only Caleb could have managed. There was no mistaking that it was me. And there was no mistaking the man in the pictures either. Especially the ones where I angled for a perfect straight shot of his lust-dazed face at the camera. I'd known if they captured his face there'd have been no hiding for Declan. As a passionate and incriminating embrace, it was convincing. The only thing suspicious about the photos were my eyes. They were downcast in most of the shots. But the ones that revealed glimpses showed clearly that there was no passion there, just cold determination. But that was a small thing when confronted with all of that naked skin. And I knew that as far as convincing Dom, it'd been overkill. But, hell, overkill had always been my specialty.

The bathroom door slammed open behind me, and I jumped.

I calmly began putting the photos back into the drawer, but of course, the damage was done. Goosebumps rose along my skin as I felt his eyes boring into me from behind.

I sat perfectly still as he appeared in front of me, wearing just a towel slung around his naked hips. The wet towel clung. I couldn't even pretend this didn't affect me. A nearly naked Dom would only stop affecting me when I was dead.

He didn't even address my lack of regard for his privacy as I'd thought he would. "How was he?" he asked, his voice low and intense.

I closed my eyes. "Dom, don't."

His hand gripped hard over one of my braided buns, pulling my head back roughly. "Tell me," he ordered.

Finally, I shrugged one shoulder. It was awkward with the way he was holding me, but I think he got the point. "He did the trick," I said cryptically. He shoved me away in disgust, and started pacing. "How often do you look at these pictures?" I finally asked him. *What have I done?* I thought to myself.

He stopped, staring at me. "Often enough. I assume you know what happened to him, what *I* did to him." His restless pacing began again. "What did you feel when you found out I killed him? That I tore him limb from limb?"

I sighed unhappily, interrupting him. "You should just burn these, Dom. It's not healthy to be so obsessed with something that happened so long ago."

He stopped, leaning in close. "I'm not obsessed with those pictures, Jillian. I'm obsessed with you. I've been obsessed with you since I was fourteen. What's not healthy is being obsessed with someone that I despise. I used to think that I could never hate you, that no matter what you did, my feelings couldn't change."

I felt each of his words like a blow, knowing that the biggest blow was yet to come.

"I was wrong," he continued brutally. "God, was I wrong. You proved me wrong.   And it wasn't just that man, Jillian.   You broke your blood oath to me without blinking.   You gave up on *us* without blinking.   You were never the person I thought you were.   You were an adolescent fantasy that I just couldn't shake."

I was still trying to let his stinging words sink in when he continued. "When I met you, you told me I was too young to fall in love.   I knew you were wrong at the time.   And what I felt didn't fade with time or distance.   But you made me wish it would." His voice was a low growl in my ear. "Now answer the question.   What did you feel when you heard I had killed him?"

I did the idiot thing and told him the truth.   I figured it wouldn't go over well.   I was right.   "Relief.   I heard you were going to fight him in the arena and I was relieved when it was over and you weren't hurt."

He smiled at me, and it was an ugly, mean smile-a bitter, heart-wrenching smile.   It hurt me as much as it was meant to. "Not hurt?   That's how you see it?"

We had a long and sordid past that spanned more than half of a normal human's life span.   He had loved me since he was barely more than a child.   His feelings had embarrassed me at first, since I was far from a child myself, but my reluctance had never thwarted his devotion.   Eventually, when he was grown, he had managed to seduce me, and my heart had never been safe from him after that.   But I had hurt him, time and again.   I broke promises, and I ran.   It was a cycle that I doubted I could ever break.

I couldn't look him in the eye for a minute.   When I finally met his angry eyes again, mine were pleading.   "I warned you, again and again, that he was going to try to kill you.   Everyone could see it but you.   And he flat out told me what he planned-"

His bark of a laugh was painful to my ears.   "I suppose I should have guessed it then, when you kept running into him and getting all worked up about his plans.   Fool that I was, I trusted you."

"You didn't trust me enough to listen to me about him. And he never would have quit making attempts on your life. Sneaky, underhanded attempts. So to answer your question, I felt only relief when you killed him. Relief that he wasn't a threat to you anymore."

His eyes went a little crazy after I finished talking, and I knew that wasn't good. "Are you somehow trying to imply that you fucked him for my sake? That you knew I'd challenge him and eliminate the threat to my own life? Please tell me you aren't trying to make me believe that you fucked him to save my life!" His voice was close to a roar at the end.

"I didn't say that." I stayed silent after that, seeing clearly that my every word was antagonizing him even more.

He paced angrily for several long moments before looking at me again. His eyes were tormented. "You wouldn't believe what I turned into when you left. I had so little control over my rage that I did things that would have made you hate me. Perhaps I did them so that you would."

"I killed Declan's guard without a qualm, just slaughtered them like sheep. I didn't know why they served him. They may have been loyal to him, or just doing their duty. But I unleashed my rage on them without hesitation, and it was a bloodbath. I had enough control not to involve any of my own people, to do it myself, but that was where my control ended. Or perhaps I wanted the carnage all to myself. I honestly can't recall. It still sits in my memories like a dark red haze."

"There were ten men guarding him. He thought to hide from me. He seemed to think that if I couldn't speak to him, I couldn't challenge him. I warned his guard once to leave or die, but they were dutiful. Misguided, but dutiful. It wasn't even a challenge to decapitate them, one by one. And then there was Declan. I was an inch away from killing him on sight, but I drew it out in the arena. I wanted an audience to see his humiliation. I wanted you to hear about it, about the brutality of it. I wanted you to hear about how I toyed with him. I drew it out, to make him scared, to make him suffer, and cry, and beg. And he did. I wanted you to know that I tore him into tiny pieces and bathed in his blood. I wanted you to know that I drank his blood, and ate his heart, and took his power as my own with no remorse. Perhaps it's better that I didn't find you early on." He came to stand above me on the bed, that mis-matched gaze boring down at me. His wolf's eye was wild with the beast. Its cobalt twin wasn't far behind.

"When we found Christian, on the verge of leaving town, I snapped. Did he tell you about what happened?"

I nodded, never looking away from him.

"I tortured him relentlessly. I did it myself. There was scarce an inch of him unscathed when I was through. I sliced him to ribbons."

That I hadn't known. I felt a sickness deep into my soul.

"I was just so sure that he knew where you were, or at least, how to get ahold of you. And I was just as certain I could break him. And when I realized that nothing would make him talk, whether he knew or not, I came so close to killing him. You don't understand how close. I could taste his severed jugular in my mouth. That's how close I was to taking his life. I even wanted you to know about it, if only to make you reappear, even if it was just so you could come after me. I still don't know what stopped me, but I think not killing him is what snapped me out of the rage I'd been living in. At least enough to function again."

"Did you know that's what you left behind?" he continued relentlessly. "An animal so wounded it didn't care who it hurt. If you had known it would turn me into a monster, would you still have done it?"

I didn't begin to know how to answer that. Though angry, he was no animal now. I couldn't picture the things he described. Dom and self-control had always just been a fact to me. And a point of pride for him. A symbol of his power. Could I even begin to imagine all I'd taken from him when I left? I'd always thought I could. The parting had cost me, as well. I hadn't had a moment of affectionate human contact since we'd parted. I simply couldn't bear it. But, of course, there were some pieces of the destruction I had failed to anticipate. Like how it would make him hate himself. I had been so certain that all of the loathing, both from him and from myself, would fall squarely on my shoulders.

"I just don't know. I felt so desperate, so powerless over the events taking place. So much of what I did was panic and instinct. And once the running starts, it's impossible to stop. It's a familiar pattern that's almost a comfort to me." My answer was quiet.

So was his response. "Get dressed and get out."

CHAPTER THIRTY-TWO

Touchy Subject

I took a quick shower, re-donning my burnt up clothes as a last resort. If Dom had any clothes I could wear in his apartments, I didn't particularly want to know about it, so I made a point of not asking. Most of my holsters were still intact, and I armed myself, my guns and knives now fully visible.

"Your phone's been ringing," Dom told me as I re-entered his bedroom. He waved in the direction of his nightstand, where my cel was sitting, miraculously unharmed by the nights violence.

I'd missed several calls from Caleb. His messages sounded borderline panicked, and I can't tell you how good that *wasn't* for my peace of mind. The gist of the messages was, "Get to Club Dante. Some shit's going down." He didn't pick up when I called.

I hung up the phone, looking at Dom. He was eyeing me coldly. "I've gotta bounce," I said. I paused awkwardly. "My kind has an enthrallment spell. I've seen humans ruined by it. It plants a pernicious, persistent devotion that holds you in its grip for a lifetime. I don't have any idea if druids can be affected by it, and I was never taught the enchantment, but I wonder if I inadvertently cast it on you, when you were young."

He laughed, and it was a bitter sound. "Wouldn't that be handy? Any spell cast surely has a counter-spell. But no, I think not. And doesn't that just say it all about us? Love is such a foreign concept to you that you think it must be an errant spell."

I flinched. Talk about a jab that hit its mark. The sad thing was, Dom was all I knew about romantic love, and I really had tried my best to show it to him. But amidst the pain in my chest, his words also brought me the beginnings of an idea. What I wouldn't give to have that counter spell, just to cast it on Dom to see if it had any effect. If I had somehow enthralled him, he had a right to be free. And I needed to know.

He nodded at the door, dismissing me. "Sloan will go with you."

"Ugh. I don't even know where my car is."

"Sloan has a car. She can drive you."

I glared at him. "I'm pretty sure Sloan won't want to go where I'm going."

His lip curled in a half-smile. "Yes, Club Dante. I heard." There was disgust in his voice. "I don't care what kind of sordid places you frequent. Sloan goes with you."

I gave a little half wave as I stormed out. I knew he wanted a fight more than anything else and it wasn't hard to figure out that having Sloan follow me around was the lesser evil.

Sloan was waiting in the antechamber, by the elevator. At my entrance, she rose from the chair she'd been lounging in. She gave me a blank face, not saying a word, just pushing the down button on the elevator. We both filed in silently.

"Any idea where I could pick up clothes this time of night for an S&M club?" I asked bluntly as the elevator began to move. I was wearing the tattered remains of my combat gear. My cargo pants still covered the essentials, but the black tank I'd worn under my armored vest was pushing it. The material that had covered my stomach had burned away completely, leaving my midriff bare. The chest area was at least covered, though the straps on the tank looked in danger of falling off.

She looked a little surprised at the question, but recovered quickly, eyeing up my tattered clothes. "What you're wearing should work, if the club is dark enough to hide the Necro blood. That torn up, shredded look is actually kind of in right now. You need different shoes though. Some black stilettos would be better."

"I don't do heels. I'm keeping the shoes."

She shrugged. "Like I care." She was silent for a moment. "Shit, does Dom know you're going to an S&M club?"

"Yes. You don't need to come, though."

"Why the hell would you tell him about it?"

"He overheard me talking on the phone. Believe me, it's the last place I want to go, and certainly the last place I wanted to tell him I was going. Just loan me a car and I'll get out of your hair.

She just gave me a level stare. "Are you saying you're being forced to go to an S&M club?"

"Yes, I am."

She just raised a brow. "I don't even wanna know. Though I suppose I'll be finding out soon enough, since I'm coming with you. Don't bother trying to lose me. I'm your shadow until I'm ordered otherwise. But believe me, I'd rather be doing just about anything else."

"Me too."

We reached the parking garage, and I waved her ahead. "Lead on."

She led me to a new black mustang with bronze racing stripes. "Nice car," I told her.

"Whatever." She slid into the drivers side, starting the car and backing up right as I shut the passenger door. "Where am I going?"

"Club Dante. Need directions?"

"Sadly, no," she replied shortly. I was more than a little curious how she knew about the club, but knew better than to press my luck and ask her about it.

Several silent minutes of driving weakened my resolve. I finally asked, "Ok, so how do you know about Club Dante?"

She cast me a cursory glance. "You need me to turn on the radio or something? I don't feel like chatting with you."

"Sounds like a touchy subject."

She turned the radio on, tuned it to the rock station, then cranked it up loud, effectively drowning me out for the duration of the drive.

I'd thought getting through the door would be a problem. I knew a little about the place from Lynn. At least enough to know you needed a password to get through the door. So I was pleasantly surprised when the doorman opened his little eye slot, widened his eyes, and the door swung gently open.

The small doorman was in full S&M getup. From the looks of it, I guessed he was a sub, covered in only latex straps. He stared at me, literally open-mouthed.

"We good to just go in then?" I asked him.

He looked like he wanted to speak, but was just kind of sputtering. I shrugged at him. "I'll take that as a yeah. Thanks, dude." I brushed past him.

I had no clue about the layout of the club, but figured I could search every room until I found Caleb or Lynn. A simple plan, but sometimes simple works just fine.

I was striding down a narrow hallway when I caught a movement out of the corner of my eye. A small figure darted around a corner to my right. I would've sworn it was a child.

My brows drew together at the thought of a child in this place.

I caught up to the child in a dark room at the end of the hallway. I switched on the light in the small room. It was a little girl, and she sat huddled on the ground in the back corner of the room, skinny knees pulled up to her chest, head down. Her streaky, ashy blond hair was a tumbled mass that touched the ground where she sat. It covered her arms and face almost completely.

"Are you ok?" I asked her quietly. She tensed at the sound of my voice, but didn't answer.

"What are you doing here? This is no place for a child."

At that she looked up. Her eyes were a startling lavender, her features lovely and delicate and unmistakably asian. Though by her streaky blond hair and lavender eyes, it was obvious that one of her parents was not. She stood. She was tall and delicate, and wore a stained, baby-blue nightgown that was close to rags. I guessed her age at maybe nine.

"Are you ok?" I asked her again.

She blinked those gorgeous eyes at me slowly. "I am learning english," she spoke carefully.

I nodded. "Ok. What's your name?"

"What's your name?" she asked me back.

I smiled. "I'm Jillian. What's your name?"

She smiled back, and her face lit up. "I'm Jillian, too!!"

I laughed at the obvious lie. "You are not. What's your name, really?"

She clutched her hands together excitedly. "I'm Jillian. We have same name. Maybe you're my mother?"

I shook my head at her, still smiling. "Sorry, sweetheart, I'm not your mother. I think I would have remembered if I had a little girl."

"Maybe you forgot."

"I promise I didn't. Can you tell me what you're doing in a place like this?"

"This is bad place."

"For children, yes, it's very bad. Where are your parents?"

She scowled, and even her scowl was pretty. "I don't know. I think maybe you are my mother."

I sighed at her persistence. "Why do you think that?"

She looked down, shrugging. "I don't know, but I wish you were."

I knelt down in front of her. "Trust me, you don't want a stranger for a mother."

Her chin set stubbornly. "You are not strang-" she was cut off suddenly by a loud crashing sound that seemed to shake the whole building.

"Um, I think we should check that out," Sloan spoke, reminding me of her presence. I nodded, standing.

"Stay here," I told the little girl. "I'll come back after we take care of some business, ok?"

She ran after me, surprising me with a tight hug to my stomach. "Be careful. They are very strong. Don't get hurt." She placed both hands on my belly, whispering something indecipherable. It was then that it occurred to me that the girl wasn't human. I had no time to ask, though, knowing my help was needed elsewhere.

"You stay here," I reminded her as I strode away. "We'll be back very soon."

We continued our search of the club, and I couldn't help but notice the increasingly strange looks I was getting. I glanced back at Sloan. "You notice people are staring at me?"

She rolled her eyes. "People always stare at you. You should be used to it by now. I hate blonds. And big boobs. Bitch."

I stopped, looking at her. "Have you seen the looks they've been giving me? They're not checking me out. Something weird is going on here."

"Um, yeah. I thought that's why we were here."

"Just watch the faces of the next people we come across."

We came across another chamber with someone getting whipped. I interrupted them without hesitation, calling out loudly as I stormed their private room. "Hey, have you guys seen a woman about my height with spiky black hair? Or anything strange at all, for that matter?"

They both turned to me, the still chained woman craning her neck. They just stared at me, confused. "She would look a little like me, my size, black hair. Ring a bell?"

"B-black hair?" the woman asked.

"Yes, pitch-black. Seen anyone by that description?"

They both shook their heads, still looking at me strangely. I let out a frustrated sigh as I stormed out.

"I see what you mean," Sloan muttered behind me.

We continued our search of the large building, until we came across a large audience chamber of some kind, with a show going on that stopped me in my tracks.

A tall blond woman was at the center of it all, barely covered in a series of latex straps that didn't manage to cover even the essentials. Nipple clamps tried but failed to help cover her nipples, and her crotch didn't fair much better, with a g-string so thin it barely covered anything. It was one of the most obscene outfits I'd ever seen, and she wore it with no shame. Her pale blond hair was done up in twin braid buns on the sides of her head. As I noticed her face, a face identical to my own, my hands clenched into fists at my sides.

"Holy shit," Sloan muttered beside me.

"I'm gonna kill him," I growled.

Two men knelt at her feet, but a cat-o-nine was only busy working on one of them . They both knelt facing us, and adding insult to injury, I recognized them right away. One was Luke, looking way too comfortable being bound and helpless. The other was the club's owner, Johnny, who I recognized because he and Lynn had gone out a few times. He seemed to be a less willing participant than Luke, as he pleaded with his torturer to stop.

"Caleb," I screamed across the room.

CHAPTER THIRTY-THREE

Mimic

Caleb heard me scream his name, but didn't bother to stop whipping the figure before him.

"I've searched the building, Jillian," he called back to me in my own voice. "Johnny here knows where she is, and he's gonna tell me."

I strode to the center of the room, standing directly in front of the stage. I stood there with my arms crossed in front of my chest until he finally looked at me, with my own eyes. It was beyond creepy. I just glared at him until he finally shrugged, saying, "Looking like this got me in the club, fast."

I eyed him up and down, portraying with a look how disgusted I was with my body in that ensemble. "You're really gonna try to tell me that this," I pointed at his near naked crotch, "was entirely necessary?"

He shrugged, "It did the trick."

"I'll help you beat the shit out of him, if you want," Sloan spoke from behind me.

I gave her a surprised look. "Thanks for the offer, but we need to find Lynn first. Maybe after." Something occurred to me, and I turned back to Caleb/Me. "Is this the first time you've mimicked me?"

His/My face went carefully blank, and I cursed out loud.

"You bastard!" I burst out. "Where and what have you been doing with my body and face?'

He held up his hands. "Don't get too excited. I've never impersonated you in public before this."

My eyes widened, then narrowed. "What the *hell* is that supposed to mean?"

"I think that means he did something worse," Sloan said softly. Her tone was deadly. It was almost like, in spite of herself, she wanted to have my back. The thought warmed me. I had the bizarre urge to win her over again. But what was the point of that? Stupid human emotions. Even a small amount of contact with Dom had made me soft again. He had always had that effect on me. He made me almost feel human. Everyone always accused me of screwing with his head, but he'd had the same effect on me, in his own way.

Caleb rolled his/my eyes. "We don't have time for this, Jillian. The Chinese dragons have taken Lynn, and I have a feeling Villi may have gotten his hands on her by now." His eyes focused very suddenly and intently on a spot directly behind my left shoulder, his hand flying to his back, for a weapon, I assumed.

I didn't even have time to react before a hand gripped my elbow from behind. Me and Sloan had our guns trained at the man's head without blinking. The man raised his hands in a non-threatening manner, backing several steps away. But there was nothing non-threatening about a man who could sneak up on me like that. And Sloan, too, for that matter. I studied him.

He was, quite simply, stunning. He was tall and slender, with an unmistakable resemblance to the dragon, Drake. That told me a lot. I could assume right away that he was one of the Chinese dragons, and related to Drake. Drake had been messing with Lynn for days, and must have helped to take her captive. So this guy was a hostile, and I had to assume he was immeasurably dangerous. Almost any other dragon would have the jump on me, since I'd had so little formal training with my dragon powers. His features were even and surreally beautiful. His long black hair hung free and long down his elegant back. Every movement and line of his body was elegant, for that matter.

His violet eyes were pale and stunning. It was hard to look away from them, they were so startlingly beautiful. Was he related to that little girl? Her lovely eyes had been so similar. Could the child have been dragon-kin?

He was giving me an almost amused, but utterly intense stare, like his gaze had a purpose. Was he trying to enthrall me? *Could* he enthrall me?

"Don't shoot," he said, in a softly accented voice, then smirked slightly. It was a crisp accent, as though he'd learned his English in England, rather than America. "Although, I'm not too worried about a few bullets. But I stayed behind to help you, Jillian."

My eyes narrowed. I gestured at him with my gun. "Who are you, and how do you know my name?"

"All of the dragons know about you and your sister. It is the sole reason we are in this city. We came here to meet with you and negotiate…things. Your relatives have, unfortunately, complicated all of our plans." His eyes flicked to Sloan, and the amusement bled from his lovely face, replaced by cold disdain. "This strange, perverted preference of yours for druids has complicated things as well. We will have to discuss that, as well, when we have a more formal, less hurried, meeting. Was it only that none of our kind were available to mate with? Is that why you mated with the druid King? You must know that such a thing has lowered your value considerably, though not diminished it completely. I would still take you, for the sake of breeding."

He was suddenly standing too close to me, and I hadn't seen

him move. Either he was scary fast, or he had me at least partially enthralled. Neither option was sitting well.

"What the fuck are you talking about?" I asked him sharply.

He was at my side, out of my gun's range now, using my body to block him from the others. I was frozen in place, unable to move. That was my answer. He was trying, and succeeding, at enthralling me.

"You are the only two draak Princesses left, Jillian. Our bloodline is dwindling, from too much inbreeding. We've decided to branch out, and you are our only options. You and your sister will be our mates."

I gave him my best, 'You're out of your fucking mind' look. He was unfazed. "How romantic," I said, trying to get my limbs to move rather frantically.

He pressed his body against my still frozen body. "You won't need romance, Jillian. I will give you so much more. You will be a slave to my passions, enthralled for my whims, and you will bear my sons.   But not until after I have punished you adequately for your depraved sins with the druid King." He kissed me then, as though he'd said something romantic.

He tasted…intoxicating. And in spite of myself, my mouth softened for him. I wanted to kiss him back. I felt compelled to. Even as I had the thought, I could move again, and my mouth opened for his onslaught. He didn't hold back, kissing me as though he would consume me.   It took me long, drugging moments to realize that the compulsion had lessened, and I could move. I bit down hard on his tongue. I was satisfied when I tasted blood.

He pulled back, looking smug. "I like spirit. I'll enjoy taming you. You may call me Tianlong. Remember the name, Jillian. I am far from done with you."

I spit in his face. It was red with his blood. He still only smiled.

"I can tell you where they've taken her."

"Lynn?" I asked.

"Yes."

"Tell me."

"I will tell you. First you must agree to an arrangement."

"Fuck you."

His smile widened, growing more heated. "Yes. But a formal meeting first, I think. If you want me to help you, you will agree to meet with me formally to discuss terms."

"What terms?" I asked suspiciously. I was old enough not to make a deal with the devil without knowing the details.

He stroked my hair. It was a mess, half up in braids, half down and trailing messily. I tried to pull away. "We will discuss them at the meeting. A meeting, that is all I ask. Is a meeting not worth your sister's life?"

My jaw clenched. "Fine, I agree to a meeting. Tell me where they've taken her."

"Swear it."

I glared. "I swear I will meet with you."

"As soon as you are able."

"I will meet with you as soon as I am able. Fucking tell me."

"You need to do a few things first, if you are to have any hope of helping her."

I glared at him. "I don't have time for any games."

He pulled a card out of his pocket, flicking it at me. I caught it without taking my eyes off his face. A single phone number was written in small letters on the card. "First, you need to get your friend Christian. You must have a slayer with you to face Villi."

"Christian is in lockdown right now. And he's in no shape to face anyone."

"Yes, I know. That's why you need to feed him your blood. Not only will it restore him, it will make him stronger than ever. Slayer blood is poisonous to us, but drinking our blood does great things for them." His lips quirked up in a smile. "Not exactly fair, but there it is. Oh, and you need to hurry. You aren't the only ones who want your slayer right now, especially in his weakened state. As soon as you have him, call that number." He gestured at the card.

"Why should I believe anything you say? Why on earth would I trust you?"

He shrugged nonchalantly. "I only want to help you and Lynn. That's all I can tell you. "

"The druids will have Christian under heavy guard. How do yo propose we get him out?"

He gestured at Sloan. "You have one of the druid leaders with you. The 2nd in command, yes? And if that doesn't work, spring him." And with that, he disappeared in front of our eyes.

"Ok, where did he go? What kind of dragon trick was that?" Sloan asked behind me.

"Hell if I know. This could be a trap. They could just be trying to distract us. And perhaps get their hands on Christian."

"I say we do what he says. Personally, I hope it's a trap," Caleb spoke as he approached. He smiled, his cold, chilling smile. It seemed to fit too well on my face. "A trap means they'll stop running, and we can finally start fighting. Let's go."

I couldn't really argue with that logic. I strode back to the stage. I began to untie Luke, completely ignoring Johnny, who pleaded for the same treatment from beside him. I ignored him. He had turned on Lynn, and put her in danger. Why else would this whole mess, and her abduction, have gone down at his club? I just knew he was knee deep in it all. I wanted to kill him, but there wasn't time, so I wouldn't touch him, either.

"Caleb, why was Luke bound?" I asked him, but thought I had already grasped the situation.

"Johnny had him like this, before I got here. Luke tried to help Lynn."

"And you couldn't have untied him?"

Caleb just shrugged, making his/my heavy breasts kind of gyrate. It was obscene. "He didn't mind being bound, so it wasn't really a priority."

I finished untying him, straightening. The thought that he had tried to help Lynn, even though there was no way that he could have stopped the ones that were after her, warmed me towards him considerably. His doe eyes met mine, and I gave him an affectionate smile. I couldn't seem to help it. "Thank you for trying to help my sister, Luke," I said.

All of my fondness died a short death as he suddenly bent and started kissing my boot. I sighed. "Get up, Luke. I have an important job for you."

He obeyed instantly. He would make a good soldier, I realized. His submission was so complete that he wouldn't question orders, wouldn't hesitate. I filed that information away.

"There is a child in here. A little blond asian girl, maybe ten years old. I want you to find her, and get her out of here. Take her to the druids. She isn't human, and she doesn't know where her parents are, so they'll take care of her."

He nodded, processing the order. "How do I find the druids?"

Sloan sighed beside me. A card just suddenly appeared in her hand. "Call this number. And the Grove is where they'll direct you, so take her there. Tell them Sloan told you to call them, and explain about the kid. They'll give you the exact drop-off location."

Luke nodded, then took off at a run to search for the girl, a man on a mission. "He's starting to grow on me," I said, breaking into a sprint myself.

I felt and heard Caleb and Sloan match my pace behind me. We were headed for the druids' lockdown.

CHAPTER THIRTY-FOUR

See You Next Tuesday

Day 5

The sun was rising gloriously over the mountains to our left. The bright morning light was almost blinding. The night had gone by, seemingly in a flash, without a moments sleep. Caleb was driving, pulling rather crazily out of the parking lot.

"We need to make a second stop, after we get Christian," I told Caleb. He shot me a look from the drivers seat. The look told me clearly that he thought I was crazy. That Caleb look coming out of my face made me glare back with feeling.

"You're crazy," he said, just to be clear, as if the look hadn't told me his thoughts on the matter.

I ignored him, turning to look at Sloan in the backseat of the small car. "I know I'm the last person that you want to help, but please, for my sister's sake, I need to know where they're keeping Christian."

She sighed. "I'll help you get the dragonslayer. But you're gonna do something for me first." I was all ears. "I want the truth about what happened with Declan. I vouched for you when it all went down. I even had myself and Dom half convinced those pictures were a fraud-" her eyes widened, an idea occurring to her mid-sentence. "Ah, fuck, was that you, Caleb?"

I couldn't keep a bubble of laughter from escaping my throat. Sloan glared at me. Caleb glared at Sloan.

"No. Unfortunately, it was really me in those pictures. And it was really Declan," I added, guessing her next question.

Her glare held a real malice this time. "Tell me why? Why would you do that to him. If you're lying, I will know it, and I won't help you."

I made a snap decision, for better, or worse. "Are you going to tell Dom any of this?"

She shrugged. "That's for me to decide, and it's not negotiable. He is my Arch. My King. I would die for him. Start talking."

I shot a look at Caleb, wondering how he'd feel about our deception being revealed. "It was a setup," I admitted. Caleb shot me a hard look. I shrugged at him. "Declan is dead, along with his Lieutenants No one that's left alive is gonna care that you took some pictures, Cal."

Her eyes widened. Something I'd said was a genuine shock to her. "What do you mean by a setup? And don't even think about being vague with me. You're wasting precious time here."

"Declan needed to die, Sloan. And I couldn't kill him myself. It had to be another druid, and a legal kill. He had been stalking me for months, threatening me and my sister. He knew way too much about us, and was trying to blackmail me into bed. That was bad enough. But then he tried to extort me to help with an assassination attempt against Dom. That's when I knew he needed to die. So we set him up. I told him to meet me in that hotel room. Caleb took pictures through the window from a ledge outside. I let it get exactly as far as what you see in those photos, then I knocked him out cold. I knew Dom would finally kill him for what was on that film. So Caleb delivered the pictures anonymously and I got the hell outta dodge. Call me crazy, but I just didn't trust the druids after all of the things that had happened."

She cursed fluently. "What a mess." After a short rant, she gave Caleb directions to the location where they were holding Christian.

"Just let me do the talking," Sloan surprised me by saying as we pulled up to the small fenced building. I'd been surprised she'd even been willing to direct us here, let alone help us get in.

The armed druid in the booth gave her a respectful nod before opening the gate for us without a word. She was second in rank only to Dom, after all.

"This might be easier than I was thinking," I muttered.

"Don't count on it. My people don't make anything easy."

Sloan started cursing again as we pulled into the small parking lot.

"What's wrong?"

"That's Cam's car." She gestured towards a black cadillac SUV. She started cursing again as she and I got out of the car. Caleb stayed inside, still mimicking me. I had personally seen to wrapping the small blanket Sloan kept in her car around his torso.

I hadn't seen him as we pulled up, but sure enough, Cam was standing in the shadow of the building, arms crossed menacingly across his chest.

"What the hell are you doing, bringing her here?" his gravelly voice called out. His eyes never left Sloan.

"We need Christian," she said quietly.

He pushed away from the wall he'd been leaning against. "Only the Arch can give the order to free him."

Sloan whipped out her phone. "I guess I'll call him then."

"He's in a meeting for another hour, at least. He won't be taking any calls. He's giving the dragon King his answer. We don't expect them to take it well."

She gave him a level stare. "Well, we need Christian now. This won't wait."

He just shook his head at her. "No go, Sugar."

It's possible steam started coming out of her ears. Sloan was one of those people that never lost her composure. She was cool and competent to the core...except where Cam was concerned. "Do Not Call Me Sugar. What are you even doing here?"

"Boss's orders. Some of the dragons slipped away, so he wanted me to personally keep an eye on our local slayer. Lucky you."

"Just let us have him, Cam. It's important."

"Important meaning dangerous, I take it. Dom wanted you to follow her, not help her get you both killed. The answer is no, and hell no."

"What do you care? If Dom is upset when he finds out, you can just put the slayer's release on my shoulders. Your problem's solved, now hand him over."

He just shook his head at her.

"Dick," she fumed at him.

He smirked at her. "And there's nothing you hate more than a dick," he remarked.

"It's true. When a dick can walk and talk and looks like you, there's nothing I hate more."

His mouth twisted bitterly. "Fucking man-hater. I swear you've gotten even meaner since you started playing for the other team."

I couldn't help it, I sent Sloan a surprised look. This was something new.

"It's your imagination. I've always hated you this much," she shot back, not denying the implication.

His smile was mean. "Not always..." This discussion was getting more and more interesting.

"Tie your balls in a knot, breeder." She sneered at him.

His smile turned rueful. "That's a new one."

Sloan changed the subject back to the issue at hand. "We need the slayer. I'm pulling rank on you, Cam. If Dom is unavailable, the decision falls to me. Give us the slayer."

He glared at her, just a cussed mean glare, for at least a full minute. I shifted impatiently on my feet.

"You know I fucking hate it when you pull rank on me," he said softly.

Sloan smiled at him, a goading kind of smile, but with the most bitter of twists. I thought that she must hate pulling rank on him as much as he hated having her do it, by that look. I didn't understand it, but I still saw it clearly in her eyes. "Please, Cam, let's take it to the arena. There's nothing I'd love more. If you want my rank, we need to fight."

Cam met that goading smile with a challenging look, his chin lifting. "Never going to happen, Sloan. Fucking *never*. Deal with it."

"You still scared of me?" she goaded.

He smirked at little at that. The pair of them really did enjoy their nasty little confrontations. They shared a long, intense look, full of a lifetime's worth of raw emotion and straight up animosity. "You know why I won't do it. Hate it and fight it all you want, sugar, but we both know why I won't fight you."

"Just give me the slayer, you ass."

Cam sighed. "He's in no shape to help you."

"Dragonsblood will restore him. And guess what we have."

I wasn't surprised that Cam didn't spare me a glance. He was silent for awhile before finally saying, "I suppose it's pointless to tell you not to do anything stupid." He disappeared into the building without another word.

"Why does Cam think you're a lesbian?" I asked Sloan as we waited, referring to one of the many insults Cam had thrown at her. I had been waiting ten minutes to ask her about it.

She rolled her eyes. "Because he's an idiot."

"Is there a reason you want him to keep thinking it?"

She shrugged. "Because it seems to piss him off, which has been my mission in life for more years than I care to count."

"Fair enough."

It was a good twenty minutes before Cam appeared again, carrying a sickly looking Christian.

"Is he unconscious?" I asked softly.

"I only wish. Little bastard keeps shooting off his mouth," Cam growled.

"I'm not little. You're just one huge mother-" Christian began, rather weakly.

"Shut your mouth, boy."

Cam handed him off to me without sparing me a glance. His weight wasn't a problem for me, but cradling a six foot plus man in my arms was awkward, to say the least.

Christian didn't open his eyes as he said to me softly. "I'm sorry I tried to kill you, Jillian. I'm glad they put this thing on my wrist, even if it knocks me on my ass."

"Don't worry about it." I told him gently. I was over it, honestly. "I've got a job for you to do, and you're gonna like it."

"Oh yeah?" His voice was half-interested. He held up his wrist, jangling a bracelet of bones at me. Druids and their geases... "It is a relief to me, like a weight off. They tell me it only applies to you and Lynn. You still owe me a lot of answers, Jillian, but when I'm thinking clearly I know I don't want to kill you. But when I found out that you were...well, I couldn't think at all. It was like a red haze went over me, like I had no control over what my body wanted to do."

I listened as he spoke, staying silent. Caleb helped me put him in the backseat without a word. I moved into the backseat with Christian, and we all watched the show. Sloan and Cam couldn't seem to help but put one on for the world whenever they got into each other's vicinity.

Cam was gripping her arm tightly, and she was attempting to pull away, to no avail. "Get your hands off of me, you cave man," she was yelling at him.

His response was to grab her other arm, leaning down until they were face to face, pushing closer until their foreheads literally bumped, and he was snarling at her in a whisper, all of his teeth showing.

"Can anyone hear what he's saying?" I asked. I started rolling down my window. I wanted to grab some popcorn and watch this little reprieve. It was a nice temporary escape from the bigger problems at hand. The way they interacted had always been more fascinating to me than any movie. I had concocted a drama in my head where they were secretly in love, but couldn't be together because they were both so stubborn and dominant. I was team Sloan, of course, but a part of me had always respected Cam for his staunch loyalty to Dom. And I couldn't help but have a soft spot for someone who looked similar enough to Dom to be his brother.

I also couldn't help but think how beautiful Sloan and Cam looked together, standing nose to nose, both tall, with straight black hair and blue eyes.

"Fuck you, Cam," Sloan was shouting, a comical contrast to Cam's fervent whispering. She was still pulling hard against him, but he was immovable. This went on for precious minutes while we watched.

I started, remembering that I had a phone call to make. I had a short, succinct conversation with a voice I didn't recognize. "The desert stadium. The druid one," it told me. That was all. I supposed it was enough. I certainly knew where that was. If it was a trap, it was a trap. I couldn't walk away from a chance to get Lynn back. That wasn't even an option.

Sloan and Cam were still going at it even after I hung up the phone.

Finally he seemed to finish his quiet lecture. He looked up at us, pointing. "You get her killed and I will hunt you down. I will gladly forfeit my life to take your miserable heads, if she is killed. Do you understand?"

We all nodded. My eyes were wide. Well, well, well. That had been revealing.

Sloan finally got free of him. She gave him the finger as she got in the car.

"See you next Tuesday, Baby," Cam called to her.

The moment she got in the car, Caleb started driving again.

Sloan and Cam had a hostile staring contest until we drove out of his sight. She punched the dashboard a few times when we were out of his sight, then fell silent.

"See you next Tuesday?" I asked her finally, dying to know.

She just shook her head, and I caught a corner of her smirk in the rearview mirror.

"C U next Tuesday. C U N T," Caleb finally explained. I couldn't hold back a laugh.

CHAPTER THIRTY-FIVE

Torst

Without further ado, I slashed a deep but small cut into my wrist, holding it to Christian's mouth. "Drink," I ordered. "As much as you can stand to."

He obeyed without argument. That's how I knew I had a contrary nature. Him *not* protesting made me antsy. But I held my tongue while he drank. It hurt more than I would have thought, but I'd be damned if I complained like a wimp in front of Caleb. He always turned everything into a badass contest, and I was in no mood for that today. Especially since I'd lose.

Christian drank for a solid five minutes, drawing hard, as though he did this all the time. Which was a little disconcerting. I'd add it to the growing list of questions I had that were definitely *not* going to get answered today.

My wrist had already made good progress towards healing by the time he finished. He drew back, looking breathless and dazed. He shook his head a few times, as though to clear it. "That is some powerful shit! Whew! Let's party!"

I rolled my eyes.

"So..." I began. "You, uh, know what to do, Christian? I know you've never, yanno, 'slayed' a dragon before. But you know *how,* right?"

He glared at me, pouting exactly as though he didn't know what to do. "Of course I do. I went through all the training. So I have a very good idea about what to do."

"A very good idea?" My brows rose. It didn't sound like quite enough to me.

He just continued to glare. My blood ringing his mouth made him look slightly more ferocious than normal. Sloan handed us a box of tissues without a word. I thanked her, and we began to wipe up.

"My father never got a chance to slay a dragon either....but he taught me all of the theories."

I looked at him incredulously for a few tense moments. "Theories..." I said softly.

He became even more defensive. "I know enough, trust me. Besides, it goes against the grain to discuss the family secrets with one of you. They've been well guarded from your kind... obviously."

I just raised a brow at him. "As long as you know what you're doing..."

He shrugged, the casual gesture not working for him as it usually did. "I guess we'll see, huh?" His response was defensive and childish, and far from the reassurance I had hoped for.

I brooded for a few minutes until I realized where we were. "We need to make a stop. Make a right on Tropicana, left on Warm Springs," I told Caleb suddenly.

Three pairs of incredulous eyes swung to me, Caleb's glaring into the rearview mirror. "Why on earth?" he began.

"Torst," I said very softly, looking out the window.

"Torst," Caleb repeated in the same voice, a wicked grin spreading across his/my face at me. "God, I love hanging out with you guys."

I rolled my eyes.

"Torst?" Sloan asked.

Christian just sighed. "I thought that thing was buried for good. But, yeah, guess that's worth a stop, under the circumstances. Torst means thirst in god only knows what language. And Torst is an...object of power that Jillian acquired, oh, who knows when? She won't share the story." He glared at me.

I half-smiled. "I'll tell you what. If we live through this, I'll give you the full story, or as full as it can be, without the when part." Age was a touchy subject, as always, and the when would reveal far too much about mine.

His bloody mouth turned up in a shit-eating grin. It just looked wrong on his face. I started attempting to clean his face again. The blood had dried too quickly, so the dry tissue could only do so much. "Hell, yeah," he said.

"Who is holding Torst for you?" Caleb asked.

I flinched. I was embarrassed. I couldn't help it. I'd done a bad, bad, thing. "No one is. I put it in storage."

His eyes in the rearview mirror were cold with disapproval. "How? Why?"

I sighed. "It's not good. I just couldn't see another way. It won't be happy."

"What kind of blood did you use?" Professional curiosity colored his tone. I was surprised, though I shouldn't have been, that he'd guessed my method so quickly.

"Necro. I was in a pinch at the time, and more than a little pissed at that stupid axe. I swear it was provoking me on purpose. Maybe it *wanted* to rot in storage." I grimaced.

"So defensive," Caleb said flatly. "It must be bad."

Christian whistled. "It's gonna be pissed."

"So it's an axe?" Sloan was asking the car at large.

I nodded. "I'm just hoping that the promise of dragonsblood will calm it down..."

"Your blood, perhaps," Caleb suggested.

I grimaced again. "That's hardly what I had in mind. It never drinks as much as you want it to."

"So it's an axe that drinks blood?" Sloan sounded dubious.

"Oh, yes," Caleb said succinctly, and in such a way that I had the strong urge to deck him. He spoke about the axe far more passionately than I'd ever heard him refer to any woman. "So many would kill to have a relic like that, and she puts it in storage. You're lucky I didn't know where it was all this time."

I rolled my eyes at him. "Why do you think I didn't tell anyone?"

"It's not going back in there at the end of this," Caleb said, his tone very final.

I glared at him. "We can cross that bridge when we get to it. We certainly don't have time to fight about it now."

Caleb just nodded. "As long as you realize that it will be a fight, if you try stash that thing away again."

It was a threat, and I wanted to take exception to it, but now was not the time. "Your opinion on the matter has been noted," I said neutrally. I wasn't neutral about it, though. Not by a long shot. Torst was a killing machine, only good for mass carnage. I sure as hell didn't intend to keep it handy when there wasn't any killing to be done. Its thirst knew no bounds. I would fight Caleb over it if it came to that, but I would curse the gods all the while for giving me shit for options once again.

"It's that storage facility up ahead, the big one on the right," I said, as we approached the spot.

I was getting out of the car right as it stopped, running before anyone else had gotten out of the car. I wanted to get the whole mess over with.

It was no coincidence that the storage unit's eighteen digit password ended in 666. I felt a punch of rage and hunger as I stepped into the small, climate-controlled space.

The axe was in my head, insinuating itself into my thoughts, before I'd even opened the giant, airtight, steel container where it resided. That was bad.

I dropped to the floor as I opened the lid and the thing came flying at me. The man-sized receptacle was bone dry. No surprise there. It had probably finished off that blood within a week, even though it had feasted right before I'd locked it in there.

The axe embedded itself into the wall before pulling out and taking another long swing at me. I rolled out of the way, catching it by the handle from where it had embedded itself into the ground. It was obviously too angry to fight well.

"Dragonsblood!" I shouted at Torst. "All that you can drink, in just a few minutes! All you have to do is calm the fuck down and wait ten minutes!"

Yes, blood. Yes, dragonsblood. Your blood. All of it. I thirst.

Like that was news. Torst always thirsted. Always. "I have three with me. You can't take us all. But we're going to kill a dragon, and if you just come with me peaceably, you can have all of it's blood that you want."

I'll have all of your blood that I want. And all of your three as well. I thirst.

Torst had a bit of an ego. There was basically no fight that he didn't think he could win, just by being thirsty enough. "Remember what's it's like to fight with me? I captured you. You were never able to take my blood by force, but I know you remember that when I go into battle, I get you all of the blood you can drink. You said no one before had ever quenched your thirst so well."

When you fight, I drink, yes. But you rarely fight, and then you locked me away. It was a horrible thirst in that metal box. Never have I known a thirst so terrible.

I sighed. Torst wouldn't be getting over that for a long while, I knew. "You tried to slaughter innocents after a battle. I warned you. I had to show you that I meant my threats. You do not feed on innocents. Not ever."

I thirst. Necro blood is vile and rotten. Human blood is young and fresh. I thirst for human blood.

I shook the infuriating axe. "Never happening. Get the idea out of your head. But I have something better. I've given you small tastes of my blood. Imagine getting enough dragonsblood to quench your terrible thirst."

Yes. Even human blood cannot compare to dragonsblood. Even druid blood cannot compare to a dragon's.

I gave Torst another little shake. "Don't go around talking about druid blood. They avenge their own. Always."

It was a long time ago that I drank my fill of druid blood.

"Lalala, I didn't hear that. How about this? You keep quiet, and I will take you to a bloody battle. We will bathe in it."

Yes, my warrior is back. Into battle, dragon warrior. I thirst.

"Yes, you thirst. I think I got that one. Shhh." I was more than a little surprised when the axe went still in my hands and actually stayed silent.

No one had followed me into the storage unit, but they all hovered near the open door, giving me strange looks.

"I missed this. Jillian talking to herself again feels like old times," Christian said, a way too happy expression on his face.

I glared at him as I passed by, Torst clutched tightly in both hands. I didn't trust the thing not to turn on me. That had been way easier than I had expected, which made me tense as I waited for the other shoe to drop.

CHAPTER THIRTY-SIX

You People and Your Special Weapons

I stood poised at the opposite end of the stadium from the creature, axe balanced on my shoulder. Caleb and Christian flanked me, posed identically, long swords held chest level, pointed at the enemy. You knew things had gotten serious when Caleb traded in his guns for a good old-fashioned sword. Sloan had shifted into bear form, and it was eery how quiet and still she stood behind us in her massive shape.

He makes an ugly dragon, I thought, my mind trying to shy away from looking directly at my sister, who so obviously lay in dire straights. My eyes, however, kept stealing glances at her body. She lay in a pool of blood, completely still. She was blocked largely from sight by the monstrous dragon almost completely in front of her, but I could still make out some worrisome details. For one, her eyes were completely missing, bloody holes all that remained of them. And lying beside her was a glowing blue battle hammer that I knew of all too well. If the hammer had somehow been used to help remove her eyes, it would be a real problem.

Villi screeched at us, drawing my attention back to the issue at hand. His mustard yellow wings flapped restlessly. The

261

awful color was darker closer to his torso, and almost brown at his chest. His scales were large, disproportionately so. He drew back, his long, too thin snout twitching like he had a tick.

Gods, he was ugly. It was ironic, because his human form was ridiculously good-looking. With long white hair, and the most perfect alabaster skin I'd ever seen, he had put even other dragons to shame. He was tall and thin, with the cold, pale-blue eyes that all of us shared. It was likely him that had turned Lynn and I off of blond men, I mused.

His dragon form was huge, appearing to cramp his side of the arena. That could be an advantage for us, though.

"My Lord, he is ugly." Christian voiced my thoughts out loud. "I sure hope your dragon form is prettier than that thing." He pointed a negligent hand in Villi's direction. I turned my head slightly to look at him. He sounded way too cheerful, considering what faced us. He was casually talking trash to me, as though we were headed to a party, and not a bloodbath. His eyes glittered as I'd never seen before, his nostrils flaring, his white teeth showing in a grin.

"It is." My voice was calm. "If I looked like that thing, I'd just ask you to trance me into a coma and go turn myself into a mountain," I joked, referring to his claim about dragons and mountains.

He laughed, a way too happy sound.

"Whenever Christian is done enjoying his slayer hard-on, we should probably get to work here." Caleb's voice was deep and quiet. He was back to his own form, to my great relief. I eyed him up. He looked just as excited as Christian, in his own stoic way. I could see it in his eyes, and I knew he had caught sight of the hammer.

"You can have it if we live through this, Caleb," I told him, referring to the hammer. If there was anyone in the world that could keep that thing in safe hands, it was Caleb. Talk about making a deal with the devil. Handing over that kind of power to a psychopath… But if there was anything I knew about Caleb, it was that he wasn't interested in any form of Godhood.

He met my stare, his positively glittering with anticipation. "I'm glad you said that, Jillian. I would hate to have to fight you for it."

I pointed a finger at him. "You better keep it secure."

"Oh, yes." He took a deep breath, as though savoring the moment. It was possibly the most animated I'd ever seen him. It was an alarming sight.

My eyes moved back to the dragon. I took a deep breath, preparing.

"Take his head. And whatever happens, don't let him touch you with that hammer," I told them, watching Villi carefully. We charged.

Villi completely ignored the others, his focus solely on me as his dragon form ran at us, letting out an ear-piercing screech before he began to breath blue fire directly at me. This was a pointless move. Half of us were completely resistant to flame. And he was expelling this force solely at me. He had to know it was nothing more than wind to me. Intimidation, perhaps? I couldn't remember a moment of my life when fire was something that I'd feared. I *was* fire.

Torst positively glowed as we drew closer to our goal. *Drink, drink, drink,* was its mantra in my head. This was the problem with Torst, the reason why I had put him away. He didn't just make me hear his thoughts, he made me feel them, until I didn't know if it was his hunger or my own. But I wanted blood, and I would have it. That was his power, and it was perfect for the problem at hand.

I jumped before the dragon reached me, swinging down with all of my strength and the force of my fall as I dropped back to the earth. The axe hacked brutally at Villi's neck, actually drawing blood with the first swing. I was shocked. Dragon scales were diamond hard and resilient. To draw blood on the first blow was a stroke of luck I had never expected.

Torst sang with triumph at the taste of blood, drawing back again quickly, hacking again and again. No human eyes could have followed the speed with which I was swinging. I would be surprised if even the non-humans with me could keep up.

Villi careened around, throwing me a good fifty yards away with the force of his push. I landed with a strong whoosh, the air knocked from my lungs. I had been so focused on just mindlessly hacking away that I'd let him catch me at a disadvantage. And that, of course, was the catch with Torst.

Villi skittered towards me clumsily, an angry bear attached to his nose, gnawing away through the scales. He tossed her off, throwing her in the opposite direction of me. It was easy to see, though, that she had done some damage, blood dripping down to the ground from his wounded nose as he approached me. Good job, Sloan, I thought, a little surprised. Getting past the scales of a dragon that quickly was no small feat.

Just short of his goal, Villi froze oddly, and I quickly saw why as a bright blue glowing sword appeared out of his belly, followed by a bloody Christian.

He had literally gutted the dragon, I saw with shock. It was then that I finally realized that Lynn must have been at him with the hammer before we got here. It was the only thing that could possibly have Villi so weak so fast. Go sis, I thought, with wonder. She had somehow laid the groundwork for a hell of a dragon slaying. Against all odds, she had managed to hand us the upper hand, even though Villi had had the hammer. I couldn't imagine how, but the how was not the important part.

Villi's head careened oddly to the side, snapping from a blow too quick for me to see. Suddenly, Caleb just appeared, wielding the hammer for another blow to the dragon's head. I should have known he was up to something. It was when you couldn't see Caleb that you knew he was up to the most trouble.

All of this had happened in the few seconds it took me to

stand up. I staggered to my feet, stalking forward purposefully to rejoin the fight.

Christian hacked at the beast's neck with gusto, yelling curses at the prone dragon between blows. He was truly in his element today. I joined my axe to his sword, knowing decapitation was our best bet. And the sooner the better.

Torst fed hungrily as I chopped away. The dragon's neck was thick, but we were making short work of it. The huge bear roared as it lumbered back into the fight, tearing great hunks from the dragon's neck.

I quickly decided that three bloodthirsty fighters were enough to take the head, and made my way to the second most important goal.

Christian had already cleared a lot of my way to the heart with his precise gutting. Finding a heart still pumping blood through a body was one of Torst's specialties. All I had to do now, really, was get messy.

I hacked at the flesh around that precious organ tirelessly from an awkward position below his underbelly. I finally just took a deep breath and waded into the disgusting, bloody depths of his insides. I submerged myself just long enough to see exactly where I needed to go. I surfaced, gasping. I pointed Torst in the right direction, and let it do the rest of the work. It was alive in my hands, chopping away at the twisting flesh and bone of the beast's ribcage. Every part of Villi was weakened, and the muscle tissue gave way in short minutes, like so much butchered meat. I finally pulled the beating mass free from its intricate cage.

It was a full armful, and I fell on my ass as I finally got it separated from the body. Still, as awkward as it was to pick up, being the size of my entire torso and heavy as hell to boot, it was smaller than I would have thought a heart would be inside of that giant, hideous beast.

"Caleb," I screamed, and I knew I was a sight, covered in

dark blood and entrails. He appeared quickly, swinging his new toy casually. He gave me a quizzical look. "Use the hammer on the heart. It will help further immobilize him, until Christian can cast his spells."

I heard a bear roar, and Christian whoop happily, and I knew they had severed the head. He still wasn't dead, but damn, it had just been too easy so far. Caleb started hacking at the heart without preamble. He pounded it again and again, and the hammer glowed that horrible, eery blue that I associated with my sadistic father.

Christian appeared from the other side of the prone dragon, dragging the severed head slowly. "Help me line this up next to the heart," he told me.

I obliged.

"I'm not sure you should be real close by for the death-spell," he said.

I nodded curtly, heading to Lynn's prone figure. It had been a struggle this entire time not to go to her.

Sloan almost beat me to her, in human form again, already re-dressed in black. She had to be the most efficient being on the planet. "Healing is a strength of mine," she told me. "Let me check her out."

Lynn was in rough shape, as I had known. She stirred a little as I sat beside her, holding one of her limp hands.

Sloan's breath hissed out in a curse when she knelt by my sister. "Can you regrow body parts? Like, say, eyes?"

"Yes." Like druids, we could regenerate body parts, eventually. "But if that hammer was involved, I have no idea."

"You people and your special weapons," Sloan said with disgust, as though I had done it.

Lynn was battered and bruised and broken. Sloan was able to help with a lot of the damage, but the eyes were a lost cause, for the moment. Possibly forever. It didn't bear thinking about. We needed to finish up and get out of there. There was no way our epic battle had gone unnoticed.

"I got the jump on him, Jillian," Lynn whispered to me as she came to.

I laughed, painfully relieved.

"We saw that. We took him out easy, thanks to whatever you did to him."

"I reversed a spell at him, then beat the shit outta him with that hammer. Christian better finish his ass."

I looked to the slayer at her words. He knelt on the ground, one hand on the dragon's heart, one on its head, which I could see they had beat to a bloody pulp, as well. With the hammer, I assumed. He was chanting. I would kill to know what he chanted, but I just couldn't hear it from that distance. And getting closer might be bad for my health.

Suddenly Christian roared and whipped out Dragonsbane, pointing it high in the air. The sword had swelled to a size I had never seen it before, the fiery blue blade as long as Christian was tall.

All at once, my lungs felt emptied of air, as though it was all being pulled like a magnet into Christian. Wind swept past all of us, from Gods knew where, rushing at the slayer in a furious tidal wave. I was stunned but pleased as Villi's blood and gore was pulled off of me, swept up with all the rest.

Dragonsbane, poised gloriously above Christian, seemed to absorb it all.

All of the gruesome pieces of Villi suddenly burst into vivid blue flame. They shimmered like that for long moments before the flames were sucked into the slayer relic like the wind. The weapon was absorbing Villi's power. The powers of an ancient being with abilities we could only imagine. Christian was naturally powerful, but now he'd be a force to be reckoned with. I was more happy than ever to have him on our side. I had a very good feeling that this wasn't the last time we'd be doing this.

As the storm seemed to pass, a sonic boom shook the valley. The Vegas Valley. All of it. "Fuck," I groaned. "We need to get out of here. There's no way that didn't bring us to their attention. We're just damn lucky we caught Villi alone long enough to take him out."

CHAPTER THIRTY-SEVEN

The Bitter Pill

I picked Lynn up awkwardly, heading back to Christian and Caleb. Sloan followed silently behind me, a solid, steady presence. Damn, but she was good backup.

The men were carefully scouring the ground where Villi had lain. There was no blood left, only what looked like tiny yellow diamonds, scattered here and there. "What the hell are those?" I asked them.

"All that's left of a dead dragon. I need to bury them quickly, for the death spell. I know just the place." Suddenly Christian looked up at me, grinning unabashedly. "I've been fantasizing about this day for awhile. Like, my whole life. I feel incredible."

I just blinked. Strange reaction, though I shouldn't have been surprised.

The men finished gathering the tiny jewels, doing an extra sweep to be sure none were left behind to resurrect the monster. Christian packed the jewels away in a small black pouch, giving us careful directions on where to meet him. It was a good two-hour drive into the middle of nowhere.

"We need to split up. We don't even know for sure how many of them there are, and we can't risk it. There's no way that magical storm didn't draw someone's attention. So we need to run fast. We'll meet up at the burial site. I'll take Lynn, and we'll go the long way. You guys take his remains. Whatever happens, don't let them have those remains, or the hammer."

"I'm coming with you," Sloan said quietly.

I nodded at her. "Thank you. This is *not* going to be pretty."

We split up, and I made it to the car carrying Lynn.

We took Sloan's car. I laid Lynn in the backseat, and took shotgun. I shot a glance at the guys, who were casually jacking a sports car from the parking lot. Damned miscreants. But hell, what else could they do?

Sloan pealed out of the stadium's lot with speed and skill.

If anyone was after us, they would undoubtedly follow Lynn and I. Which gave Christian the opportunity to finish the death spell, no matter what.

Sloan made it quickly out of the stadium parking and onto a small dirt road, speeding like the demons of hell were behind us. It was a good possibility that they were.

Her ridiculously fast driving didn't make me the least bit nervous. There was nothing Sloan didn't excel at, I knew.

We hadn't made it five miles before I saw the black SUV following us, and I knew, just absolutely knew, that it was my relatives. Every hair on the back of my neck raised, and I gasped. How many of them were in that car? As if the thought had manifested it, another, identical car turned onto the small road behind them. "Holy shit," I muttered.

"What's going on? Try not to distract the driver here, please. Especially if you're not being particularly informative," Sloan snapped.

"It's them," I said, feeling an almost overwhelming sense of despair. How could we outrun them with no head start at all?

Sloan had spotted the cars in the rearview mirror. "How do you know? Those cars could be druids sent to help us."

Lynn spoke for the first time from the backseat, her arm flung over the spot where her eyes should have been. "It's them. I can feel it. And if it was druids, I bet you would be able to feel *that*. Can you see how many there are? We know there were at least three other Norse dragons in town with Villi. At least. And the Chinese dragons had at least three."

"The windows are tinted too dark. That's gotta be an illegal tint," I muttered.

Lynn laughed, albeit weakly. "Yeah, I'm sure they're real worried about it."

Shit, shit, shit. "Guns. Everybody give me guns. I'm gonna blow out some tires, buy us some time."

I rolled down my window. Not surprisingly, Lynn was unarmed. Sloan had two small pistols. I only had one small handgun from my usual ankle sheath. Neither of us had extra clips on hand. Guns hadn't been the order of the day. There was an arsenal in the trunk, but it didn't do us any good back there now.

At the back of my mind was always Torst, chanting about stopping and facing them, to drink all of their blood. As always, the axe had a very high opinion of his own abilities.

I started with my own gun, the most familiar weapon. I leaned out of the window, facing our tails, and took careful aim.

Bang. My first bullet took out a front tire of the closest car. It careened sideways wildly. I shot twice more, taking the two tires facing me fast. I shot the car five more times, aiming for the fuel tank, but had no luck with a big explosion, like in the movies. Dammit, but that would have been convenient. And I'd always wanted to do it. If only we hadn't gone through all of the explosive rounds in the necro fight. But the first car was in a ditch now, out of commission. I immediately took aim at the second car. It was careening back and forth, trying to avoid the same treatment. Oddly, no one was firing back at us, not even one shot. Why weren't they? It's not like they could possibly care if we were injured.

They had underestimated my aim. I took out the tires of the careening vehicle nearly as quickly as I had the one before.

"Well, that bought us at least a five minute lead."

"Five minutes is better than what we had before," Sloan reassured me.

She was right. Anything was better than having them right on our ass.

I was feeling marginally safer as we made it a good twenty miles farther out of town, unmolested by any further pursuit.

A sick feeling entered my stomach as a huge shadow fell over the car. It was a stiflingly hot and sunny Vegas day, without a cloud in sight. And then I sensed its presence. I could even smell it. The old, familiar, stench of dementia that tainted my family. The shadow got bigger and bigger as the dragon lowered over us ominously.

"Fuck. Is that what I think it is?" Sloan asked. I would have had to stick my head out the window to see it. I did not want to do that. Seeing it would only make the panicky feeling more acute.

"Yes. Just keep driving, fast."

"Dom is gonna kill me if I let you get killed," Sloan muttered.

I snorted. "If either of us survives this, it is Cam that will be killing *me*."

She grimaced. "Overbearing son of a bitch."

We barely made it into the unpopulated part of the desert before a huge weight crushed the front of the car. The back end of our car shot straight up in the air, and we were rolling.

We all just lay there, stunned, when the car stopped rolling. It was turned wheels up. My chest hurt where the seatbelt had abused it. Lynn was lying below me, unmoving, so I knew she'd felt the collision even worse. I looked over at Sloan, and she met my eyes calmly. Damn, I thought, yet again, but she was a good fighter to have at your back.

As though we had choreographed it, Sloan and I released our

seat belts, dropping to the ground.

I dragged Lynn's still form with me out of the burning car. Sloan rolled out of the shattered back window like she did it ever day, casually brushing off her dusty black clothes.

I looked around frantically, but saw no sign of the dragon, no sign of any of them. Lynn began to stir as I took off running, Sloan close on my heels. "What's happening? I can't see."

I glanced down at her bloody eyes, and cursed. That's when I felt them behind me. "They're catching us, Lynn. We're going to have to fight them."

She was still dazed as I set her on her feet. "I can't see anything." Her voice was weak. She wouldn't be much help in a fight, in this shape.

"Don't let them take you without a fight." I turned, saw them, and cursed again. "There are seven of them." I hesitated. "Three are Chinese. One of those is Drake. And one of the Scandinavian ones is in dragon form. He's a pale blue dragon. I've no idea who it is." I put a gun in her hands. She was badly wounded, and we were hopelessly outnumbered. "Give em hell, sister," I told her, cocking the weapon and pointing it.

The men fanned out as they approached us, as though they planned to flank us. The dragon stalked behind them, a slight distance back, its wings outstretched. It was colossal in size, far larger than Villi had been. But then again, I didn't suppose this dragon had been beaten with a God's lightning hammer before it shifted.

I shot Sloan a look. She was a silent presence beside and just behind me. "You should run." I pointed toward the highway, out of sight now. "They might not chase you. It's us they want."

She just curled her lip. "Fuck that. I have *never* run from a fight. Dragon-kin don't scare me."

I sighed, selfishly relieved. It was so reassuring to have her as backup. And now it was almost certainly going to get her killed.   But I knew better than to waste time arguing with someone as immovable as Sloan at a time like this.

I turned my attention back to the task at hand.

Seeing the Chinese there had surprised me enough that at first I didn't see our brother, Sven, among the three viking draak.   Of all the people they could have sent after us, he seemed the unlikeliest choice.   He was flanked by two of our nastier cousins.   Those two I had expected, but seeing Sven felt like yet another betrayal.

Sven was a strong telepath, the only dragon-kin that I knew of with that particular skill.   He was not much older than I, born sometime between Lynn and I.   Growing up, he'd always been a kind brother, a stark contrast to the treatment I'd received from the other men of the clan.   He was the only one, besides my bespelled mother, who I had regretted leaving behind.   And he had even helped us escape, in his own way.

He had known our plans.   I'd seen it in his eyes, the night we planned to leave.   He had picked them cleanly from my mind.   I had been trembling in terror that he would be our undoing as I gazed at him across the long trestle table where the family was sharing the nightly feast.

The feasting hall had been as loud and boisterous as always, with both laughter and casual violence.   If one of the human serving girls committed the grave offense of dropping a tankard or tray, she was almost certainly raped and beaten.   If the offended party was in a particularly foul mood, one of the always present axes or swords the men carried would thoughtlessly hack her to pieces.   It would usually draw a round of laughter from the bloodthirsty men.

But Sven's look at that dinner so long ago had been quiet and intense.   It had confused me enough to abate my terror through that never-ending feast.   When I'd been excused from the table, I had walked quickly from the hall.   Sven had caught up to me as I left the hall.   Silently, he had hugged me, and given me a soft kiss on the forehead. He was much taller than I at the time, though still not fully grown. He'd had to bend down far to whisper in my ear, "Be careful, little sister. Godspeed," and walked away.

I had treasured that memory over the years. Whenever I had felt betrayed, as I had many times, I'd thought back to Sven and thought, *See, there is someone out there who loves me and wishes me well.* It had hovered in my consciousness like some kind of beacon of hope, when there was little. Now, it only made this latest betrayal all the more acute. *This* was the bitter pill of immortality. Living long enough to see every happy memory you've ever had turn to ashes.

He gave me a tentative smile when our eyes met. I glared back. "What are you doing here, brother?" I asked him bluntly.

He raised his hands, palm up, saying, "They thought I was the one most likely to get you to come with us peaceably. Any chance of that?"

"Any chance you're all gonna turn around and leave us alone?"

He shook his head, that kind smile still on his face. "Afraid not, little sister. But we have no wish to harm you. And you have to see that fighting us at this point is futile."

"Come a little closer and say that to me," I told him, drawing the axe, and bringing it to front of my body in a defensive stance.

"You would raise a weapon against me, sister?" he asked sadly, his irises so pale, and his pupils so small, that his eyes looked almost completely white.

Before I could answer, a gunshot went off from behind me. It didn't hit anyone, but it wasn't a bad shot for someone who couldn't see a thing. "Does that answer your question, brother?" Lynn called out unsteadily. "If you were wondering, I was aiming at you." I smiled in spite of myself.

"Just tell her," a cousin said quietly to Sven. "It's obvious she

Rebecca K. Lilley

doesn't know. If she knew, she'd be much less hesitant to hurt herself."

"Shut your mouth," Sven told him, in the most murderous tone I'd ever heard come out of my kindest brother's mouth. "If she knew, she'd fight us twice as hard, you imbecile."

"I can hear everything you're saying, you knuckleheads. What are you talking about?"

Sven met my eyes, his panicked now. "Please, dear sister. Please just come with us. Don't get yourself harmed more than necessary."

"Why are you helping them take us in? If you don't want me harmed, then just walk away. The elders have gone insane. I know you know that. Villi was demented-"

His mouth tightened as he interrupted. "Was?"

I smiled, savoring the moment. "Oh, did I ruin the surprise? We took his head and heart not long ago. And left him to the tender mercy of a slayer." Sven shut his eyes at the revelation. The rest of them just stared at me, shocked.

"And the hammer? What have you done with the hammer?" Sven asked.

I shrugged. "I musta lost it. Oh well."

Sven sighed heavily. "That was very unwise."

"Why are the Chinese dragons here? What do they have to do with this?" I asked him.

He sent them a quick look. "We've...temporarily allied ourselves with them. They helped us to find you." Lynn started cursing at them, aiming her gun wildly. They looked more comfortable than they should have, with a blind woman pointing a gun at them. Bullets still hurt like hell, even if they couldn't kill us.

I sent Drake a scathing look. His eyes met mine with a blank stare. I mouthed a few choice words at him. Still no reaction.

One of the men with Drake spoke to him in chinese. He just nodded, starting towards Lynn. I stepped up beside her, smoothly sheathing my axe as I moved. "I'm going to try something. Don't shoot me, k?" I said in a whisper.

I started moving before she could answer, picking her up, and running. I grabbed a silent Sloan by the hand as I passed. I closed my eyes, concentrating hard. I never would have tried it on purpose if it hadn't happened by accident just a day before. Still, I was shocked when it worked a second time. I hovered above the earth with little more than a thought. Transforming was usually a long and arduous process, but apparently I'd found a loophole. My wings of flame beat up torrents of wind as I fought hard to lift far off the ground. The extra weight of two bodies didn't help.

It didn't last long, of course. I'd had little hope that it would, but I couldn't help trying.

The arm holding Sloan started shaking first. My heart skipped a beat when I looked down and saw several fist width poles impaling her chest. She was just staring at them, dazed. My whole body started to shake, dropping slowly to the ground, against my will.

"Drop me, Jillian. I can fend for myself down there. It's you they want. I'll hold them back to give you a lead."

I sent her an incredulous glance. "Fuck that," I said, quoting her own favorite phrase back at her. Sloan's death on my conscience hurt my heart to even think about. I only made it about fifty more feet, however, before the choice was taken from me. The world went black as I felt myself dropping back to earth.

CHAPTER THIRTY-EIGHT

I Still Think You're A Bastard

SLOAN

I woke up with my chest on fire, and the certainty that I was done for. I was lying on my back, every part of my body paralyzed except for my left arm. Agonizingly, I fished around for my cell. I was vaguely surprised when I actually found it. They must have assumed I was dead to have left me a life line. I punched in a number instinctively, before clearly thinking about it. But as I struggled to lift the phone to my ear, I knew there was no one else I would have made my last call to. I barely got the phone to my ear as a gravelly voice barked at the other end. "What's up, Sugar?" Cam's voice was curt. "To what do I owe the honor of this call?"

My first attempts to speak came out as gasps. I was assuming this was due to the gaping holes in my chest. Druids could survive just about anything save a beheading, but being stabbed in the chest repeatedly with an object bigger than a fist could do it, too, if the heart was pierced. I knew by the blood pounding out of me that mine was.

"Cam," I gasped out.

His tone altered drastically. "Sloan, what's wrong?" All of the normal antagonism was gone from his voice, replaced by something akin to panic. We'd known each other for most of our long lives, and I'd never heard his voice like that. "Tell me where you are. I'm coming to get you."

"It's too late for me, Cam," I finally got out. "But you need to get a message to Dom for me. I don't have another call in me."

"Shut the fuck up with that. Tell me where you are."

"Tell him that the Chinese dragons took Lynn, and the Viking dragons took Jillian. They were both in bad shape when I got taken out. Call him right away please, but talk him out of doing anything crazy. If you can."

"Tell. Me. Where. You. Are."

"It's no good, Cam. They filled my chest with holes the size of my fist. My heart's spilling out of my shirt. It's a mortal wound. This is the part where you get to tell me it's my half-blood weakness that did me in."

He cursed fluently on his end. "I'm going to wring your neck just as soon as I find you. I have someone working on tracking you by your cell, but for the love of god, give me some kind of direction!"

"Shit, I don't know. We took a dirt road off the 215 somewhere west of town. We went off road after that. The tracks should be pretty clear from there. I think I can make out the ruined car in the distance. It's north and west of me. They tore it to pieces."

"I'm on my way. I'll call Dom now. Keep your phone in your hand, and don't black out," he ordered.

"Easy for you to say."

"Just hang in there, Sloan. Just think of the shit you can give me if you survive. It'll be even better than that time you wiped the floor Siobhan."

I grunted into the phone. "Thanks for reminding me. What a nice memory to think back on in my last moments. In case I don't get another chance to tell you, I still think you're a bastard."

He barked out a laugh. "I know I am, sweetheart. You can tell me that every day for the rest of our lives. Just don't die." If I hadn't known better, I would have sworn that his voice was thick with tears.

"Cam-" I felt the world going hazy. "I always wanted to tell you that-"

"You can tell me when I get there, sweetheart."

"I won't make it that long. I just wanted to tell you that I'm sorry, Cam. I'm sorry for everything. And don't ever call me sweetheart."

"Baby, cut it out with the apologies. I'll be there in ten minutes, and I know you'll regret apologizing to me as soon as you're better. I'm not above gloating at an injured woman." Strangely, I still heard those thick tears in his voice. I was really losing it.

"I have so many-" the world went hazy, but I gripped onto consciousness to finish, "regrets. Goodbye, Cam."

His gravelly voice raised to a panicked shout on the other end of the line as the world went black.

CHAPTER THIRTY-NINE

Infamous

I came to, fully aware that I'd been captured. I was surprised, however, to find that I was not alone, though Sloan and my sister were conspicuously absent.

Two pairs of eyes tracked me warily as I sat up inside of a small cage. The cage was positioned in a line of similar enclosures, set behind a huge dark red curtain, and hung so far off of the ground that I had no concept of how high I actually was. Only two of the other strange human birdcages were occupied. My gut twisted when I saw that the other prisoners were two very young teenage girls.

The girls clutched hands tightly across the space that separated their cages. They were opposites in looks, but obviously had some close relationship, and were of a close age, perhaps twelve or thirteen years old. It was obvious to me at a glance that neither was human, though I had no clue what they *actually* were.

The bolder of the two spoke first. She had red and gold hair colored like no hair I'd seen before. It looked more like trails of crimson and gold flame than actual hair, and tumbled down just past her shoulders. Her bright golden eyes were piercing and accusatory. "You-you're one of them! Don't try to deny it! We heard them talking about you when they thought we were asleep. If you're here to try to trick us, you can just forget it!" Her young voice was defiant, but held an obvious tremor.

The other girl, a pale contrast to the girl beside her, made a soothing noise. "Don't get worked up, Nix. It wouldn't be good for either of us. Whatever their latest trick is, we won't let it affect us. Remember, we resolved not to let them feed off of our rage and terror any longer." The girl spoke in a voice that could break any heart, the despair soft but prevalent, despite her bolstering speech. As she finished speaking, she raised watery eyes to mine. They were startling and lavender, and every bit as heartbreaking as her soft voice. Her hair was white and looked soft like feathers. It hung almost to her waist. Her skin was palest alabaster and, combined with her white hair, seemed to create a white glow in the darkness around her.

Both girls wore thin white slips that didn't cover nearly enough. "How long have you two been held here?" I asked as my mind began, with dread, to connect the dots of their situation.

"Why would we tell one of *you* anything?" the one called Nix spit out.

"Well, if I was working with them, which I'm not, I would already know the answer to that. So you have nothing to lose by telling me," I said reasonably.

"Long enough," Nix said.

"Too long," the pale one stated.

"Care to elaborate?" I raised a brow at them until they spoke again.

"Months," the pale one said.

Nix followed with, "Weeks for me."

I clenched my eyes shut, rubbing my throbbing temples. "So the red one is Nix. What's your name, white one?"

"Leona," the heart-achingly soft voice answered me.

"Well, Leona, Nix, to answer your statement, yes, I am one of them. That's the bad news. The good news is that I hate them as much as you do-"

"Impossible." Leona's soft voice surprised me with its vehemence.

"And I'll help you in any way that I can," I continued. "Oh, and I have some help on its way."

"You look terrible," Nix said softly. "I doubt you could even help yourself."

I couldn't really argue with that. I felt like crap, too, dirty and bloody and weary to the bone. And oh yeah, like my skin was about to burst, my other form was so close to the surface. It was an alarming development, to say the least.

"What are you two? You're obviously not related to each other, and of course you aren't human."

They looked at each other, trying to decide without speaking what to tell me.

I just stared at them, waiting. They shifted their eyes and feet nervously. I could tell I disconcerted them. "Do the dragons already know what you are? If so, it's pointless not to tell me."

"I'm a phoenix," Nix stated tonelessly, shocking me speechless for a moment.

"I thought your kind were extinct," I told her honestly.

She shrugged, obviously having heard that before. "If they manage to kill me, then as far as I know, we will be."

I nodded at Leona. "And you?"

Her watery eyes were pointed at the ground. "Just think of the most useless creature in existence. I bet you can guess it." It's not an exaggeration to say that her despairing tone brought tears to my eyes. She was powerful at evoking emotions in others, that much was obvious.

I thought for a few moments, but came up blank. "You're a necro, then?" I shot back.

She smiled, just the tiniest bit, and hope bloomed inside my chest.   She seemed to have no idea that she cold affect emotions with her slightest move. "No. A unicorn."

I whistled softly.   "I knew unicorns weren't extinct, but just barely. Do you know of any more of your kind?"

She shrugged.   "My dead-beat dad's still breathing somewhere in the world, but my mother's human. I don't know of any other relations."

"What are these bastards up to?" I asked softly.

"Collecting pets is the only idea we've come up with," Nix told me.

"They like to have things around to torture," Leona added.

"Are you the only ones they're holding?"

They both shook their heads.   "We don't think so.   We've heard them talking about other captives.   They tell us all the time that we're their favorites.   But we haven't actually seen anyone except our captors, you, and each other."

"Do they move you at all?   Or have you been in this room for months?"

"Oh, they move us all the time," Leona spoke.   "We've traveled almost constantly since they captured me.   I was in Florida when they grabbed me, walking home from school."

"They took me in Ontario, Canada," Nix added.   "They snatched me out of my bed."

"Have you heard them talk about the two women I had with me?"

They exchanged a wary glance. "They said something about a druid woman…. They said she was dead.   They seemed to think it was funny how they'd killed her."

I shut my eyes tightly against a sharp rush of emotion. Rage, anger, and pain, oh yes, pain, washed through me. Pain for the death of a woman I had always liked and respected.   But most of all, I felt guilt, that she'd died for my fight.   The rage seemed to help some of the pain in my body. Revenge had always been my best motivator.   Heads were gonna roll for what had happened to Sloan, of that I was sure.

"Did they mention anyone else? My sister was with me, as well."

They shook their heads in unison, and I cursed. They both cringed. "I'm not mad at either of you. And, though I know it's hard to believe at the moment, I will get us all out of here. My kind don't stay conscious and captive for long."

Nix had a thoughtful look on her face. Thoughtful and determined. "So if you're a dragon, can't you make fire?"

I studied her for a moment, trying to see what she was thinking. "Of course."

"Could you set me on fire from that far away?"

I just stared at her, a little shocked.

"Oh no, Nix! You can't! You told me you'll lose your memories! And it will hurt! You said you wake up in total agony."

Nix shrugged. "I only lose some of my memories. As it stands, there are quite a few memories I'd *love* to lose. And I can take the pain. The only thing that worries me is how long it takes to recover from the change. It's just so hard to predict when they'll check on us."

I shook my head at her, meeting her gaze squarely. "I couldn't do that. I'm sorry, but I just can't torch a little girl. I'm capable of some pretty dark stuff, but not that."

She glared at me, but didn't speak. I decided to cheer them up a bit. I pulled off one my faux black pearl earrings. I waved it at them. "My reclusive family must not know too much about druids and their tracking devices. Guess what these are, girls?"

They both just shook their heads at me, looking at me like I was crazy. I just smiled. "I'm being tracked by the druids, which means that, any minute now, we'll be rescued."

Nix and Leona both glared at me, as though I'd said something offensive. "The druids only care about their own. Why would they help us?" Leona asked, her tone accusatory and bitter.

My brows rose. "I'll agree that the druids can be elitist bastards, but they would help you if they knew of your plight, that I can promise."

Nix snorted. "These monsters have been working with some druids. We've heard them talk about it."

That was a bit of a shock. I filed that away with things I needed to tell Dom the next time I saw him. Hopefully that would be very soon, like when he was busting the door down to free me. "That's strange and disturbing information, but it won't stop our rescue. The Arch himself is tracking me, so I guarantee our rescuer outranks whatever druids you're talking about."

Nix gasped suddenly, her hand flying to her mouth. She pointed at me. "You're her. I've heard of you. Leona, remember the stories about the mysterious supernatural woman that the Arch is obsessed with. Everyone knows the story, how she bewitched him with some dark magic, and then betrayed him with the last Arch. She actually caused the one to kill the other."

Leona's lovely brow furrowed. "No, it can't be her," she said softly.

I sighed. I really was famous, far and wide. Infamous, rather.

"Yes it is her. You can tell, even with her all beaten up and dirty, that she's exquisitely beautiful. Her long golden hair, and her pale blue eyes. She's tall, with comic-book curves. I've heard her described tons of times. The druids hate her, every single one of them."

Leona was still doubtful, but studied me intently. "No," she said softly, less certain now.

"Tell us the truth. Are you Jillian?" Nix was nearly glowing in her agitation.

I grimaced and nodded. "Yes, I'm Jillian."

Leona looked crushed and defeated at my admission. It

made me feel bad just looking at her. "No," she whispered. "But you're...evil. The druids won't be rescuing you. They *hate* you."

"She gets off on tormenting people. I've heard that about her," Nix spat. "She gave us hope, just so she could crush it."

"Don't believe everything you hear. I'm no angel, but I'm not evil, either. Dom put this tracker on me himself, and I swear to you that he will come here to free us." I reached the device across the distance between our cages. It covered two-thirds of the distance, but Leona would have to reach to grab it. "Take one of these. That way, even if they separate us, the druids will still find you." She hesitated, and my patience snapped even as the roaring in my ears grew with the huge presence trying to overtake my body. "Take it! What do you have to lose?"

My tone frightened her into obeying, but she backed away from my cage the instant she got ahold of the pearl.

"You'll be okay," I reassured the young girls, as well as myself. "No matter what happens, they'll find you now." I was folding into the corner even as I spoke, my body turning on me, as it tended to do lately.

The change started like a raging torrent in my blood. It was faster and more violent by far than any I had experienced before.

The girls looked on with horror as I lost all control of my body. I think my eyes went first, because my vision changed to dragon between one blink and the next. It's impossible to say what changed next, it all happened so fast.

I tried to reassure the girls in the other cages. I just wanted them to know that no matter what I turned into, they didn't need to fear me, but there was no time.

Blue flames engulfed my body, which was normal. My wings expanded in one huge flap, quick as flight. That was not so normal.

The steel bars on the cage that had seemed so sturdy just

moments ago snapped like twigs.

I was suddenly too big for the oversized theatre. There was no exit that would come anywhere near fitting my full dragon form. I would have to make one.

CHAPTER FORTY

The Return

I landed softly on top of the vaguely familiar building. My shift to human form was more difficult than any I could remember. But also faster. I had been submerged in my other form for over six months. I had never stayed changed for such a long period of time. But I'd had a lot to do as my dragon self.

I just lay on the textured concrete pavement of the roof for what could have been hours while I acclimated to my new form. I lay wrapped around my precious burden. It was carefully bundled inside a thick leather hide that I had been clutching securely the entire flight here.

Finally, I stood on wobbly legs. My skin still glowed gold, and I could see from the strands of my hair that lay against my chest that the dragon-trance still claimed that as well. I knew from experience that these effects would last for days or even weeks.

My landing perch was the posh balcony that I knew connected to the presidential suite of the casino that was my destination.

I didn't make a sound as I slipped in the door. The first four rooms I moved through were empty, but I followed the sounds of voices and easily found my target.

I found him holding court in a palatial dining room. The room was dark and beautifully decorated, all dark wood and marble. Dom sat at the head of a massive table, his back to me. I'd obviously arrived at a bad time, during some kind of business dinner, but I couldn't leave until I'd completed my mission. Dozens of druids faced me, staring with mixtures of shock and contempt. Siobhan sat to Dom's left, obviously his hostess. Hers was the only glare I returned. She clutched a steak knife in her hand like she intended to use it on me. I half-wished she would try. The draak still held enough sway over me that I knew I would show no mercy. Consequences be damned.

Dom had frozen at my entrance, but hadn't turned. He addressed his dinner party. "I assume by your silence that whoever just entered is posing no threat to me." His tone was sardonic. I heard him take a deep breath. "Jillian," he said, his voice dangerously soft. I wasn't myself enough yet to have any idea what that tone of voice meant.

"Dom." My voice was hoarse from disuse. I worried that the faint sound hadn't reached his ears, but suddenly, he turned. He stood at the sight of me, and it was only as he stared at me with shock and fury that I remembered clothes. Or rather, my lack of clothes. I was nude, of course. Dragons have no thought for clothing.

"Everyone out!" he roared, his voice going from human to beast in an instant. They obeyed. All except for Siobhan. She sat where she was, as though she were immune to his order. He turned to her slowly, growling in his throat. "Did you hear me?" Menace inundated every word.

She swallowed hard. "There's nothing you can't say to her in front of me, Dom." Brave woman.

"OUT! You don't want me to remove you myself!" She was gone in a blurred flash, door slamming hard behind her. She cursed colorfully on the other side of it as she stormed away.

I drank in the sight of him. He was enraged, but I felt no fear. Perhaps it was my other form's hold still on me, or maybe I had just never been afraid of his rage.

He studied me closely, visibly shaking. His voice was calmer than I would have expected when he spoke. "I didn't think you were coming back." Abruptly he turned and sat. I sat to his right. He had his head in his hands, rubbing his temples wearily. His hair had grown since I left. He obviously hadn't cut it. It hung nearly to his shoulders now. Druids grew things back quickly; hair, nails, limbs. He looked wonderful. I drank in the sight of him, starved to the point of pain.

"Me neither." My voice was getting stronger. "I thought I was flying north to perish, to tell you the truth."

"But you didn't perish."

"No." I surprised myself by laughing.

He looked up, startled and angry. "Something funny?" he asked coldly.

I shook my head, but a little smile still lingered on my lips. "No, it just feels good to know that I'm not going comatose or crazy for the foreseeable future."

"So what have you been up to for the last seven months?"

"I thought it was closer to six," I mused out loud, though I was sure he had tracked it more closely than I had.

"Trust me, it was seven. You know, we raided that place they were holding you in. I even let the slayer and the mimic in on the action. We got there just one hour after you had escaped. We were so close to rescuing you. But you never were one to wait around long enough to be rescued."

My eyes widened in surprise This was all news to me, of course. "Did you see the other captives? Where they okay? Was Lynn in there somewhere?" I still felt bad about that, about leaving them, even though I'd had no control over it at the time..

"No signs of Lynn. The slayer believes a different group of

dragons took her. But we found the other captives, and they are fine. The dragons left in too big of a hurry to take them. They were both orphans, so they're in druid custody now. They are acclimating as well as can be expected, considering all that they've been through."

I shut my eyes, laying my head back against the large, comfortable headrest of my chair. The elaborate chairs at the banquet table were closer to thrones.

It was a relief to hear that those girls were okay, and hardly a surprise that they hadn't found Lynn in that place.

It felt like at least one huge weight had been lifted from my shoulders. I hadn't realized what a burden of guilt I had been carrying for that. My desertion of those girls hadn't been deliberate on my part, but that was little reassurance when I knew first-hand what the monsters who held them were capable of.

"The dragons were in such a hurry, in fact, that we captured one of them mid-flight."

My eyes snapped open, and I leaned forward to look at him more closely. I had been trying to avoid looking into his eyes up to that point. Those mercurial, mis-matched eyes had such power over me. "Who was it? What did you do with him?"

He smiled at me enigmatically. "At last, I have the answers and you are the one asking the questions. Perhaps we can bargain, then. Let us trade information. I ask you again. What have you been up to for the last seven months? We've been looking for you. I'm sure that's not surprising to you. I feel like I've spent most of my life chasing your trail. So I must admit to some curiosity as to your whereabouts these past seven months."

I licked my lips nervously. Where to start... "That's why I'm here actually. I have a favor to ask you. I have something very important that I need you to protect for me."

He raised a brow at me. "Let me guess. You'll ask me for a

favor, I'll agree, and then you'll leave in a rush, giving me no information, as usual. Whatever you were up to, it didn't change you much." Bitterness dripped from every word.

"Actually, I plan to tell you everything. I'm just trying to figure out where to start." I could tell I'd surprised him, but he was still wary. "I went north because of something that happened years ago, back when we were together."

He removed his jacket suddenly, throwing it at me. "Put on some clothes, for god's sake. Why the fuck are you naked?"

"Sorry, that wasn't intentional. I forgot about clothes. I've been my other form almost since I left. My mind doesn't work the same when I'm changed." Still, I let his jacket fall to the floor.

Suddenly, his nostrils flared, as if picking up a scent. Before I could blink, he had me on my back, on the table, his weight pushing me down. "You provoke me, as always."

"Wait." My voice made him freeze. His body started to shake as he straightened up.

I ran my burden to the corner, turning to smile radiantly at him. "Sorry, it's delicate." I was back to him in a flash. Just the smell of his neck made me shake with need. "I missed you," I whispered in his ear, and felt him tremble.

He splayed me on the table, more carefully this time. He set to work on my body slowly with his lips, tongue, and teeth. I gripped his hair in both fists, its silken texture a wonder to me.

I tried to guide his head lower, but he just ignored me, chuckling softly against my skin. The sound was sinister, and it drove me crazy. He always took control in this fashion when we made love. He would take no orders, and I could refuse none of his. He was dominant to his very core. I doubted there were any truly powerful druids that weren't. They melded their souls with the beasts. It was the nature of their power. And I had never seen a druid more powerful than Dom. Or more controlled. He could tamp down his dominance when needed, but when we were like this, letting go completely, he didn't even try. I would have hated it if he had. His power spread over me like a mist, and every part of me loved it.

He buried his face in my neck, biting down hard. I whimpered, but not in pain. He kissed the bite marks he'd made, soothing me, then kissed his way from my throat to my breasts. He kneaded one in his hand while his mouth set to work on the other. He sucked my flesh into his mouth so hard that it would have left a lasting mark, if I was human. He gave the other one the same attention, then moved south, kissing across my ribs, and into my naval. "Stroke your breasts," he ordered roughly into my skin. I obeyed, but made a sound of protest in my throat. I didn't want to stop touching him, didn't ever want to let go of him again.

When he finally buried his face between my legs, I was sobbing with need, begging for it. He licked me, and thrust three long fingers into me with one smooth motion. He had me coming in moments. I screamed loud enough to have someone knocking on the door.

"Sir?" An uncertain male voice called from the other side. "Is everything all right?"

Dom straightened, unbuttoning his severe black robe as he answered. "Yes, I'm fine. Do not interrupt us again."

He made short work of the heavy buttons. I'd been so wrapped up with the sight of him, so lost in his enchanting eyes, that I hadn't even noticed what he was wearing. It was some sort of druid ritual robe. They had been either coming or going from something very important. Druids wearing anything other than three-piece suits meant serious business.

I bit my lip apologetically as I asked, "I came at a bad time, didn't I?"

He laughed, and it was the most carefree sound I'd heard come out of that beautiful mouth in years. My moody Dom.

I released my right breast and raised a trembling finger to his lips, tracing his soft lower lip in wonder. "Oh, Dom, how I've missed your smile." I was horrified when a tear slipped down my cheek.

He nipped my finger playfully, smiling into my eyes as he wiped my tear away. "Perhaps you shouldn't work quite so hard at running away from it, then."

The hand on my face traced down my body swiftly. He parted my thighs wide apart with sure hands. "Don't move," he ordered, as he parted his robe. He was gloriously naked underneath, and I drank in the sight of the body I had missed so desperately. He didn't bother removing it completely, just opened it enough to bare his tanned, muscular torso, and his heavy arousal. Just the sight of it made my insides clench.

"Please, Dom, I want you naked. I want to see you."

He just grinned at me. His wicked grin. "Maybe next time." He thrust to the hilt in one perfect motion of his hips, his masterful hands holding my legs wide apart. "Keep your hands on your breasts," he ordered, and started up a hard rhythm. He had my legs pinned so that I couldn't even wiggle against him, holding me in perfect stillness for his penetration. The sensations were nearly too intense, and I screamed again as I came. "Don't look away," he told me roughly. "Maybe I should fuck you 'til you can't walk away tonight."

He finally leaned his chest against mine as he grew closer to his own release, and I plunged my fingers into his hair with relish, pulling his face to mine in a fierce kiss.

I lay with my ear over his pounding heart when we finished, stroking his hair. I knew this was far from a reconciliation, but I still felt a raw part of my heart heal. "I haven't been with another man since long before I met you." I felt him freeze at my confession, his heartbeat jackhammering. "I know you think that doesn't matter now, since we're over," I continued hurriedly, not letting him speak. "But it's significant because it pertains to what I have to show you. You see, the thing I need you to guard belongs to us both."

He sat up, dragging me upright by my arms to look him in the eye. "Tell me what it is," he demanded, his voice hoarse.

I brought the satchel to him, unwrapping it carefully. I cradled the large bronze egg to my chest as he stared at me in shock and confusion. "He says he's not ready to be born for a while yet," I whispered as I stroked the egg of our unborn baby. "He told me there are some things I need to do in the time before he's born. He's our son, Dom."

"He?" His voice broke on the word. His eyes were softer than I'd ever seen them as he stared at the egg. His hand was trembling as he touched it ever so softly, with just the tips of his fingers, tracing the intricate patterns etched along its surface.

"Yes, he speaks to me already. He's an incredible telepath. I've never known one who could communicate so clearly. And he's very strong, even for a dragon. He told me he can speak to you, too. So....be prepared for that. We conceived him about twelve years ago...i think. I had no idea what was happening. I'd been told draak could only conceive with draak. And, of course, the gestation period was a bit of a shock to me. I was the youngest of my kind when we left our village, so I was never made familiar with the breeding process."

I handed him the heavy egg, helping him settle it into his arms. He cradled it like the precious burden that it was, wonder in his eyes. He sank to the ground, folding his body gracefully and effortlessly. I couldn't help myself; I joined him.

He shifted the bronze egg and made room for me in his arms. I didn't hesitate, curling against him and around our son. I was loathe to waste a moment of the bliss of having the two of them surrounding me, but exhaustion from long days of flying with no sleep, and the toll of shifting were a heavy weight on my body, and I quickly drifted off.

CHAPTER FORTY-ONE

Reflections

I awoke to an intense feeling of safety and warmth that was both familiar and foreign. But I knew whose arms held my naked body cradled. Who else?

I opened my eyes and was surprised to be looking at..myself? It took me a few confused moments to make sense of it. I was looking at a mirror that lined the entire wall in front of us. Tall, lit sconces lined the large room around us. The candlelight played across my skin teasingly. Dom was wearing a black robe with such a high neck that it almost looked like a soft, floor-length coat. He cradled me naked against his chest. The contrast of his darkness with my golden, glowing body was startling.

My hair had grown much longer than I had realized while I was away, falling against our bodies in soft, golden waves. His own blue-black hair fell against his face as he looked down at me, his eyes glowing intensely at me from our joined reflection. His expression was closing off quickly, but I thought I'd seen something there for just an instant, something that made my chest hurt with a yearning I hadn't allowed myself to feel since I'd ended it between us in such a destructive manner.

"How long have I been asleep?" I finally asked. My voice was whisper soft. I hadn't wanted to break the spell we seemed to be under. We had both been staring at our melded figures in the mirror, as though entranced. I loved the sight of us. I loved the thought of him watching me like this, with a tender look on his face, while I slept naked in his arms, loathe to even set me down.

"A few hours. Not nearly long enough for you to already have that look back on your face."

I saw my face set into familiar neutral lines as I schooled my expression. "What look?"

His face was sad but rueful. "Your running look. As though you've rested too long and you're about to get up and start running again. That look makes me want to tie you to my bed. I would, if I thought it would keep you there. For someone who can fly, you sure love to run. Do you suppose you'll ever stop?

I smiled at him sadly. "I hope so. But it's all I know. We've always been running. And hiding. And scheming. And lying. But I'm sick to death of it all. It's no life we've lived, for all of these centuries. Leaving behind or destroying the things we love." I swallowed hard past the lump in my throat, trying not to let my feelings show in my eyes. His contrasting eyes were so intense, cutting into my soul.

"Not today, though. I need to find Lynn. And get her back. I have my work cut out for me. I'll be running, as usual, but this time I'm running into the fight, and not away from it."

His mouth hardened. "Yes, I know. The druids can help you. You have but to ask. And no more lies, Jillian. I'm sick unto death of your lies."

He was silent for a long time after that, and I lay unmoving against him.

Finally, he spoke again. "I've lost count of how many women I've been with since you left seven years ago." Ouch. "And it wasn't even for comfort that I turned to them. Not even for lust. It was all to punish you. To remind myself that we were done for good. And that you were dead to me."

Ouch. Ouch. Ouch. He didn't let me lick my wounds before he continued. "And, sometimes, when I was really having a bad time of it, it was even a misguided attempt to find you. Some part of me just couldn't believe that you would let me get away with defiling our love like that. I had some dysfunctional fantasy in my head that you might come back to me, like some avenging angel, to punish me for what I was doing. But it didn't matter how many times I did it, or with who, every *single* time it felt like I was breaking faith with you."

"That may have been what enraged me the most. That it still felt like breaking vows for me, even though you were the one that betrayed us. I felt like a bastard, when you were the one who had moved on, long before I."

"And even hating you so much, all the while, I was still sick with worry, because I knew that, even with your betrayal, fear is what had made you run. It was my last thought before I slept, for *every single night* of your absence. There was something that you feared, and I had no way to know if it had caught up to you, or even if you were alive. It killed me, *every single day,* that instead of staying where I could protect you, you had left me in purgatory, and made yourself more vulnerable. And made me think that you had fucked my nemesis on your way out the door..."

"And now I find out that it was all an elaborate lie." His mismatched eyes had turned positively malevolent in the mirror by the end of his confession. The golden one was glowing like a torch. "Sloan told me, when she finally regained consciousness, about your little scheme with Caleb."

Tears had started running down my cheeks at the beginning of his speech, tears of pain. But they turned to tears of relief at news of Sloan. "Sloan is okay?" My voice was raw, holding back sobs. How I'd hated myself for dragging her into my mess, and thinking it had gotten her killed.

He stroked my wet cheek, his expression softening at my tears. "She was in real rough shape when we found her, but she's fully recovered now. It will take Cam far longer to get over it." He smiled slightly. "You might want to avoid him for awhile."

"I usually do. Those two are something, huh? They almost make us look stable."

A corner of his mouth kicked up. "I wouldn't say that. But their story goes back just as far. The same year, in fact. 1947 was the year for tempestuous lovers to meet, perhaps."

This was news to me. My brows shot up. "I didn't know that. I would pay good money for that story."

His gaze turned speculative. "I'm sure we can come to some sort of agreement. Some other time. I had something else in mind for the moment."

He lowered my legs, one at a time, very slowly, to the floor. They felt like jelly. I leaned back heavily against him. He watched me, his lids heavy, while he arranged my uncharacteristically wavy golden locks around my torso, curling them around my breasts just so. "Put your hands on the mirror," he ordered hoarsely. I did. "Spread your legs further apart." Another order. I complied.

He stepped away from me, moving to my left and closer to the mirror. I could see him more clearly now in the reflection, but he was out of arm's reach. His exquisite eyes never left me, his hair falling against his face as he bent forward slightly to unbutton his long, dark robe. I noticed for the first time all of the intricate patterns embroidered into it, in a deep purple thread. It was covered in runes. Powerful ones. Whatever the druids had been up to tonight, it was strong magic. Something that required the most powerful druid I had ever seen to also have to dress himself in power. "That is an intimidating piece of clothing. Am I allowed to ask what it was for?"

He smiled enigmatically. "It's best if you don't. Druid business. Some things gain power when you speak of them."

I thought immediately of that terrifying grove I had witnessed. "The grove," I guessed.

He gave me a level stare. "There is a binding ritual that the guardian must perform in order for us to maintain...peace. I am the guardian. That is all I can say about it. Please, speak no more of this. As I said, words give it power."

I nodded slightly. Giving that thing more power was the last thing I wanted. It had been added to the very small list of creatures in the world that scared me shitless. And I had only had one run-in with the thing...

I gasped, my mind going suddenly, perfectly, blank. Dom had finished unbuttoning the robe and let it drop to the floor. He stood gloriously naked now, and I was transfixed. My eyes soaked in the sight of him. He was massive, of course, towering over my own six foot height. And his muscles bulged in a most distracting fashion. But for all that, he was lean and sinewy. There wasn't an ounce of fat on his entire, perfect frame. He was almost..elegant, for all of his monumental size. That perfect body combined with his aristocratically beautiful face. He was an exquisite work of art. How many hearts had he broken since I'd left? At least one, I knew firsthand.

I bit my lip as I openly ogled him. He was tan from head to toe, and I wanted to lick every tan inch of him. My eyes ran down his chest, past his sculpted abs, to his glorious, jutting erection, and all the way down his long, muscular legs.

"You said you wanted me naked. Well, here I am." His voice held a playful taunt. I practically panted.

"Don't move an inch," he told me, sensing I was about to jump him. Dammit.

Without warning, he started to stroke himself. I gasped. I was in for a doozy, if he was in this kind of a mood. He knew just what would drive me mad. I licked my lips. "I want to do that," I told him. I didn't even recognize my own voice.

His eyes were heavy-lidded, his lips sensually amused. "Do

you? Is that *really* what you want?"

I nodded, then thought about it, and shook my head. He laughed, stroking faster and harder. "Tell me what you do want. Or I may just make you watch me finish myself."

"I want you to take me against this mirror. I want to watch your eyes while you do it. I want it to be so hard, and so deep, that you wonder if you're hurting me. But I want you to be so far gone that you don't stop, even if you are."

That did the trick. He was behind me, bending over me in a dizzying move. He pulled my head back by the hair, so I was looking up at him.

He didn't hold back, ramming into me in that oh so smooth way he had. He thrust, again and again, and I could see my hair shifting through colors out of the corner of my eye. His eyes turned from playful to ardently serious, and he started speaking in a language that sounded like Gaelic. His voice was a deep lilt when he did this, and it drove me mad. How had I never learned to speak that language?

Tears pricked my eyes, then ran down my cheeks freely. What I wouldn't give to have him love me again, the way he used to. That kind of love was addictive. I had simply known that, for him, the sun rose and set with my presence, and I had felt the same for him, though I had never been as good at showing it to him. Not like he had for me. Was that love he'd once felt still salvageable? Were we? I was terrified to ask. So scared that I knew I would run from the answer until it chased me down. And so the tears flowed freely down my cheeks, tears of hope and despair.

He moaned loudly. It was rare for him to get loud. It simply wasn't his way. But he loved my tears. Some memory from long ago, he'd once told me, when my tears had moved him deeply. He said I'd been crying the first time he'd realized that he would love me forever.

He moved a hand to my face, the other still gripping my hip

like a vise. He traced my tears with an unbelievably soft touch, never stopping his hard thrusts. He licked his finger, then bent forward and started kissing the sides of my face from behind, licking and sucking at my tears. That did it, and I came. He followed me, like he'd been waiting for my cue, which I knew he had.

CHAPTER FORTY-TWO

Epilogue

When I came to again I was laying on a warm, hard chest. I could feel Dom stroking my hair. What had woken me? I couldn't put my finger on it. A feeling, maybe. An instinct. A sound? I looked up at Dom's face. His head was tilted back, his eyes open wide and staring at the ceiling, lost in some faraway thoughts.

A cel phone started ringing on the beside table. I lifted my head, glancing around the room, vaguely recognizing it as the room Dom had been using the last time I had been at the druid casino. The bed was different. "Did you get a new bed?" I asked him. He seemed to be getting more distant by the second, his face closing off completely as he continued to stare at the ceiling.

His mouth twisted. "I did. I tore the last one to pieces after I found out you'd been captured by the dragons."

Oh. The phone stopped ringing for a few seconds then started up again. "Aren't you going to answer your phone?" I asked him.

"It's for you," he said, his voice hollow.

I blinked at him. "I don't have a phone. I don't have anything, for that matter. This is the first place I've been since I came back from the dragon-trance."

"It's my phone. But it's for you."

"How do you know?"

"I just do. Are you going to answer it?" His eyes stayed glued to the ceiling.

It stopped and started again. I picked it up. "Hello?"

"Jillian, we're in Summerlin. You need to get here, fast. We have a lead." It was Caleb's voice, sounding a little animated, for him. He was acting as though I'd been gone for a day, instead of seven months.

"How did you know I was back?" I asked carefully, glancing at Dom. He hadn't moved a muscle.

"I have the casino under 24/7 surveillance. The pale dragon landing on the roof was a dead giveaway."

I shot Dom a worried glance. "Do you think that's a wise move? You do not want to fuck with the druids."

I heard a snort through the phone, then Christian's voice in the background. "Look who's talking!"

I pushed up on my arms, becoming momentarily distracted by the sight of my gold hair trailing across Dom's naked torso. I might have drooled a little. I'll never tell. I shook myself out of my distraction.

"While you've been playing dragon, to fly around the world, we've been trying to find Lynn. We finally have a lead, so get your ass over here," Caleb was saying impatiently. "We've got Luke spying for us, and he's actually damn good at it. But he wants to talk to you before he goes back undercover. He's insisting. Your sub is becoming a little too assertive here. It's too bad we need him..." Caleb's voice trailed off in a threat that I knew was directed at Luke, who I assumed was in the room.

"He's not my-" I shot a worried look at Dom. He was still in the same pose, but his expression was positively arctic now.

Christian took over Caleb's end of the phone, his excited

voice making me smile. "We've missed you, girl. Especially Luke. He's written you a stack of love letters that I read for you. For future blackmail purposes, of course. Chop, chop, Jillian. He's dying here, and he's been bloody helpful. He's earned at least a kiss. Dinner and a blow job would be even more appropriate, considering that he's been risking his life."

I shut my eyes tight in annoyance, knowing Dom was hearing every word of this, and would take it all wrong. Christian knew Dom was with me, I was on his phone, but he just didn't care. He liked to stir the pot. Damned instigator.

"It's tiresome, Christian. Give me your location."

At my words, Dom got up suddenly, spilling me from his chest in the process, and not directing so much as a glance in my direction. He strode, naked, out of the room. I admired the view, unable to help it. He had the most magnificent ass in the world. I wondered where the door he'd left out of led.

I shook my head, telling Christian to start over. I got it down this time, memorizing the address. "Shit." I suddenly realized I had nothing. No clothes, no phone, no car. My mind went blank.

Christian was still chatting happily on the other end of the line. I could tell he had missed me, by his excited chatter. Even Christian wasn't normally this ADD, jumping from one subject to the next before I could get a word in.

My mouth went dry when Dom strode back into the room, still completely nude, and carrying a large duffle bag. He was semi-hard and getting harder while I stared, open-mouthed, at his perfect cock, with absolute fascination.

Abruptly he threw the bag in my lap. He handed me a phone. I studied it dumbly. It was the updated version of the top of the line cel I'd had before I was captured. Apparently a new model had come out while I was away.

"There's a cel phone kiosk in the shops downstairs in the casino. It's yours, all set up, with a new number, and an alias, of course. I figured you wouldn't stay long before you were running again, so I ordered it while you slept. My number is programmed in, and I have yours."

"I assume your friends have some kind of a plan for finding Lynn, but the druids would like to become involved, as well. The dragons have declared themselves rogue, even launched a few attacks that were hard to cover up. I'm calling some people into town who will be useful to your endeavors. I will be putting together a task force designed specifically to combat the rogue dragon threat. I'll let you know the time and place of the meeting."

I nodded mutely. I couldn't exactly turn down help, with my sister's life on the line. And the druids were officially in the fight now, with or without my consent. "That bag has several days worth of toiletries and clothing, all in your size." He pointed, exuding the coolness and command of his Arch position, a position that had always intimidated me. "The bathroom is in there."

I showered and changed in record time. The running shoes and jeans fit perfectly. They were the dark colors I favored. I fished out a small black t-shirt, zipping up the bag. He had even remembered the shampoo I liked.

I walked out, fully dressed, carrying the bag, and froze. Dom stood where I'd left him, still gloriously naked, his jaw clenched hard. His eyes were grave. He pointed to another door. "That's the exit."

I paused. "Where is my-our, um, egg?" I knew the egg would need to be guarded, day and night. I couldn't begin to imagine what the wrong people would do with such a thing. My enemies, or even harvesters with any knowledge of what it was, would go to great lengths to steal it.

His mouth tightened. He pointed to another door. "I set him up in there, for now. That is the only door in or out. I'll set him up in a well fortified vault, first thing in the morning. I'll keep him safe. I swear my life on it."

I swallowed, hard. I didn't want to leave him, not even for a second. I didn't want to leave either of them. But I had to do this. "Thank you."

"There's a car for you downstairs. Like I said, I knew it wouldn't be long before you were running again. I made all of the arrangements." There was a world of bitterness in his voice.

I stepped toward him, wanting to touch him, but his forbidding manner dissuaded me. The fear that Dom would reject me was always enough to have me turning away first. I tried for a weak smile. "At least this time, I'm running towards the fight. It's an improvement, I think."

He gave me a hard look out of those magnificent mismatched eyes. "Not to me." He turned away first. "Good luck."

It was a dismissal.